Winding Roads

Brenda O'Bannion

Winding Roads

Brenda O'Bannion

Tranquility Press, 2025

Tranquility Press
723 W University Ave #234
Georgetown TX 78626
TranquilityPress.com
TranquilityPress@gmail.com

This book is a work of fiction. Historical figures are used fictitiously, and any scenes, situations, incidents, or dialogue concerning them are not to be inferred as real. Any other similarity to real persons, living or dead, is entirely coincidental and not intended by the author.

ISBN: 978-1950481521

Publisher's Cataloging-in-Publication data

Names: O'Bannion, Brenda, author.
Title: Winding roads / by Brenda O'Bannion.
Description: Georgetown, TX: Tranquility Press, 2025.
Identifiers: ISBN (trade) 978-1950481521
Subjects: West Virginia (WV). |Trauma. | Family. | The Vietnam war. | Faith.
BISAC FIC014090: Fiction/Historical/Post-WWII | FIC042030: Fiction/
Christian/Historical | FIC071000: Fiction/Friendship | FIC066000: Fiction/
Small town-rural
GSAFD: Historical fiction. | LCGFT: Novel
Classification: LCC PS3620.033665 L36 2023 | DDC 813/.6—dc23

This book is dedicated

to the 58,220 men and women
who gave their lives in the Vietnam War
and to the thousands of others who came home.
We honor your service.

*I am with you and will watch over you
wherever you go.
And I will bring you back to this land.*
Genesis 28:15

Chapter 1

1970

Kathleen watched as Cody woofed down two hamburgers, a massive serving of fries, and a monster shake while keeping his eyes on the red-and-white Dr Pepper clock on the facing wall. She wished countless times he would stop and see her. And listen—really listen.

Placing her half-eaten burger back into the basket, she breathed in. "Cody, we need to talk."

"No time for talk. We gotta go, Katho. Coach is a stickler about being at the airfield on time." Cody stood and threw a five onto the table, then turned to the waitress with a wink. "Keep the change."

She followed him out of Micky's Diner to his dark blue 1964 Chevy. Several students who were grouped around their parked cars outside the hamburger shack shouted comments, wishing Cody good luck. Kathleen observed as her boyfriend's shoulders went back and his chest thrust forward. A stark contrast from the young boy she'd dated for four years in high school and two at Marshall University.

Kathleen approached the passenger door and waited, watching him shake hands and high-five his admirers. She gave a headshake and whispered, "He's not the same Cody Machek I fell in love with." Resolute about her recent decision, she tried again once they were in the car. "Cody, please listen."

"Shh," he said, turning the radio louder. "They're talking about tomorrow's game."

She opened her mouth to try again, but before she spoke the first word, Cody quieted her as he made a left turn. "Hey, baby, turn it louder. It's about me."

Several hateful replies started in her brain but never reached her lips. Why try? He stopped listening long ago.

At the small airport, Cody skidded the car into a parking place and met Kathleen beside the vehicle to toss her the keys. "Thanks for taking care of my car. Don't take it on any joy rides!"

"Wait!" she said to his back when he pivoted toward the waiting plane.

Cody turned and squared off with Kathleen from several feet away. "You know I can't be late."

"I understand, but I have to tell you something." Kathleen moved closer. The irritated expression on Cody's face ignited a flame of anger from what had been an ember. Words poured from her mouth. "Never use the phrase 'Gotta go, Katho' again! And never walk out of Mikey's or any other place ahead of me!"

"Is that what this is about?"

Kathleen hung her head long enough to regain her composure. Eyes back on his, she lowered her voice. "It's time for us to take a break."

"A break? If this is a joke, I really don't have time—"

"It's not a joke," she said. "What we had in high school was special, but we've changed. We need to stop seeing each other. It's over between us."

When the plane's propellors buzzed into movement, Cody spun and ran toward the tarmac. But not before she saw the confusion and hurt registered on his face.

"Ouch." Kathleen jerked her brush through her hair, struggling to untangle the matted strands. Why had she let Sarah talk her into a teased hairdo before her date with Cody? She preferred her long blond curls to fall naturally. On the next swipe, the brush stuck in a rat's nest. She yanked hard, horrified by how many strands of hair came out.

Breathless, Kathleen stopped and stared into the mirror above her vanity. Last night's scene slid backward through her mind like rewinding a tape recorder. Now she replayed every moment.

To her amazement, her thoughts then pivoted to a scene she remembered from long ago. She was six years old and starting first grade the next day. Kathleen marched into the kitchen where her parents were cleaning up after their evening meal. "I've decided something," she announced, striking a pose.

When her parents turned from the sink, they both gave a small laugh. Her father spoke first. "Really, have you now, Daughter? Would you mind sharing this decision with us?"

"Tomorrow, I start first grade. I'm too old to have a baby name like Tilly. Starting today, I want Kathleen to be my name." When she saw the smiles leave their faces, she dropped her hands from her waist and added a meek, "Please."

"But you've been our Tilly since the day you were born. Remember, you're named after my Aunt Matilda." Mom said softly, as she moved closer to her daughter, hands dripping from the dishwater.

"Kathleen is my middle name, so it's okay to call me that." She looked pleadingly from her mom to her dad.

"Emily," her father said while keeping his gaze fixed on Tilly, "our daughter is growing up and I think we must allow her to choose the name she's most comfortable with."

Why had this crossed her mind now? Suddenly she knew. Her mother had the same look of confusion and hurt that she'd seen in Cody's eyes last night.

It'd been almost twenty-four hours since Kathleen watched the plane filled with the Thundering Herd football team, staff, and fans lift off and gain altitude to clear the mountainous terrain of West Virginia.

She'd spent much of the day sleeping—a tactic to avoid remembering what happened last night. Her door flying open notified Kathleen her best friend had arrived. Sarah Lawson had only one speed—fast.

"Did you forget the Kappa Phi Society gathering is tonight?" Sarah stood in the doorway, hands planted on her hips, mouth pinched. "You promised to go."

"That's before I hurt Cody—before I saw his expression when I told him."

Sarah closed the door, then walked over to pick up a comb. "First, never try to smooth teased hair with a brush. Use a comb. Second, I drove here to get you since your car is in the shop, so you can't break your promise to be at the meeting with me. As for your ex-boyfriend, you did the right thing last night!"

Kathleen knew Sarah had disliked Cody but, out of loyalty, her friend rarely said anything negative about him. Sarah also never reflected on the past. She always moved forward with a kind of hope that eluded Kathleen.

Kathleen ran her hands over her curls before pushing them back with a black headband. "I still can't believe I let you talk me into a tease."

"Honey, I just wanted you to look gorgeous when you gave him the axe."

Grimacing at Sarah's choice of words, she protested, "I didn't give him the—"

"No time for this now," Sarah interrupted, glancing at her wristwatch. "It's too late for you to take a shower. Just spray on some deodorant and get dressed. I don't want to miss P-I time."

Kathleen groaned inwardly. Not prayer and inspiration time again. That's the last thing she wanted to hear today. Yet, she kept going back each time Sarah asked, though the reason escaped her.

Twenty minutes later, Kathleen sank into the passenger seat of Sarah's bright red Dodge Charger. "I hope you realize I only came because I made you a promise. All I really want is my favorite pajamas and my bed!" She crossed her arms over her chest, waiting for Sarah to respond.

When no response come, Kathleen sighed and said meekly, "I guess a promise is a promise." Sarah smiled with a slight nod. From the radio, gospel songs spoke of hope, faith, and grace. Kathleen grabbed the radio knob and turned it off, ignoring their rule, "my car—my music."

Kathleen wished her Volkswagen Beetle wasn't in the shop. She'd thought briefly about taking Cody's car so she could keep her promise to Sarah and then make a quick exit. But it felt wrong to use the car of someone she'd broken up with.

"I'm sorry you're miserable right now, Kathleen. But give it some time. You'll find your real self—not the person who has followed the campus football hero around for the past two years. You deserve more than just being a jock's girlfriend." Sarah turned the radio back on, lowering the volume.

Kathleen stared at the windshield wipers as they swiped back and forth, wishing she could wipe away her confused feelings. *Jock's girlfriend? Is that what everyone thinks?*

"Watch out!" She screeched and grabbed the dashboard when a man stepped off the curb and into their path.

Sarah slammed her brakes, causing the tires to skid on the wet street. She corrected the wheels and eased the car to the curb before putting it into park. "Thank goodness you saw him! This fog is getting thicker." Her white knuckles released from the wheel and fell into her lap. She inhaled deeply and lowered her head. "Lord, thank you for your protection."

Turning to Kathleen, she asked, "Do you want to go back to the dorm?"

Nothing would make her happier, but Kathleen knew how much Sarah enjoyed hanging out with her Christian friends. Feeling more charitable than before when nothing suited her, she replied, "No, we're only a few more blocks from the Kappa Phi house."

Under way again, they diligently watched the road as the rain came down harder. Sarah parked her car in the driveway of a large two-story house on a tree-lined street. They exited her car with umbrellas overhead and sloshed their way up the sidewalk. Sarah took the lead, with Kathleen behind her.

"Let's still make it a short evening, okay, Sarah?" Kathleen said when they reached the front door.

"Why don't we wait and see what blessings are in store for us?"

Kathleen sighed. Her friend always brought faith into their conversation. She usually ignored it, but now her nerves quivered like a worm on a hook, making her paranoid. What kind of bait would the Kappa Phi sisters throw her way?

With prayer and inspiration finished, the group settled before the television to enjoy American Bandstand and snack on popcorn, peanuts, and soda pops. For the first time since last evening, Kathleen's body relaxed as she munched on popcorn.

The girls soon lost interest in the show and chatted with each other. Kathleen's eyes remained on the TV, pleased the group didn't pull her into their conversations.

When the station cut to a news bulletin, she alerted the others with loud shushing.

Breaking News. At approximately 7:30 p.m. tonight, Southern Airlines Flight 932, carrying the Marshall University football team, crashed. The DC-9, attempting to land in rain and fog, missed the runway at Huntington Tri-State Airport and sheared off trees before plunging into a hillside. According to Fire Chief Dusty Rhodes, it is unlikely anyone will survive the severity of this crash. This is Barry Smith reporting from WSAZ-TV, Channel 5.

"Sarah, we have to go!" Kathleen knocked her bowl of popcorn to the floor. She hurried toward the front entrance. Jerking on her coat as she opened the door, she gasped at the blare of sirens—lots of them. Kathleen had her hand on the handle of Sarah's car when someone gripped her arm.

Chapter 2

"Wait! I'll take you." A young man yelled over the cacophony coming from the rescue vehicles.

Kathleen stared at the muscular hand tightened around her forearm, then up to the face towering over her.

"I'm Walt Johnson, the teaching assistant in your investigative writing class."

He released her arm. "Sorry to frighten you, but I recognized you from class. I have press credentials to get close to the crash." Walt stopped and exhaled, causing white frost to circle his face. "If you want to go with me, decide now. I should be there as soon as possible."

"Kathleen, wait!" Sarah yelled from the door of the sorority house. "Please stay here. We'll pray for everyone on the plane."

Kathleen ignored Sarah's pleas. She let go of her death grip on the door handle, then fell in beside Walt as he jogged to his car.

In short order, they approached a bright orange junker parked under a streetlamp. The car had to be ten years old. It had more than its share of rust spots, making it look like an orange that had gone bad.

Walt took her hand and pulled her to the driver's side. "You'll have to get in on this side. The passenger door only opens from the inside."

When she resisted his pull, he continued, "She may be a mess, she'll get us where we're going. Get in. I need to hurry."

Kathleen hopped in and slid to the passenger's side. After two grinding starts, the engine settled into a purr. Walt avoided the major streets that were packed with emergency vehicles.

By twisting and turning through residential streets and a few alleys, Walt turned onto the road leading to Tri-County Airport.

As they moved closer, the northern skyline came into view. They stared at the orange glow with black smoke billowing into the night sky. Suddenly, the old car filled with the putrid smell of burning jet fuel and another unidentifiable foul odor.

"Oh!" Kathleen whispered as she covered her nose with the collar of her blouse. She looked at him with incredulous eyes.

"I apologize. A back window doesn't roll up all the way." Walt paused. "I'm afraid it's going to smell even worse when we reach the scene. There will be sights beyond what you can imagine. You'll have to be strong." He watched her out of the corner of his eyes as she nodded several times.

Cars dropped out of the line as they found parking places along both sides of the road. People of all ages exited their vehicles and walked uphill to the site. Kathleen recognized a few students, then gasped at the sight of Cody's parents emerging from their car and joining the others.

She swiveled her head to watch them. Her chest seized, squeezing the air out of her lungs.

"What's wrong?" Walt asked as she struggled.

She waited until her lungs offered enough air to speak. "It's Cody's parents. They came to visit him for his birthday on Monday."

Walt took his eyes off the road long enough to glance at her. "Kathleen, are you certain you want to cross the yellow tape? I can drop you off and you can be with your boyfriend's parents."

"No. If he's hurt, I must be with him." She wrinkled her brow at Walt. "How do you know my name and that Cody is my boyfriend?"

"I know your name because I have a seating chart for Professor McKnight's class. You ask interesting questions. I wanted to know who you were." He paused, coming to a stop to let a group of people pass. "When I found your name, I knew Cody was your boyfriend. Everyone who follows the Thundering Herd knows."

Choosing not to respond, Kathleen looked from Walt to the carnage. "Oh, my God. How could this happen?" She pushed one fist into her lips to hold back a scream.

Firefighters blasted water onto the pieces that once had been a DC-9 jet. Medics rolled gurneys with body bags to ambulances. Other firefighters worked to kill the fire in the forest around the crash. Multiple rescue teams searched the scene, taking pictures and marking potential evidence with orange placards. She squeezed her eyes shut, willing it to all go away.

When the cars ahead of him came to a halt, Walt locked eyes with Kathleen. "Are you okay? Can you do this?"

She grabbed his arm and leaned toward him. "I think it could all be a mistake. What if this isn't the team plane? This could be any flight coming into the airport. Maybe Cody's plane was rerouted because of bad weather." She let go of Walt's arm and asked, "It's possible, right?"

Kathleen desperately needed him to agree. Her eyes filled with tears when he shook his head and responded, "This *is* the team's plane. Air traffic control confirmed the flight number."

Walt softened his voice. "Hear me out. This is a tragic crash with many casualties. If you lose it, they'll throw us out. I won't get my story. I'm asking again if you want to get closer to the scene."

She surveyed the crash. Something deep within her turned hard, like the boulders knocked loose when the plane barreled into the mountain. "I can handle it."

Walt coasted to a stop at the checkpoint. His window creaked and made a few stubborn stops before it was down far enough to show his press credentials.

The police officer scrutinized the card. "What about her?" The man's voice raspy from inhaling the smoke-filled air.

"She's my assistant—helps with my equipment."

"All right. Stay clear of the first responders and don't bother the investigators unless they come to you with news."

"Yes, sir." Walt tried to roll up his window. When it resisted, he pounded on the inside of his door. "Lousy piece of junk. I should take you to the metal yard where you belong!"

Kathleen placed a hand on his arm. "Let's go."

"Right." Walt passed through the opening and parked beside a row of vehicles.

Her sight took everything in with a wide sweep. She'd watched movies about plane crashes. Now she was embroiled in a real one. Kathleen's emotions raced from repulsion to determination.

Walt fished through a backpack until he found a small camera and a notepad. He unzipped a side pocket and retrieved a half-sized pencil. "Take these. At least you'll look official."

"Surely you don't want me to…"

"No, but someone may question if you don't look like a reporter. Pretend to take a few pictures and write something in the notebook." He paused. "If someone questions you, tell them you're my assistant and you left too quickly to get your press pass."

Kathleen nodded once and put the camera strap around her neck, then grabbed the notepad and pencil. "Cody could still be…" She stopped herself. Saying his name made her chin tremble. She gulped down an unsteady breath, struggling against the urge to pound on something.

"Try to stay in view of me. Once I'm on a story, I become a one-man show."

Outside the car, Kathleen found herself immersed

in a horror scene. There was an eerie quiet that chilled her bones. The first responders and others spoke in low voices, almost reverent whispers. She eyed the crowd of onlookers standing beyond the yellow tape. They were silent except for the occasional muffled sob.

Kathleen carefully stepped around smoldering unrecognizable bodies lying haphazardly on the ground. Some lay at a weird angle—half in, half out of torn pieces of the plane. She willed herself to keep her eyes open. Her breath came in shallow bursts to quench the awful smell. She listened for any sound of distress. Suddenly, she tripped on an evidence placard and fell to her knees in a sea of dead bodies. She fought against the scream traveling through her throat. *Don't faint. Find Cody!*

When she raised her head, Kathleen was inches from the face of a body. She scrambled to her feet, staring at the badly burned person. Smoke rose from it to join the thick layer hovering overhead.

Revolted, she took a step back when her boot crunched on an object. She moved her foot and glanced down. Hidden in the debris was a metal necklace. Her heartbeat drummed in her ears. Even as she reached down, she knew it belonged to Cody.

Kathleen picked it up with trembling fingers. She read the inscription on the dog tag. *Power, Courage, & Wisdom.* Turning it over, she saw their initials.

Silent tears trailed rivers down her face as hope flowed from her body. Kathleen went back to Cody's lifeless body. She lay the tag on his chest, then checked the number on the evidence placard placed next to it. Number 92. Ironically, it was the month and day of their first date. Unable to produce words, her thoughts spoke. *I'll always regret my last words to you.*

Kathleen made it to the closest living tree before throwing up. She wiped her mouth using the back of her hand. Retrieving her notepad from the ground, she wrote, *I know what the foul smell is.*

Chapter 3

"Thank you for this information, Officer McCreary," Walt remarked as he closed his notebook and placed a stubby pencil behind his ear. "My newspaper appreciates the fact you let us into the restricted area."

The tall, burly officer placed his hand on Walt's shoulder. "Son, I reckon this is more about those who know Marshall University and Huntington than any of those big-time reporters who are arriving faster than flies to a picnic." His eyes were moist when he extended his right hand. "You write a story that will honor those on the flight."

Walt nodded and returned the handshake. "I have to find my assistant. I'm afraid I've abandoned her."

"She's over there, sitting with her back against a tree. I think this was too much for her. For everyone, if I'm honest."

His heart sank when he saw Kathleen. She sat on a small patch of unburned grass, turned away from the rubble, her body folded over with her arms locked around her legs.

Walt walked slowly, not wanting to frighten her. When he stopped in front of Kathleen, her facial expression frightened him. She had the vacant stare of someone close to shock.

"Kathleen?"

No response, not even a glance upward. He kneeled and tried again. "It's me, Walt. It's time to go."

When she didn't acknowledge him again, he panicked. "I need to get you home. You must be freezing. Let me get your coat." He was halfway to his feet when he heard a panicked yell.

"No! It's covered in ashes from… them."

Observing the anguish in her face, he lowered his voice. "It's okay. I won't touch it." He was slipping off his coat when she rocked her head.

"Okay, I understand," Walt said, letting his own ash-covered coat slip to the ground. He reached for her boots. "Here, get these on and I'll help you into the car."

Kathleen shoved the boots out of his hand. "They're covered too." Her eyes landed on his face for the first time. "Cody's dead. I found his body. It was…" Her face crumbled into soft sobs.

He leaned closer, putting a hand on each of her shoulders. "I'm sorry." He could feel her shivering. "It's too cold out here. Let me take you to the car."

"I can't leave him here." She mumbled as her shoulders stiffed against his hands.

Walt took a long breath. "He's gone, Kathleen. The

National Guard has transported all the bodies they found to a temporary morgue." He would eventually tell her everything, but not yet. She was too fragile for the lead he'd uncovered.

"Let's think of you now, so please listen to me. I'm going to carry you to the car. Can I do this?"

He noticed a slight nod. "Okay, I'd like you to put your arms around my neck." He waited as she did what he requested. The tight grip she exhibited surprised him—like he was her lifeline.

Guilt poured through him. *What was I thinking to bring her to this place?* His next thought added to his guilt. He did it because he was attracted to her and saw an opportunity. Walt sent up a silent prayer. *God, forgive me for considering only myself and not others. Help me now to make this right by Kathleen.*

He lifted her into the driver's seat and waited until she slid over to the opposite side, then grabbed a blanket from the back seat. "I'm sorry. The heater went out last winter. That's why I have a blanket. Sometimes I wrap it around me when I'm driving."

He looked at her, but she wasn't listening. Instead, she'd covered her face with both hands, shutting out the surrounding view.

Behind the wheel, he heard cries rising within her that soon became spine-shattering sobs.

Never had he felt so helpless and so responsible. "Kathleen, I d-don't kn-know how to h-help you," he stuttered, something he'd done as a young boy but stopped years ago.

Moisture accumulated in his eyes as he resisted an urge to bang his hands against the steering wheel. *Lord, help me. I caused this and I'm unsure of what to do!* In the blink of an eye, peace filled his heart, slowing it down. It was then he heard the soft words, *Trust me for your next steps.*

Walt put the car in reverse and left the sight as quickly as possible. He listened as Kathleen's crying slowed and lowered several pitches. Eventually, he heard soft sobs, the kind that follow a torrential outpouring. When he pulled up to her dorm, only sniffles and hiccups filled the front seat.

Before exiting the car, she gazed at her tightly gripped hands in her lap. "I did something terrible. Something I can never forgive myself for." Her voice was raspy, like one whose throat had released powerful emotions.

He stayed silent, waiting to hear if she planned to say more. Finally, he reached over and placed one hand over hers. "Sometimes it helps to talk about a burden."

When she finally found his face, he saw eyes filled with such pain it hurt to keep his gaze on them.

"Yesterday, I went to the airport. Just before Cody boarded the plane, I broke up with him. After almost seven years of dating, I chose that moment to tell him we were over."

Before he could respond, she shucked off the blanket, swung the door open, and hurried to the front door of her dorm, clad only in her bell-bottom jeans and sweater top.

Walt watched as the large door opened. A woman enveloped Kathleen in her arms and moved her inside.

He stared at the closed door through the passenger window, resisting the urge to barge in and help. But he'd done enough damage. He drove to the newsroom, his mind full of the things he'd witnessed. He tried to sort out the facts he would use in his story, but all he could think about was the coatless girl leaning against a tree.

"Walt, wake up," Liam said while shaking his coworker's shoulder. "You been here all night?"

Walt sat up and wiped the drool off his face with his sleeve. "What time is it?"

"It's 7:45." Liam gave him a once over, then said, "You look a mess, man. You get your story in?"

"Yeah, sent it to press around three this morning. There's going to be a special edition out today."

"Horrible thing. How was it at the scene?"

"It was ..." Then he remembered Kathleen. "I must go, Liam. Tell the boss I'm out on another story about the crash."

"What else is there to write about?"

"If my information is correct, plenty." He took his coat from the back of his chair and snatched Liam's fresh cup of coffee.

"Hey, that's mine."

"Not anymore. Thanks."

Chapter 4

Huntington Tri-State Airport will get you there faster and bring you home happier.

Walt stared at the sign above the door of the terminal, sickened by the reference. Grabbing his notepad, he scribbled the logo before exiting his car.

He pushed hard on the double glass door, his jaw jacked, ready to fight for a story. The check-in counter stood straight ahead. To the right, uncomfortable blue plastic chairs sat empty of passengers.

"I'm sorry, the airport is closed today. No flights in or out." The woman behind the desk, dressed in slacks and a double-knit top with a guru collar, had mascara-smeared eyes resembling those of a raccoon.

Walt pulled his press credential out of his ever-present canvas bag. "I'm from the *Herald Dispatch* newspaper. I'd like to—"

"No press. Direct order from the administrator."

"I'm not here for an interview. Toby Hardin is my

cousin. There's a family emergency. He's needed at the hospital. The relatives asked me to make sure he gets there." He felt the weight of the lie but pushed it aside.

"All the office staff is in a meeting. I'll try to get him out." Her voice broke and tears pooled in her eyes. "It's such a sad day. I hate for anyone to get more bad news." She disappeared through a door behind the counter.

A stab of guilt flashed through him. Walt's heart told him not to lie—a career conflict he wrestled with often. Yet, he loved reporting. None of the lies had bothered him before. Now, he was different. Last year, when his coworker, Dora, invited him to her church, he went for one reason—her lovely blue eyes.

Unexpectedly, the words of the pastor touched him that day, and he continued to go back. Before long, Walt began dropping by the church office to visit with the reverend, seeking answers.

The pastor patiently answered his questions and shared scripture from the Bible. Finally, Walt knew he had resisted enough. He accepted Christ late on a Tuesday afternoon in the church office.

Walt's thoughts dissipated when he heard Toby's voice. He reached into his bag and pulled out a notepad.

"Walt? Where's my cousin?" Lines of concern creased his friend's forehead, his face drained of color. "Gail said it was a family emergency."

Toby's fearful face changed to anger when he saw the notepad in Walt's hand. "You're here about the crash, aren't you? That's a low stunt, even from a reporter."

Walt cringed, knowing he deserved his friend's

anger. "I'm sorry, Toby. I just need a few answers about—"

"We aren't answering questions about the flight until the FAA has given us their report."

"Are you answering questions about the failure of this airport to make recommended safety improvements from as far back as 1967?"

"Leave it alone, Walt." Toby sighed. "Don't throw the past in now."

Walt's eyes peered into his friend's. "You know I can't do that."

Toby took a step closer, lowering his voice. "Look, I can tell you preliminary reports are pointing to an improper use of cockpit instrument data or an altimetry error. But there's no way to verify this because of the explosion of the plane. We haven't found the black box yet, may never find it. You'll only cause trouble for the airport if you dig into the past— an airport vital to not just this state, but also to parts of Kentucky and Ohio."

"You know I won't let this story go. My source tells me—"

Toby shook his head, twirled around, and vanished through the door.

Walt stared at the closed door, hoping the clerk would come back out. Maybe he could wrangle some information from her. Ten minutes later, he gave up and went to his car.

He sat in his car staring at the logo again when a light snow started. "Great," Walt said to no one. The snow grew heavier, and a fifteen-minute drive turned into thirty. Finally, he parked in front of the city library.

Once inside, after trying to ignore the black wreath on the door, Walt walked straight to the microfiche machines on the far back wall of the library. He moved to the file cabinets to the right of the two machines. Opening the drawer labeled *Herald Dispatch*, he searched for the reel from 1967. But which issue might hold news about his scoop? *I could be here for hours.* Two hours later, he re-rolled the tape. Nothing.

He returned the spool and pulled out one labeled 1970. Bingo! Buried on page seven in the June 9th issue, five months before the crash, was a story about a meeting between the Federal Aviation Administration and key business owners from the surrounding area, including the two states that bordered West Virginia. The headline: *Installation of Safety Measures at Tri-State Airport Rejected.*

Walt scratched out notes in his crumpled notepad as he scanned the article. He stopped writing when he came to an instrument called the visual approach slope indicator, commonly called a VASI. A system of lights sits on the side of the airport runway to provide visual descent guidance information up to twenty miles away during a plane's final approach. The lower paragraph stated a discussion had been held about extending the one and only runway at the airport.

The last words made him see red. *Since the group of business executives declined to match the federal funds allocated for the improvement, the meeting ended in a stalemate.*

Walt slouched in his chair. Six inches of print—all that was allocated for this story. He returned his notebook to his bag and grabbed his coat. It took all his restraint not to run out of the library.

Outside, the snow had stopped, leaving at least two inches on the ground and on his car. He pulled his coat sleeve over his right hand and swiped at the pile on his front and side windows.

Once inside, Walt prayed the battery wasn't dead. A few cranks later, the motor grunted into life. He wrote his story in his head, eager to get it ready for tomorrow's morning edition.

Wait.

Walt looked at his radio. Did it work after six months of silence? He dialed up the volume. Silence. Confused, he concentrated on his driving, more than a little freaked out.

Wait.

This time he pulled over, unable to concentrate on maneuvering the wet streets. He sat in silence, trying to believe it was nothing.

There's enough pain and suffering.

Suddenly, it hit Walt. God was speaking to him. It was the first time he'd heard anything so direct from the Lord. Humbled, the words became clear. He was being asked to wait on printing the story. Conflict warred in his head. As a reporter, he'd been trained to chase down and print news. And this was news— big time! The crash may have been avoided with additional safety measures in place.

Peace entered his heart as he understood his next move. He had a job responsibility to tell Joe Rickman, the newspaper editor. He'd always thought of his boss as hardshell—not one to bury a story. Walt had to believe God would impress upon him to wait as well.

Thirty minutes later, he exited the newspaper office, amazed by the editor's decision. The story would wait until after the campus memorial service and the many funerals. The hurts of so many would be compounded with the truth about the airport's negligence.

Walt's stomach growled, reminding him he hadn't had breakfast. He headed to his favorite diner, just a block from the newspaper office.

He threw his backpack in the seat of his car when he remembered the ash-covered coat and boots still in the back. Should he return them? Would Kathleen want them back? Guilt flooded him once again. He needed to apologize for taking her to the crash scene and tell her the truth about why he offered her a ride.

When he reached Mikey's, Walt ordered two cheeseburgers and a couple of Dr. Peppers to go.

Chapter 5

Kathleen's eyes flew open. Was it the bright white coming through the open blinds from the dorm window or the soft knock on her door that interrupted her sleep? Either way, she coveted more. Facing the day was too harsh.

The knocks at the door intensified. "I know you're in there. I talked to your dorm mother. Mrs. Crawford said she helped you get into bed late last night."

Scenes of the night before flooded her head. She squeezed her eyes tight, hoping to make the memories go away. Tears stung the back of her lids and threatened to spill out.

"Sarah, please go away," she said in a croaky voice. "I don't want to talk to you."

"But I need to talk to you, and I can't do this from the hallway. Please let me in."

Kathleen could hear the desperation in Sarah's

voice. "Okay, I'm coming. But make it quick. I going back to bed."

She threw back her covers, surprised by how tired her muscles were. Kathleen rubbed her eyes. The thing she least wanted was to cry in front of Sarah.

On her way to the door, her big toe hit the leg of her desk chair, and she tumbled to the floor in pain.

"Dang it," she cried out, grabbing the smarting toe. Sarah didn't like it when she used this phrase. Too close to cussing, her friend always said. She didn't care about what Sarah liked or didn't like.

Where were her beliefs last night when I needed her? Aren't Christians supposed to be there for their friends?

Holding on to the desk, she stood up and stumbled to the door. Her toe throbbed with each step. She paused before opening the door as a sudden anger convulsed through her body—so strong it frightened her. Instinct told her it needed a source, and Sarah was as good a person as any to receive it.

She opened the door only far enough for Sarah to see her body. With steely eyes, Kathleen spoke in a harsh voice. "Make it quick, Sarah Buckley. You're the last person I want to see." It took all her strength not to snarl her teeth at the girl standing before her.

Sarah's forehead wrinkled. "Can't I come in? I'm frightened by the way you look."

Kathleen turned and took a few steps to the mirror above her small vanity. She blinked at the reflection staring back. Was this even her? Could a death make such a mark on one's appearance?

She noticed her eyes first. A deep redness rimmed them, and mascara made tracks down her face. Her hair, still teased from the night before, stood out in little tangled pieces like the frayed end of an old rope.

But it was the look in her eyes that stunned her. They held a dullness she'd never seen before, as if the light in her world had been turned off. Her heart plummeted to the bottom of her chest when she visualized Cody as he sprinted toward the plane. When she turned from the mirror, Sarah stood in the middle of her room.

"Please. Let's talk," Sarah begged.

Kathleen moved to the bed, sitting on the edge with her quilt wrapped around her trembling body. Turning, she stared out the window, ignoring Sarah, who stood next to her.

"Kathleen, are you listening? I'm trying to apologize for last night." Sarah raised her voice a notch.

She swiveled back to Sarah, her face taunted with anger. "Apologize? For what? For choosing to stay in a prayer circle instead of helping me when I needed you?"

To Kathleen's dismay, a swell of tears cascaded down her face. She needed Sarah to see her anger, not her pain. The last thing she wanted was pity from this girl she thought was her friend. "Did you think you could change things with a prayer circle?" Her voice grew shrill. "They were all dead the minute the plane hit the mountain! Where was God then?"

Kathleen lowered her voice to a whisper and looked down at the floor. "I found Cody's body. It was still smoking."

Sarah gasped. No words materialized.

She stared straight into Sarah's eyes. "That's

right. There are no words for it." She paused and put her focus on her hands. "I can still smell the ashes."

Sarah took a step toward Kathleen, who stuck out her hand. "No. I refuse your words of hope and faith, or your hug!" A tremor shook through her body. "I'll get through this my way."

"But there is so much God can—"

"You're not hearing me. I think it's time for you to leave." She moved to the door and opened it wide.

Sarah watched her for several seconds, cheeks wet from tears, and left without a word.

The shrill ring of the phone on the bedside table caused Kathleen to jerk. She glared at it. Another intrusion! On the sixth ring, she gave in.

"Hello?"

"It's me, sweetheart. I'm so saddened by this tragedy. Cody was such a wonderful person. How are you?"

"I'm okay, Mom."

"How can you be? Your boyfriend for so many years has died."

When Kathleen didn't respond, Emily continued. "Your father and I think you should come home temporarily. We can go to Cody's funeral together. I'm sure the university will give you consideration for missing some classes."

Cody's funeral. Wasn't it just yesterday she and Cody sat eating a burger together? She surveyed her room again, wishing to be anywhere other than here or on Marshall University campus.

"All right, I'll come home." She needed her mother's arms. "I'm leaving as soon as I get packed

... and, Mom, I love you." Her voice broke on the last words. She hung up without saying goodbye.

Kathleen packed haphazardly. Her suitcase bulged with a selection of clothes that made no sense. Summer clothes with those for winter. She paused when her hands touched the formal dress she had worn to a dance with Cody. She jammed the hanger to the back of the closet.

Next, she snatched the toiletry bag her mother had given her two years ago when she left for college. Kathleen filled it with random items from her dressing table and the bathroom and scanned the room for anything she had forgotten to pack. Her eyes fell on the pink teddy bear Cody gave her in 1966, the first year they dated when she was a freshman in high school, and he was a sophomore. Leaving it, she tied her knot-filled hair into a ponytail with a rubber band she'd found on her dressing table.

Pushing a knitted hat onto her head, Kathleen pulled on her wool WVU letter jacket and stuffed her feet into sneakers, then growled when she realized she'd not put on socks. Starting over, she remedied the situation. Grabbing the suitcase, Kathleen rushed down the two-flights of stairs to the lobby. Stopping at the reception desk, she wrote a brief note to the housemother and dropped it into the message box.

Once out the door, she gasped. The air was frigid and the rain from the night before had turned into snow. Rats! She'd forgotten her car was in the shop. Leaving the suitcase inside the door, she raced back upstairs and called the auto repair shop, then for a taxi to take her there. Before leaving the room a second time, she retrieved the teddy bear—a reminder of sweet times.

Outside, she paused when she realized there were no students scurrying about as usual. The eerie quiet thundered in her ears. When a lone student passed by her, she shouted out, "Hey, where is everybody?"

"Haven't you heard? Classes are canceled because of yesterday's crash," she responded, pulling her wool cap lower on her head. "I'm headed to find lunch somewhere. The cafeteria is closed. Gotta go. The news said the snow will get heavier later today." The girl stuffed her hands into her coat pockets and hurried on.

Was it only yesterday? Visions of the sight threatened to pull her down to the wet ground. *Get ahold of yourself, girl. You've a long drive ahead and in snowy conditions.* Kathleen realized this was her first rational thought since she woke.

She was unlocking her car door when she heard a voice.

"Kathleen, wait. I've brought you lunch. Maybe we could talk a min... wait, are you leaving?" Walt glanced at the suitcase in her free hand.

"I'm going home for a few days," she answered in a sad voice.

"Home? Aren't you staying for the campuswide memorial service tomorrow? And the joint funeral service for the seven unidentified bodies?" Walt questioned. "Then please stay long enough for lunch. I need to talk to you about something."

Kathleen stared at the bag and drinks in Walt's hands and crawled into her car without replying.

She concentrated on the wet road leading off the

campus while trying to keep Walt's words from her head. At University Highway 152, she turned south and headed home. Usually, she loved the winding road that took her home, but today it required slow and deliberate attention not to go pummeling into one of the canyons between the mountains. Thirty minutes later, she looked at her gas tank. "Dang it!"

The sign for the town of Wayne was barely visible in the heavy snowfall when she pulled into the first gas station. The attendant was at her window almost immediately.

Kathleen rolled down the window just far enough to speak. "Fill her up, please." She sat in the car thinking about what it would be like when she arrived at home. Her thoughts crashed into each other until they landed on one word—pity. How could she face that on top of the guilt she had over her breakup with Cody? *I can't go home.*

"Ma'am, ma'am! You're all set," the attendant said as he rapped on the window.

"Oh, sorry. What do I owe you?"

"Eight dollars and thirty cents. Any more miles and it would have been more like $10.00. You were nearly empty," he said, still smiling even though he stood in freezing temperatures.

Kathleen shoved the money through the half-opened window and started the car without responding to the young man's "Thanks, and you come back."

On the edge of the asphalt, Kathleen looked down the road leading home and turned her car north, retracing the route she'd just traveled.

Chapter 6

By the time Kathleen reached US Interstate 64, she had a plan. She pulled in at a Shoney's Restaurant for three things: a bathroom break, a cheeseburger with fries, and a payphone.

She'd deal with the most difficult one first—the call home. As soon as she walked through the door of the restaurant, she spotted a phone on the back wall and hurried to it.

After putting a dime in the slot, Kathleen quickly dialed her parents' number before she lost her nerve. She hoped to hear her mom's voice, not her father's.

Kathleen's father had been a prisoner of war during the Korean War. When he finally came home, broken and racked with anxiety, it was her mom who had seen him through the nightmares, the extended silences, and the bouts of crying. With her sweet spirit, she reminded him of the love of Jesus and how he could lean on the Savior.

Her dad slowly improved, and by the time Kathleen was a year old, he was back at his role as superintendent of the coal mine in Farrowlee. The miners and their families couldn't believe the change in him. Before he left for the war, he had been distant and demanding, with no regard to the miners' needs. Afterward, he treated his employees as family and took every opportunity to make their lives better.

Kathleen knew her plan to run away would send him into a frenzy. Even though he was a changed man after he returned from the war, he was still furiously protective of her and Mom.

The phone rang three times before her mom answered. "Hello."

Her stiff shoulders relaxed slightly when she heard her mother's voice. "Mom, it's me," Kathleen whispered.

"Who is it?" Emily spoke louder into the phone.

Kathleen raised her voice over the din from the diners. "It's Kathleen."

"Where are you, honey? We're expecting you within the hour."

"That's just it, Mom. I'm not coming home. I don't know where I'm going, but it won't be Farrowlee or Marshall University."

A full thirty seconds went by before Emily responded. "But, sweetheart, you can't just leave. Where will you go? And what about Cody's—"

"Mom, I'm hanging up now. I'm having trouble hearing you." Kathleen hung up the phone and leaned against the wall.

Her limbs felt leaden and the sting of tears hit her eyelids. *Pull yourself together, girl. You can't burst into tears in front of all these diners.* She pushed herself to a standing position and willed her feet to move. Inside the ladies' bathroom, she ducked into a stall, flipped down the toilet cover, and sat there until the threat of tears was gone and her heartbeat moved to a normal range.

Memories of her childhood swirled through her mind. She thought of how she raced halfway down the hill from their house to meet her father as he walked home from the mine. He'd ask about her day and she'd ask about his. And how Mom always waited by the front door, smiling.

Kathleen shook her head to erase the scenes from her mind. She was on her own now. As soon as she exited the bathroom, a waitress approached her.

"Honey, you look as lost as a little kitten. Can I show you to a table?" She had gray hair and a full, curvy figure. Her friendly smile almost broke Kathleen.

She nodded, afraid to trust her voice, and followed the woman to a nearby booth.

"I'm Thelma. Here's the menu. Peek at it while I get your drink. We have a great root-beer float."

Kathleen responded quickly. "I already know what I want—a cheeseburger and a Dr Pepper." She realized how urgent she must sound. She slowed down her speech and said, "I'm in a hurry."

Thelma's smile bent into a frown. "Sweetheart, is everything okay? You seem very flustered. Anything I or maybe our sheriff could help you with?"

Kathleen knew she needed to calm down before things became sticky. "Oh, no. I'm just tired and hope to make it to Charlestown before dark."

With a slight tip of her head, Thelma continued to investigate. "You headed home, or visiting a friend?"

"I'm headed home," Kathleen lied. The woman's barrage of questions was causing the anger just under her surface to rise. She produced the prettiest fake smile she could muster. "My parents don't like me to drive after dark."

"In that case, I'll put a rush on your order." The waitress said with squinted eyes, communicating to Kathleen she didn't believe a word.

Maybe I should tell her to make it a takeout order? No, that would make her even more suspicious. What had been a small headache ratcheted up to a full-blown ten. She dug a couple of aspirins out of her purse to take as soon as her drink arrived.

"Here you are, dear." Thelma said, as she placed a mammoth-sized burger in front of her. "I put your drink in a to-go cup so you'll have something for your drive. Can I interest you in a piece of apple pie? Plenty of truck drivers claim it to be the best on US 64."

"No, thank you. I have a candy bar in my car." She lied again, wishing the lady would leave her alone.

"Oh, which one is your car?" Thelma asked, straining to see the parking lot.

Does this woman ever stop? A third lie slipped through her lips like melted butter. "That blue, two-door Chevy." She'd spotted it when she came into the restaurant. Hoping Thelma had finished her interrogation, she took a large bite of her burger.

"Well, have a safe trip home." Thelma responded as she placed a ticket on the table. "Pay at the register."

Kathleen mumbled a thank you through a mouthful of food. When she finished, she grabbed her aspirins and took them with a big drink of Dr Pepper. Fifteen minutes later, she was back on the road.

The lights of Charleston could be seen several miles from the city limits. Too many slow trucks made it impossible for her to make it to her destination before dusk. Destination? Where would that be? She'd only planned to get to Charleston, not what she'd do once she was in the city.

She thought again about the "emergency fund" money her mother had given her every time she left for school after a visit home. Kathleen had never used it and planned to give it back to her mother when she graduated. In two years, it had become a bird's nest that would provide her a few nights in a motel and beyond.

She began looking for a place where she'd feel safe. After passing three different ones, she picked the fourth, *Do Drop Inn*, because it looked safer than the others.

Kathleen pulled her car into the drive-through in front of the office. She stared at the clerk behind the check-in counter and heaved a sigh of relief. She'd envisioned a parolee with a bracelet around his ankle.

The night clerk was a grandmotherly type with short, permed hair sprinkled with gray. She wore a print dress with a princess-style collar and covered buttons down the front. A thin belt circled her wide girth at the waist. She looked like Aunt Bea from Mayberry, RFD.

Kathleen giggled, then clamped her hand over her mouth. It seemed irreverent to laugh after what had happened. Pulling her purse from the passenger seat, she exited the car, locked it, and looked around. She headed for the glass door at a fast clip, head down.

This was a first—checking into a motel alone. Kathleen steeled herself with determination. Whatever happened in the days ahead, nothing could be more terrifying than the last two days. With a force greater than necessary, she pushed the door open and approached the check-in counter.

"Hello, dear. How can I help you?"

The kindness spoken by her eyes took Kathleen unaware. She paused, hoping the tears that had taken up residence behind her eyes would not betray her. "I …uh… I need a room?" The statement came out like a question. She felt her cheeks burn with redness.

"You're blessed. I only have two rooms left. How about I put you in the one closest to the office? It has the best outside lighting." The clerk turned around and pulled a room key from a hook on the wall. "That'll be $19.50 for the night."

Kathleen fished the cash from her wallet. Her hands shook when she made the payment.

"You know, dear. There's no reason to be frightened. I'm here until midnight, then Clarence, our security guard, will park close to your room."

Now tears that had held off flooded her eyes.

The clerk grabbed a tissue for her and said, "My name is Mary Anderson. Here is my home number." She grabbed a notepad and scribbled her name and number. "I don't know how long you plan to stay in our city, but if you need anything, please call me."

She could only nod as she took the slip of paper. Back in her car, she checked the number on the placard that held her room key. Room 103. She checked the row of rooms and saw hers was right beside the office, just as Mary had stated.

Once inside her room, she looked around. It resembled a motel room similar to many she'd seen on *Dragnet.* A single bed with what had once been a maroon bedspread, now a faded pinkish color, was pushed up against the wall. A metal clothes rack stood on the short wall leading into a bathroom with a small sink, tub, and plastic shower curtain with ocean waves and flamingoes scattered on it. Next to the bed sat a small desk that did double duty as a bedside table. But it would do. She went back to her car and grabbed her suitcases. As a last thought, she grabbed the pink teddy bear.

Kathleen turned the door lock, stepped inside, and quickly strapped the chain into place. Still not feeling secure, she grabbed the chair from the small desk and pushed it onto the underside of the doorknob. Still anxious, she grabbed the bear and held him tightly to her chest.

She lay on the bed, fully clothed and in need of a shower. But her legs wouldn't move. She clinched a pillow with one arm and the teddy bear with the other, eyes glued to the door.

At some point, she drifted off into a fitful sleep, only to be woken by a screeching noise outside her window. She sat straight up in bed, her heart rate hammering in her chest.

Fear propelled her from the bed to the window. She fell to her knees and lifted the edge of the blind. Suddenly, a huge black cat leaped from the outside windowsill. Kathleen fell back on her rear end. She sat on the floor until her breathing returned to normal.

Rising to her knees, she straightened the displaced blind when she noticed a large green Ford truck rolling slowly by her room.

Chapter 7

*W*hen Kathleen woke, the sun was high in the sky and the mist over the mountains had evaporated. At first, she didn't know where she was. Slowly, like the unfolding of a new bloom, she rewound all the events that had brought her to this run-down motel room.

Kathleen lay in bed thinking about what her day should be—take a quick shower, grab her bookbag, and rush to the common cafeteria for a quick breakfast before heading to a full day of classes. When her thoughts moved on to the typical evening, she cringed. She usually met Cody at the student center after football practice to help him with his studies, then they had a quick bite to eat before he walked her back to her dorm. Date nights were rare with both their busy schedules.

Every fiber of her body wanted that life back, yet here she lay in a lumpy bed in the same clothes she'd thrown on yesterday. She turned her head and sniffed under one arm. Phew!

Kathleen reached for her watch on the bedside table. Already 2:30 p.m. Shocked to have slept so late, she stood and turned to the bathroom. After a quick glance at the condition of the tub, she deemed it clean enough.

She flipped the shower knob, turning the hot handle all the way to the right, and climbed over the edge of the tub. Under the spigot, every molecule of her body tingled as her mind skittered through many scenes. Tears shed in great torrents. She moaned, screamed, and whimpered in stages. The water went from hot to lukewarm to cold before she finally stepped out. Though spent physically, she felt better.

After dressing, Kathleen walked the few steps to the motel office. The clerk, a gentle-looking man with a receding hairline and an inviting smile, greeted her.

"Good afternoon. I'm Charles. Are you checking in?" he asked in a strong English accent.

She crossed both arms on her abdomen to counter the attack from her gut. The accent instantly put her in mind of her father. *Will he ever understand what I've done?*

Swallowing several times, she finally responded. "Uh, I'm already a resident. I'd like to add a few more nights, please."

If Charles had questions about Kathleen being young and alone, his manners prevented him from querying her. "Of course. I can book three more nights if that suits you."

A chill walked over Kathleen's body when she pictured herself spending that much time in Room 103 at the Do Drop Inn. Yet she had put on these shoes—now she had to walk in them. "Yes, that would be fine."

She turned to leave, then back to Charles. "Do you have a newspaper I could borrow? I want to check the classified ads."

"I do, love. Just finished it, so please keep it." He reached under the counter and placed it on the counter before continuing. "I hope it's not too imposing to ask if you're looking for a job and what type. The reason I ask is that Lombardi's needs a waitress. It's a diner about five miles from here."

A waitress? Could she be a waitress? She'd never given a thought about what job she'd look for. All she knew how to do was go to class, take notes, and study. She faced another first in her new life.

It was several moments before she realized she was standing silent with her head down, not responding.

Charles folded the newspaper in half and handed it to Kathleen. "Good luck, Miss."

She mumbled a thank you as she turned and left the office with the newspaper crumbled in her left hand.

Back in her room, she spread the paper on the bed and kneeled beside it. It took a moment to find the classifieds. She ran her finger down the page, stopping at the header, *Employment*. The rock in the pit of her stomach grew as she scanned each ad—paralegal, dental hygienist, medical assistant, veterinarian tech, and the list went on. She paused at an ad looking for a housecleaner. "Ugh, I'd rather dig ditches," she said to no one.

Then Kathleen spotted an ad for a waitress.

Lombardi's Diner. She scratched down the address, combed through her unruly hair, grabbed her purse and the newspaper. Rushing back to the office, she laid the paper on the counter and looked at Charles.

"Can you give me the directions to get to Lombardi's?"

"Of course. It's quite easy. Just turn right out of our parking lot and stay on this highway until you see Main Street. Turn left, and it's about two miles down. You can't miss it. It's painted in the colors of the Italian flag."

"Thank you, Charles. You've been very kind." Kathleen's eyes glazed over, wondering when this need to cry would end.

"My pleasure, m'lady." He smiled as he tipped an imaginary hat.

Ten minutes later, Kathleen sat in her car staring at Lombardi's Diner. Charles was correct when he said it couldn't be missed. The bricks were painted red with dark green trim and a stark white double door. Compared to the neutral colors of the other buildings, it stuck out like a frog at a track meet.

She didn't know how to ask for a job and decided being blunt was the best way to go. Shyness overcame her bluntness the moment she walked inside. She searched for a place to sit when she spotted the last booth at the far end. Hurrying to it, she sat on the side that allowed a view of the diner.

Red booths lined three walls with the same color stools placed along the counter. Mounted above the pass-through to the kitchen hung a large Italian flag. Green and white tiles covered the floor. Since it was after the lunch rush, only a few customers were there.

Kathleen looked down at her hands folded on the table as she debated about whether to go or stay.

"Hello, sweetheart. What can I do you for?"

She swiveled her head to the left. A tall, skinny waitress with enough makeup to sink a ship stood patiently waiting for her response. Curly black hair was working its way out of a poorly made bun, despite the abundance of fancy hair pins—everything from bees to sewing machines.

Unable to leave with this woman between her and the door, Kathleen peered at the menu and ordered the first thing she saw—a grilled cheese with a Dr Pepper.

"I'll have this right out. My name's Joselyn, but everyone calls me Jazzy. How about a piece of pie?"

"No, thank you." She watched the server spin around to head for the counter, her hair flying to all points on the compass.

In a short time, Jazzy was back with her order. "Here you go. Is there anything else I can do for you?"

"No... yes. What I mean is—"

Jazzy sat on the other side of the booth, leaning toward her, eye to eye. "Honey, it doesn't take a rocket scientist to know you have something on your mind. You aren't in some kind of trouble, are you?"

"No, nothing like that. I... uh... read in the paper that you had a job opening for a waitress. Is that position still open?" Kathleen worked hard to keep her voice steady.

"It sure is. And the sooner it gets filled, the happier I'll be. Been running my legs off since Cindy left us last week. I'll tell Joe and Bella you're here." She stood and nodded her head at the food. "Eat up, now. Nothing worse than a cold grilled cheese."

Kathleen picked up her sandwich and took a bite, sure she'd never be able to swallow it. To her surprise, it was a delicious combination of cheeses on what had to be fresh-made toasted bread. She found herself not only able to eat it but had to remind herself to slow down.

"Hello. We're Joe and Bella Lombardi. Jazzy tells us you want to apply for our opening," Bella said with a smile as she squeezed her large girth into the booth. Joe scooted in beside her, his face stern.

Kathleen was so wrapped up in her food, she hadn't seen them coming. She held one finger in the air as she grabbed her drink to wash down the bite of sandwich. "Excuse me. I was enjoying the food."

"So, tell us what experience you have as a waitress," Joe said in a heavy Italian accent.

"I don't have any experience, unless you count how many hours I spent in diners while in college." Kathleen hoped it didn't sound as flippant to them as it did to her.

Bella and Joe passed a look between each other, then Joe's gaze turned back to Kathleen. "I think my wife wants to give you a chance and what Bella wants, Bella gets." He shrugged his shoulders and continued. "So, we try you for a few weeks and see how it goes." He shook a finger in her face. "But no breaking Joe's dishes." He leaned in and placed the tips of all ten fingers on the table. "Capisce?"

Kathleen nodded her head, unable to think of a suitable response.

"Good, you start tomorrow. We see how no experience works out. Heh?" He slid out of the booth without saying another word.

Chapter 8

"Don't worry." Bella laid her hand on Kathleen's arm. "He seems gruff, but he has the heart of a kitten." Her accent was much less pronounced than her husband's. "I'll bring you a uniform. Get up and stand in the aisle."

Surprised but determined to be compliant, Kathleen stood, feeling foolish.

Bella looked at her from head to toe. "A size eight should fit you. I have two of them already washed and ironed. Joe's mama, Nonna, lives with us and she does this for me, and a lot more. She's a saint, God bless her soul. Sit back down and finish your sandwich. I'll bring you some cannoli. I make them myself. Don't tell my Joe, but they're better than Nonna's." She gave Kathleen a wink and hefted her body from the booth.

Kathleen carefully laid her uniforms in the back of her car and pulled out of the parking lot. Another first—she had a job.

Then the past few days rushed through her brain, each one playing like a short teaser on a local news station. *"Local firefighter saves puppy from drainage pipe. More on this story when we return."* Or *"Investigation is ongoing in the Tri-County crash. Hear the latest on tragedy after this advertisement."*

Guilt filtered into her being like flour through a sieve, reminding her why she'd left Marshall State. Now, a new regret settled over her. She'd also left her home in Farrowlee.

Her hands tightened on the steering wheel as resolve returned with the determination to make her new life work, one not involving the pain of her recent past.

Honk! Honk!

Kathleen jerked her head up. She was first in line at a traffic light that had turned green. How long had she sat there? Where was she?

Quickly driving through the intersection, she pulled into a convenience store on her immediate right. Inside, Kathleen searched the map selection lined up at the bottom of the counter until she found a street map of Charleston.

She laid three quarters on the counter and shook her head when the cashier asked if she'd like a bag. When had she stopped talking to or even looking strangers in the eyes? Was this another part of grief?

Determined to stay focused, she opened the map on the hood of her car and searched for a street sign. Maple Street. Yes, it would take her the direction she needed to go. Satisfied, she returned to the driver's seat, turning her car around in the parking lot until she could exit on Maple.

Ten minutes later, she arrived at the highway. One right turn and she was back at the Do Drop Inn. Crisis averted, she parked in the same spot in front of room 103 and hurried to the office.

"Hello, you look like you have news," Charles said.

"I have the job at Lombardi's. I start tomorrow." She gave him a genuine smile. The first in three days.

"Well done!" He smiled back. "What's next?"

"Uh, look for an apartment?"

"Good answer." He reached beneath the counter and placed another newspaper in her hand. "I just finished the crossword puzzle. You might find an apartment in there, although I warn you, there aren't many to choose from and they're on the expensive side."

"Thank you, Charles." She paused, then said, "And thank you for being so nice to me."

His smile disappeared with his response. "Being nice is far easier than being hurt or angry. There's a word in today's crossword that reminded me of you—tenacious. A good quality if you let it lead you down the right path."

Her lips pressed together firmly, and she left with the impression he knew more about her life than she had told him.

She craved college life where everything was orderly, and she knew exactly what path she'd be on each day. Until that moment, she hadn't considered how much she loved her classes and looked forward to getting a degree.

Back in the room, Kathleen opened the newspaper to the apartment rentals. Disappointed by the lack of choices and the cost, she refolded the paper and sighed heavily. She eyed the crumbled piece of paper she'd tossed on the bedside table the night before. Reaching for it, she smoothed the note on her knee. *Mary Rose Anderson.* Kathleen grabbed the phone's receiver and dialed the number on the note before she chickened out.

A voice came with the first ring. "Hello. Mary Rose speaking. The Lord has given us a beautiful day to praise His creation."

Kathleen moved the phone to hang up. She didn't want to hear from a Bible-thumper, but something pulled the receiver back to her ear.

"Uh… this is Kathleen. We met last night when I checked in at the Do Drop Inn. Do you remember me?" She held her breath, half-wishing the woman would hang up on her.

"Of course I remember you. I've been waiting for your call."

Waiting for my call? How can that be? She paused long enough for Mary Rose to speak again.

"I just made a coffee cake expecting your visit. Why don't you come over and we'll have coffee and a delightful visit?"

Wait. Was she really being asked to make a visit? "Well, I thought I could speak with you on the phone to see if you might know of—"

"Oh no, dear. Our conversation is much too important for a phone visit. I'm taking the cake out right now. Come while it's still warm."

"Okay," her voice squeaked out a response,

wondering if she'd fallen down the rabbit hole and would soon meet the Mad Hatter.

"Wonderful. Turn left onto the highway and exit where the crepe myrtles grow. They look like twigs this time of year, but in the summer, they have lovely soft pink blossoms. I live on Lavender Street, third street past Parsley Lane. Just look for the rose sign."

Kathleen hung up and stuffed the piece of paper into her pocket in case she couldn't find the address. She picked up her purse and stepped out into the sunlight. Walking to her car, she repeated, "Crepe myrtles, Lavender, and Parsley," hoping no one could hear her.

True to Mary's words, Kathleen found the exit with the row of dormant crepe myrtles and was soon turning onto Lavender Street. She braked her car when she spotted a wooden sign with a single red rose painted on it and the words *Rose Garden Boarding House*. With her jaw gaped, she noticed the sidewalk to a pale yellow Victorian house. On both sides of the sidewalk and encircling the house were rows of rose bushes, meticulously pruned, waiting for spring.

Kathleen rolled forward until she could turn into the circle drive. She stopped her car when she noticed Mary walk out the front door, looking much like the night before but with the addition of an apron and a colorful flower scarf over her hair. She waved her guest to come inside, then turned and reentered her house.

Kathleen sat anchored to her seat while air spewed from her lungs. After a moment, she inhaled and spoke to her clinched hands. "I have no idea what's happening here. This can't possibly be a place to live." Then she remembered Charles's words about a path.

Mary reappeared in the entryway. "Well, come on then. Coffee's dripping."

Unlocking her door, Kathleen slid out and walked, eyes down, up the sidewalk. When she moved her sight to the door, Mary had disappeared again. She paused at the threshold, then stepped through into the most sunlit house she'd ever seen. Plants flourished on every windowsill and table. To the left, overstuffed furniture, crocheted dollies, and kick-knacks of every sort filled the living room.

Kathleen couldn't help thinking about her grandmother's living room in England, where she visited every summer as a child.

"Come straight down the hallway. I'm in the kitchen."

She moved forward, glancing at the pictures and framed cross-stitch scriptures that covered the hallway like wallpaper.

"There you are. Have a place at the table," Mary said as she poured two steaming cups of coffee.

Kathleen sat down, staring at the mug her hostess put down in front of her. The aroma hit her nose as she clamped her hand around the warm cup. She'd missed the comforting drink. Her friends often went to a coffeehouse near campus when their classes were over.

Mary placed a large piece of cake in front of Kathleen. She stared at it as tears threatened to show up once again. Why was this stranger showing such kindness to her? She lifted a hand from her lap and took the fork. The first bite was a combination of sweet vanilla, savory cinnamon, and home. Kathleen took a drink of coffee and continued eating the delicious cake while listening to Mary rattle on about the weather and her roses.

Cake finished, she held her fork in her hand and asked, "Why are you being so kind to me?"

Mary smiled and reached across the table, placing her hand over Kathleen's free one. "Because you're one of God's children, and if God loves you, so do I." She removed her hand and pushed back from the table. "Now, let me show my new boarder her room."

Chapter 9

Kathleen banged on the bedside table trying to find the alarm clock, which had to be the loudest one in West Virginia. Wham! Her hand finally found its mark. In the silent motel room, she moaned and pulled her covers over her head, fully prepared to drift back to sleep. Her next thought jolted her into a sitting position. She checked the time on the clock—5:30 a.m. She had exactly one hour before she started her new job.

Her fingers knotted together as fear wound its way through her body and the phrase *no experience* shot from her brain. In less than twenty-four hours, she'd found employment and somewhere to live. Next, she needed to prove she could do the waitressing job. It was overwhelming. How did that saying go? Just go with the flow.

Kathleen pushed back the covers and put her feet on the cold linoleum. Sprinting to the bathroom, she jumped into a hot shower, dressed, and was out the door within thirty minutes.

She met Charles on the walkway outside the rooms. "Congratulations on finding a place to live. He always provides." He kept moving as Kathleen stared at his back.

Her eyebrows clinched as she mumbled a weak, "Thanks." *How did he know I found a place to live?*

Kathleen pulled into the diner's parking lot with exactly five minutes to spare, amazed she felt so calm, as if wearing the uniform would make her a waitress. She pulled her coat tighter and stepped into the early-morning coldness.

When she pulled open the large white door, the aroma of bacon and vanilla wafted into the cold air. She stood inside the door, wondering what to do next.

"Good morning, sunshine," Jazzy said from a nearby booth where she worked to fill salt and pepper shakers. "Put your coat on the hook in the back room, and there's a locker for your purse. You're on napkin duty. Collect the holders from each table and make sure they're full." She never took her eyes off the saltshakers. "We open at seven and usually have a large breakfast crowd. Bella's pancakes are a wonder to behold."

"I thought I smelled vanilla," Kathleen remarked.

Bella lifted her head from where she was whisking a huge pan of pancake batter. "Look, Joe. Our new help has arrived."

Joe grunted and never looked up from the massive amount of bacon frying on the grill.

Kathleen gave them a slight wave and headed back to work on the napkins. The day flew by in a blur of big mistakes and minor victories. The worst was when she cleared a table and dropped a plate.

When he heard the crash, Joe stuck his head out of the kitchen. "Humph!" he commented, shaking his head.

Jazzy appeared at her side with a broom and scoop. "Don't worry, honey. We've all broken dishes, including Joe."

Shortly after noon, an older gentleman entered the diner and headed for the booth in the back—the same one Kathleen had sat at yesterday.

"That's Owen," Jazzy said, nodding toward the man. "He comes in every day for a late lunch. Why don't you take his order?"

"Is he particular? Maybe you should—"

"No, something tells me he might be exactly what you need."

Confused, Kathleen took her order pad from her pocket and approached the booth. "Hello, what would you like today?"

She raised her eyes from her order pad when no reply came. The man was staring at her—not rudely, more like an assessment of who stood before him.

The gray hair and the lines making pathways across his face signified he had age on him. But his hazel eyes caused a hitch in her breath. Never had she met anyone with such a calm, peaceful look. For the first time since the crash, she wanted to know a stranger.

Maybe he couldn't hear well. "What would you like from the menu?" she asked in a voice two decimals above normal.

She watched his wrinkles become more pronounced as a grin spread cross his lips.

"No need to yell, young lady. I heard you the first time. Please excuse me for staring. I was trying to decide if we would become friends."

Kathleen had no idea how to respond, so she pointed to the menu.

"Oh, of course. I should order. I'll have my Wednesday usual."

Baffled, Kathleen gave him a pleading look. She needed to show Jazzy and the owners she could handle this customer.

"I'll have the meatballs and spaghetti with salad and Italian bread."

Relieved, she scribbled down his order and hurried back to the counter when she realized she'd forgotten to take his drink order. She turned panicked eyes toward Jazzy, who'd heard the entire exchange.

"Don't worry. He always orders a cup of hot tea. You did fine."

Kathleen delivered the cup of tea, hoping her shaking hands didn't spill the hot substance on the man. "I'll be back with your order soon," she said, as she successfully placed the drink in front of him.

"Please call me Owen. Thank you for the tea. I'm sure Jazzy filled you in on what I always drink. Old habits are hard to break."

His accent seemed familiar to Kathleen. She'd heard it from many of the miners back in Farrowlee. But she couldn't place it. She pushed back the thought, not wanting to think about home.

"I'm Kathleen. This is my first day."

"I would have never guessed that. You're doing a fine job."

She smiled, touched by the compliment. *Maybe I can do this*. The heavy cloak that had weighed her down for the past days seemed lighter.

By the end of her shift, every muscle in her body begged for a rest. With Jazzy's help, she'd made it through her first day.

When she retrieved her coat and purse, she turned to find Joe standing behind her. "So, maybe tomorrow you won't break any dishes."

Tomorrow? Even with the many stumbles she'd made, Kathleen still had a job. She left the diner with a sense of accomplishment.

She rolled her window down when she pulled away from Lombardi's. The fresh cold air was a welcome relief from the cooking smells in the diner. She'd love to take her stiff muscles for a jog, something she did almost daily back on campus.

Then she remembered—she was moving to The Rose Garden Boarding House today. She groaned, wondering if she'd regret her decision to become one of Mary's boarders. Kathleen pressed the gas petal. Might as well get it done and over with. In short order, the few things she'd taken into the hotel room were loaded into her car. She entered the office, holding her room key, hoping Charles would be there so she could say goodbye.

This thought stopped her in her tracks. Two days ago, she didn't want to even look at anyone, much less speak to them. Still, she knew that deep in her soul, a volcano lay simmering. Grief, hurt, regret, and anger each had its own smoldering rock.

The sunlight was waning when she entered the circle drive at the boarding house. She had so many questions. Where do the other boarders park? Would they all eat together? Would it be like a sorority house where everyone was all cuddly and acted like family? Kathleen hoped not.

She tugged her bag from the trunk of her car when the porch light came on. Mary came down the path to Kathleen's car. "Here, let me help you carry something in."

Kathleen responded by placing her dirty-clothes bag into her landlady's waiting arms, then berated herself. *What if it stinks?* If it did, Mary didn't seem to notice.

"Dinner's at six. I hope you like beef stew with homemade biscuits," Mary said when they stopped in the foyer. "I'll put your laundry bag on the washer. It and the dryer are just off the kitchen. Use them anytime. I'll let you get settled in now."

Kathleen started up the stairs, then turned around, "Mary," she asked, "Where do the other boarders park?"

"Oh, God only sends me one boarder at a time. The last one He sent was late last year. Poor child. She only stayed for three months, but we had some wonderful conversations. I think she left on the right path."

Did everyone in Charleston talk about paths? More questions with no answer.

Before Mary left for the kitchen, Kathleen asked another question. "What time do you leave for your shift at the motel?" She wasn't looking forward to staying in the old house alone.

"Shift?" Mary's forehead wrinkled. "Oh, you think I work at the motel? I was helping my nephew. His wife thought she was going into labor with their fourth. False alarm. I'm his backup when he needs off. I'd rather be behind the counter at the Do Drop Inn than caring for his kids. They're a handful." She paused before stating, "I'm glad I was there the night you checked in. Providential, don't you think?"

Chapter 10

Kathleen woke before the alarm went off, glad to be rid of the reoccurring dream about planes crashing into mountains. She slid out of the warm covers, grabbed the top blanket from the bed, and tiptoed across the cold floor to peek out the window. Unbelievable! The forecast said there would be a sprinkling of snow. There had to be at least four inches on the ground.

She put on her robe and slippers and tiptoed down the hall to the bathroom. The shower made a growling noise when she turned on the spigot. She hoped it didn't wake Mary.

In Charleston for two weeks, Kathleen had adjusted to her job and living in the boarding house. She often went to the park beside the Kanawha River that ran through the city where she watched the children play and the older gentlemen fishing. Wondering through Woolworth's on Capitol Street, she tried to fill her thoughts with the present. Anything to occupy her mind.

But she still struggled not to think of her past. Her pain sprang up again and again, sometimes making it difficult to endure Mary's endless cheery chatter, especially when she turned the conversation to God.

Shivering when she turned off the hot water, Kathleen grabbed the towel for a quick dry-off before putting her robe and slippers back on, then rubbed her hand across the steamy mirror and spoke to herself. "I can't believe I have to drive to work in this snow." She'd started talking to herself when loneliness walked around with her like an unwanted friend. Speaking out loud helped.

Back in her room, she dressed in her uniform, then put on her warmest coat and a pair of rubber boots. She shoved her working shoes into her large macramé bag and tiptoed down the stairs. She was almost out the door before hearing a voice from the kitchen.

"Good morning, love. God has blessed us with a beautiful snowfall. When the sun shines next, we'll see a splendid sight of glistening snow, almost as breathtaking as the sights of heaven." Mary appeared in the doorway and said, "Come on, dear. I've made a big pot of oatmeal and some cinnamon toast. Something that will stick with you in this weather."

Kathleen rolled her eyes. Did this woman ever sleep? She knew there would be no escaping the fuss Mary would make if she didn't do as requested. It always amazed her how her landlady could reprimand her in such a loving way.

She woofed down the oatmeal and toast

half-listening to Mary's chatter about how good the snow was for her rose bushes. "They'll get an extra dose of water when it melts."

Kathleen put down her spoon, unable to finish her food. She had to escape all the prattling. *How can anyone be happy about four inches of snow?* "I must leave, Mary. It's going to take longer to drive in this snow and I can't be late."

"Of course, dear." Mary nodded. "Though not many customers will brave this weather. It's snowing again."

Ugh! Kathleen pulled the hood of her coat over her head. With only a nod to Mary, she walked out the doorway and stopped on the porch. Frigid air hit her face and hands. She wished she'd remembered her gloves but didn't dare go back inside. Kathleen could take no more of her landlady's cherry disposition when she felt so grumpy.

The porch suddenly filled with light when the front door open. Mary stepped onto the porch and smiled. "Here's a pair of my gloves. Godspeed." With that, she turned and hurried out of the cold.

Kathleen stared at the gloves in her hand as her eyes moistened. Any act of kindness made her want to cry and, worst of all, tell her story. She knew she could never do that. What would the new people in her life think of her?

Gloves on, she stepped off the porch, surprised to find the sidewalk shoveled. Surely, Mary hadn't come out and done this before she was even awake. When she arrived at her car, an ice scraper lay in the hood. Who put this here? So many strange things had happened to her since she arrived in Charlestown—things she couldn't explain. She grabbed the scraper and attacked the ice on the windshield.

After scraping the front, side, and rear windows, she jumped into her car and turned over the key. Nothing but a growl. "Come on, Bug. Don't fail me today." She waited a moment and tried again. This time, the car's engine hummed. She looked back at the house to see Mary, head down, standing in the front window.

She pushed the stick to drive position and left with such force the tires spun and the little car bounced twice before it moved forward.

Her ten-minute drive turned into twenty because of the icy roads and falling snow. Fortunately, the snowplows had already made their pass on the streets. By the time she arrived at Lombardi's, her hands cramped from their tight grip on the wheel. Kathleen pushed open the door of the restaurant, depositing snow from her coat and boots all over the green-and-white floor. She looked around to see if Joe was watching.

"Well, welcome. We didn't think you'd brave the weather to come in today," Jazzy said from the place where she sat filling the salt and pepper shakers. "Don't worry about the snow on the floor. If we get any customers in this mess, they'll be track it in as well."

"I'm late," Kathleen whispered, looking toward the kitchen where pots and pans banged around.

"Don't worry about that, either. Joe and Bella will just be happy you're here."

As if on cue, Bella walked from the kitchen. "Child, I can't believe you braved this weather to come in. Thank you. If the snow stops, we're hoping for our usual crowd." She walked as she spoke and soon had Kathleen locked in a bear hug.

"Uh… I'd better get to work before Jazzy starts fussing about the napkins not being ready." She freed herself from the hug. Human touch was not something she welcomed now.

"The chances of having any breakfast customers are about as slim as me winning the state lottery," Jazzy commented, then looked at Kathleen. "Why don't you give the tables and booths a good cleaning, and I'll do some cleaning in the stockroom?"

This was fine with Kathleen. She didn't want to go through the kitchen to the stockroom with Joe in there. She wasn't convinced he'd be okay with her late arrival at work.

Just then, he walked out of the kitchen and took a few steps toward her. "Bravo, donna forte." He twirled around and headed back to his kitchen.

Bella came out next. "He just said 'good.' And he called you a strong woman. He is a nice guy, yes?"

Kathleen, mouth agape, could only nod. Then, the door opened, bringing a gust of wind and their first customer. She grabbed her order pad and followed him to a table.

The next three hours offered only a sprinkling of those who wished for Bella's pancakes more than they minded the weather. By mid-morning, Kathleen sat on a stool wondering what to do next.

She spotted the large calendar that hung on the wall at the end of the counter. Jazzy had flipped it to December. Relief made a journey through her body. Now she didn't have to look at the date of the crash. It was no longer November, with all the pain that month held.

Then her eyes moved to the end of the month. December 25th. She'd been with her parents every Christmas of her life. What would her Christmas be like this year?

Before lunch, the snowstorm had moved on. The sun fought with the lingering clouds to shine. Kathleen was peering out a window when the sky cleared. The snow glistened and sparkled just as Mary had said. But she knew that in just a matter of time, it would be brown and ugly with dirt from crowds trampling it. It suited her mood to think about it that way. Her life had become messy, like dirty snow.

She looked at Jazzy, who was also peering out the window. "Hey, looks like our first lunch customer is here. There's a truck pulling into the parking lot."

Kathleen returned her gaze to the window and watched as a green truck drove slowly through the parking lot, then turned around and exited the same way it had entered.

Sudden fear caused her breath to stick in her throat. Was it the same green truck she'd seen her first night in Charleston?

Chapter 11

"That's our lunch wrap," Jazzy stated. "Not a bad crowd, given the weather."

Kathleen bent to pick up the dustpan from the floor, then straightened and looked out at the snow while shoving a strand of hair behind one ear. She stopped sweeping and leaned on the broom to glance at the big clock over the door. Two more hours and she'd be on her way home. She astonished herself by considering the boarding house as home. Would she ever feel at home anywhere again?

She jerked around when their faithful customer, Owen, appeared in the doorway. "You're here," she commented while she followed him to his booth.

"Where I was raised, this snow is only an insignificant blip." Owen smiled and added, "But an extra-large cup of tea would be nice on a day like this." He shed his coat and removed his scarf and wool hat. "I came because it's part of my routine. My wife taught me that doing the same things in the same way is good. Life is easier if one isn't bouncing around like a ball in a Ping-Pong machine. That and Joe's good cooking is why I come here every day."

Kathleen noticed the shadow that crossed his face each time he mentioned his wife. She assumed the woman must have died. Since her first day, she'd been his waitress. He always said something that would come to her thoughts at night when sleep eluded her. Sometimes his words felt like a compliment, but others seemed to be an admonishment. She often felt he could see right through her.

"I'll have—"

"I know. It'll be lasagna because it's Tuesday."

"That's correct. It's Tuesday." Owen smiled. "And Wednesday will be?"

"Meatloaf."

"Very good. You're an excellent student!"

Kathleen smiled, but it left her quickly as she thought of being a student at Marshall University. She missed learning. "I'll get this order put in and be back with your tea." As much as she liked Owen, she wished he'd leave his thoughts at the door. They haunted her— as if he knew her better than she knew herself.

Kathleen placed Owen's drink on his table, then twirled around when the door burst open and three rowdy college-aged boys entered. They sat at the booth near the entrance.

"Where's our service?" the largest boy questioned, thumping the table.

"Be right there," Jazzy yelled over their din of chatter.

They looked at Jazzy and laughed. The short one

with long hair spoke up. "No way! We'll take that one." He pointed at Kathleen with a grin that turned her stomach.

"Be careful. I suspect they're stoned," Owen whispered as he stared at the boys in the booth.

Kathleen wondered how Owen even knew the word *stoned*. She wasn't worried. *Get their order and get away as quickly as possible.*

She went to their booth, standing slightly farther back than usual. Kathleen asked in an even voice, "What can I get for you to drink?" She laid three menus on the edge of the table.

The long-haired boy, dressed in a tie-dyed T-shirt and a jacket with long fringe down the bottom of each arm and across the bottom, spoke first. "Well, sweetheart, you can start by coming closer to the booth. You're out there in no-man's-land. I'm Tommy and we call him Moose." He pointed to the large one who wore flared, plaid pants with a jacket that bore a peace sign. "That's Kenny." He jerked his thumb at the one sitting on the inside of the booth next to Moose. "Why don't you step up and tell us who you are?"

Sighing, Kathleen took a step forward and repeated her question, not offering her name.

Kenny, who had a huge afro and wore a shirt with a Nehru collar, responded first. "I'll take a root-beer float and a large order of fries."

Moose jabbed him in the ribs. "Not so fast. We want to keep this beauty here as long as possible." He reached out and put his hand on Kathleen's arm.

She snatched it away and said in an icy voice, "I'm assuming you two jokers want nothing. I'll get your friend's order going." She started walking away when

Tommy leaned out of the booth and squeezed her by the waist, pulling her closer to him.

Joe was at the table before she could jerk away. He grabbed Tommy's arm with his massive hand, squeezing it hard. "I think it's time for you to leave."

Tommy released Kathleen and wriggled his arm from Joe's grip. "Take it easy, old man. We're just having some fun." None of the three made a move to leave.

"Bella," Joe yelled. "Call the police."

Everyone could hear the slow rotation of the rotary phone as Bella made the call.

"Wait a minute," Kenny said, holding a palm in the air. "We're leaving. Let's go, guys. This man means business."

The boys scrambled out of the booth and headed for the door. Turning back to Kathleen, Moose grinned and said, "Don't worry. We hang around in this area all the time. We'll see you again, pretty girl." He winked and exited to join his buddies.

Bella hung up the phone as Joe looked at Kathleen with eyes that seemed to say *I'm sorry*. He went to the kitchen, muttering a string of words in Italian.

Jazzy walked to where Kathleen stood. "I'm sorry, honey. You didn't deserve that. Don't let it bother you," she whispered, giving her a sideways hug.

"Don't let it bother me? Are you serious? Did you not hear one of them threatening to find me?" The loud words spewed from her mouth. "How can I feel safe now?" She suddenly realized she hadn't felt out of harm's way since the day of the crash. Now a new fear had a face—three hippies from Charleston.

Kathleen heard Owen's voice as if it came through

a tunnel. Her ears still rang from the unsettling dialog. She turned to see him pointing to the pass-through.

"My order is ready, if you'd be so kind as to deliver it."

Kind? The last thing she wanted was to be kind. Every fiber of her body needed to scream and throw something. Kathleen took a deep, slow breath and gathered Owen's order.

At the table, he motioned for her to sit on the bench across from him. "Since I'm your only customer, Joe and Bella won't mind if you sit with me for a bit."

She raised one eyebrow and set her lips in a firm line, not wanting any more of Owen's thoughts. But when Kathleen saw the care in his face, she glanced back at Jazzy, who nodded and disappeared to the back. She slid into the booth and peered at her folded hands.

"Kathleen, what those young boys did wasn't fair. This life is never fair, but God always is." Owen paused, then spoke in a low, compassionate voice. "Your eyes hold a great sadness even when you smile. I suspect you've had a tragic event in your past. But I'll save that for another time."

She lifted her eyes, anger and humiliation boiling inside her. Silent tears coursed down her cheeks.

Reaching for a napkin from the holder, he handed it to her.

Kathleen wiped her face, then drew in a breath. Her tears dried up as if someone had closed a main waterline. "My past is my past—one I don't plan to share," she declared in a clipped voice.

"Please remember that life can be cruel, but

there's a path to peace and even happiness," Owen added when she stood up.

"I should return to work." Kathleen left the booth and busied herself vigorously wiping tables Jazzy had already wiped. What path could lead her to peace, much less happiness, with all that had happened?

As she went from one table to the next, she searched her memory for the kind of car the boys were driving. After wiping the surface of the last one, she remembered.

When her shift was finally over, Kathleen drove a different route to the boarding house, checking often in her rearview mirror for a red Ford Mustang.

Chapter 12

Kathleen grabbed the first umbrella her hand landed on from the full container by the door, where at least a dozen of all sizes and patterns were crammed into the holder. *Why does Mary need so many if she only has one boarder at a time?*

Once she was on the porch, she opened the black umbrella covered with yellow ducks, each with a different silly face, splashed across the top. The words *I love a Rainy Day!* repeated itself around the edge. Kathleen rolled her eyes. How like Mary!

She sprinted to her car, grumbling about the heavy rain that had replaced the multiple snowfalls the first few weeks of December. Kathleen sat in her car, holding the keys in her right hand but not inserting them into the starter. Her thoughts captured her body, holding it still.

It was December 22nd. Kathleen hoped the rain would stop soon and they'd have snow for Christmas.

She gave a single guttural laugh. Why did she care if it snowed? Her Christmas promised to be bleak.

Last night at dinner, Mary announced she planned to visit her sister in Beckley for the holidays. "I rarely travel that far. But my nieces and nephews, along with Flora's new grandbaby, will be there," Mary told her. "I assume you plan to head home soon to be with your family."

Kathleen nodded, regretting lying. But she didn't want her landlady to change her mind. She preferred to be alone this Christmas.

The heavy rain continued during her drive to work. Once parked at the diner, she grabbed the umbrella, hoping she could close it before her coworkers saw the ridiculous ducks. She sprinted quickly through the many puddles on the asphalt.

Even walking on her tiptoes didn't prevent her shoes from getting wet. *Why didn't I put on my rain boots from the closet?* She didn't grab them because, like every day since her arrival in Charleston, she struggled with a hazy brain, as though she were walking in an early-morning fog.

Kathleen stepped into the diner, then swiveled back to the open door and shook her umbrella hard before snapping it closed, not worried about the wet folds being compressed together. Mission accomplished. She turned her attention to her soaked shoes. Why didn't she keep her extra pair in her locker? This pair would just have to dry on her feet.

"Kathleen, is that you?" Bella called from where she was kneading dough.

She walked into the kitchen, her shoes squeaking

with every step. "I'm here. Where's Jazzy? She is usually here before me."

"She just called. There's a low water crossing on the road out from her house. With this torrential rain, the water is too high to cross." Bella stopped working on the dough and extended her palms outward. "It's just you until this heavy rain stops and the water goes down."

What if there's a large crowd for breakfast or lunch? How can I manage this alone?

Bella laid a flour-covered hand on Kathleen's arm. "*Mia cara*, God will give you the strength you need. Just give it to Him, my dear."

The sting of tears hit her eyes. Her bruised heart told her she didn't deserve anyone's kindness. She hurried to get ready for the breakfast customers.

The hard rain kept the breakfast crowd low. She handled everything with ease. When the rain stopped and the sun peaked through the remaining dark clouds, Kathleen's hands curled into fists and she closed her eyes. *Please keep raining until after lunch.*

Kathleen blinked and forced her eyes to open. Did she just pray? *No, I was exercising my will!* She hoped the thought would remove her apprehension. It didn't.

The sun continued to shine as cars filled the parking lot with hungry customers. Soon, the diner didn't have an empty booth. Kathleen rushed from table to table to help disgruntled patrons frustrated by the long wait to be served.

"I'm here!" Jazzy's loud voice announced her arrival to everyone in the diner. She rushed to the counter and grabbed her order pad. Looking over the crowd, she said, "Who hasn't ordered yet?" Hands went up, and she hurried to the closest table, giving Kathleen a wink.

Soon dark clouds moved in again, shutting out the sun. A second wave of hard rain followed. Despite the downpour, Owen arrived at his usual time, decked out in rain gear from head to toe.

Jazzy saw him before Kathleen. "You look like a wet dog. Give me that dripping raincoat to hang in the back. I'll get you a towel from the kitchen for your hair and face." She couldn't suppress a grin.

"Thank you, Miss Jazzy. My hat fell off when a wind came. Most of this wetness is from when I chased it down. It kept tumbling away from me." His soaked hair sent streams of rainwater down his face.

Kathleen was waiting at Owen's booth when he'd dried off enough to sit down. "You know I could deliver a meal to you after I get off work. Just call it in." Kathleen's voice became airy at the end of her statement. She surprised herself by offering an act of kindness. Was she getting better? The slightest glimmer of hope grew deep within her body like a rose opening. Yet, roses had thorns and Kathleen still had too many of those in her life to accept hope.

"I couldn't let the rain stop me today. I have an important invitation to extend to you." Owen waited for a response. When none came, he continued. "I'd like you to share a meal with me on the 25th. My wife and I always cooked the Christmas Day meal together." He chuckled. "Actually, it's the only meal I know how to cook."

"I... uh, I can't. I'll put your Thursday order in." Her heart thundered like a herd of wild horses.

She'd been rude to someone who'd become her friend. Thoughts of past Christmases spun around in her head. In high school, Cody always came over after the noon Christmas meal. He spent the afternoon playing games with her family; then, before dark, the two of them took a walk. That's when they exchanged gifts. One year, he gave her a charm bracelet holding a single heart with her name inscribed on it. She turned it over to find his name on the other side. Where was the bracelet now? No, she couldn't go to Owen's.

Kathleen begged Jazzy to finish serving Owen. Jazzy's eyebrows formed a question, but shrugged one shoulder and picked up his dinner plate. Kathleen busied herself with jobs usually done by the night shift.

Before Owen left, he walked to where Kathleen worked folding napkins. "If you change your mind, I live at 223 Red Oak Lane." He tipped his hat and turned for the door.

Kathleen watched him leave, hating the person she'd become. She checked the clock, relieved to see it was quitting time.

Chapter 13

The cold from the wooden floors hit Kathleen's feet the moment she stepped out of bed. By the time she was at the window, they felt like two bricks of ice. Yet, she didn't turn back to retrieve her slippers. Something drew her to the window. She pulled back the heavy curtains and gasped. A beautiful soft snowfall, the kind with large flakes, drifted to the ground.

Hot tears stung her eyes. Snowing on Christmas Day. Her mother came to mind. What was it she once said? The memory came to Kathleen as clearly as if her mother were standing beside her.

It's wonderful when it snows on Christmas. It reminds me of the manna God gave the Israelites when they were wandering in the wilderness. This day we must thank Him for all his provisions, especially for His Son, our Savior.

Kathleen had rolled her eyes and asked where her sled was. Why hadn't she been kinder that day?

Homesickness hit hard. She felt her middle clinch into a tight coil as she leaned her head against the cold window, soft sobs causing the pane to frost. Her desire to be at home with her parents consumed her body. With weak legs, she slid to the floor and wrapped her arms around her knees. *What have I done?*

Kathleen didn't know how long she sat there, but slowly her hardened heart returned. She didn't deserve to be at home with her parents. She'd hurt them deeply.

Suddenly her stomach grumbled, and Kathleen glanced at the beside clock, surprised it was 2:00 p.m. Did she really sleep that long? She grabbed her fleece robe and slippers and headed to the kitchen. A quick survey of the cupboards and refrigerator was less than encouraging. She briefly thought of going to a restaurant, but didn't know if any would be open today.

I'm inviting you to my house for Christmas dinner. The words came softly. Alarmed, Kathleen stood and looked around the room as though Owen were there. *Silly!* Back upstairs, she sat on her bed and pulled her feet under herself. When she heard more rumbling from her empty gut, Kathleen regretted not accepting the invitation. Was it too late to accept now?

Without his phone number, she couldn't call to ask. Still, the desire to go grew stronger—not just for food, but for companionship. The surrounding stillness threatened to choke her. *I can't stay here by myself for another minute!* Racking her brain, Kathleen finally remembered his address.

She took a quick shower and dressed in corduroys and a heavy sweater. Kathleen grabbed the address she'd written on one of Mary's rose-printed notepads and her coat.

Once in the car, she snatched a map of Charleston from the glove compartment and searched for the route. Satisfied she wouldn't get lost, Kathleen started her car and turned on the windshield wipers. The snow still fell in soft, large snowflakes that floated to the ground with grace.

A short drive soon placed her in front of an older brownstone on a tree-lined street. She sat for a moment as nerves threatened to break her resolve. "I'm sure he won't mind. I'll leave as soon as we eat," Kathleen whispered, doubtful she believed her statement. Kicking down the fear of coming unannounced, she opened the car door and raced up the steps to Owen's front door, knocking hard before she could change her mind.

Owen was there almost immediately. "It's so good to see you. Come in out of the snow."

Kathleen relaxed immensely when she saw he was beaming with delight. "I'm sorry I didn't let you know. I only decided to come today."

"Not to worry! I'm blessed you're here. Make yourself comfortable near the fire. I must check on the latkes." Owen gestured toward the living room.

Not sure what he meant by latkes, Kathleen pulled off her coat and hung it on the rack by the door. Looking around, she saw a cozy room with a hodge-podge of overstuffed furniture. Heavy curtains hung on the room's two windows, opened wide to reveal the snowfall.

Drawn to a bookshelf between the two windows, she found a collection of books from the classics to modern day mysteries. The top shelf held books about Christianity, and Judaism, and a large Bible.

A sudden chill sent her to the blazing fireplace. Kathleen stood facing the fire, watching the wood burn into ashes. Lightheadedness hit her when she thought of the ashes that horrible night. She grabbed the mantle, steadying herself. Looking up from the offensive cinders, she found a double row of framed photographs. Each contained a picture of Owen and a woman she presumed to be his wife. Her eye landed on a black-and-white photo in an antique-looking frame.

With care, she lifted the faded picture. Closer inspection revealed the couple standing on a dock in front of a large steamship. They wore old clothes that hung on their slender frames like a little girl playing dress-up in her mother's clothes. What struck her the most was the great depth of sadness in both their eyes.

"Beata insisted we keep this picture." Owen stood in the doorway, holding two steaming mugs.

Kathleen twirled around, nearly dropping the frame. "I'm so sorry. I shouldn't be snooping."

"It's all right," Owen said as he sat the mugs on the coffee table, then closed the distance between them and took the picture into his hands. "My wife was emphatic to include this one with the others as a reminder of how good God has been to us." He reached around Kathleen and returned the frame to the mantle.

"Come, join me on the sofa. I've brought us hot apple cider."

She could still feel the redness on her face as she made her way around the coffee table, hoping her host wouldn't see her blush when they sat next to each other.

"So tell me. What prompted this last-minute decision to accept my invitation?" Owen asked. He took a sip of his cider and waited.

Kathleen looked at the fire and hesitated. Why did she come? She couldn't tell him he was likely her only source of food for the day. To her surprise, she blurted out, "It was the snow." Embarrassed, she knew he'd think she was crazy.

"Ah, that makes sense."

She searched Owen's aged, wise eyes. "How can it make sense to you.? I don't have a clue why I said that."

His wrinkled face creased into a wide smile. "God wanted you here. That's enough for you and for me." He paused and his face became serious. "Maybe He'll tell you why today, or maybe He has this time planned to store as a memory for later. Drink your cider. The brisket will be ready to cut in a few minutes."

When a timer buzzed in the kitchen, her host stood and asked, "Will you join me in the dining room?"

Given no time to process what he'd said, Kathleen knew it would plague her sleep when she went to bed.

Owen turned and gave a small smile. "Come and help me bring the food to the table. We're having brisket, latkes with applesauce, and challah bread." He grinned and shook one finger from side-to-side. "And for dessert, fried jelly-filled doughnuts."

"Latkes?" Kathleen regretted the impulsive

question. *Beggars can't be choosers* came to mind. "I'm sorry. I'm just happy to join you at this meal."

"Latkes are potato pancakes. They are traditionally eaten with applesauce." As he filled her plate, he continued. "I must admit I bought the bread and the doughnuts. My sweet Beata cooked the entire meal from scratch. I should have paid more attention."

"Don't be confused by the menu," her host said. "I realize it's not what you expected."

Understanding filtered through her brain. "You're Jewish."

"Yes and no. Beata and I became Christians not long after we came to this country. We always celebrated the birth of Christ by making a traditional Jewish meal on Christmas Day."

Unsure how to respond, Kathleen took her fork and ate. At the first bit, she closed her eyes and moaned silently. It was delicious! Every bite was better than the one before. In minutes, she had finished the entire plate. She glanced at Owen, flustered that he was watching.

"I'm glad you enjoyed my simple meal. The coffee percolator has completed its job. Let's get a cup and have our doughnuts in the living room." His eyes brimmed with tears when he continued. "But first, it has been a blessing to have you share my meal today. Never do I miss my beautiful wife more than when I eat this meal alone."

Not comfortable with the conversation, she spotted the doughnuts on the table and picked them up. "I'll take these if you'll get the coffee."

"Excellent." Owen responded as he rose and

headed for the kitchen. He returned with two hot cups of coffee.

He took a swallow of the dark, steaming liquid, as did Kathleen, who couldn't stifle a small cough.

Owen chuckled. "Polish coffee is very strong."

Polish? Was this where they were from? She wanted to ask, but Owen spoke first.

"Beata and I are from Poland. I was a professor of English at the university in Warsaw. My wife owned a small bookstore. When the Germans invaded Poland in 1939, it took only a week before they were in our city. In early 1940, we were arrested because of our jobs. We were sent to Auschwitz." Owen stopped, rubbing his hands on his thighs, his gaze downward.

Kathleen's heart dropped a beat as her mouth went dry. A concentration camp. Scenes and words from history classes flooded her mind. She searched for a reply, but nothing seemed adequate.

Still in the same position, her host spoke again. "It was difficult. Beata and I were separated and assigned to hard labor. My wife never recovered from the backbreaking work and the serious lack of food. She died two years ago, still suffering from the long-term effect of being in a concentration camp."

Owen swiveled his head toward Kathleen, who noticed the weariness on his face. "I'll share the rest of our story soon. And I hope you'll share yours. Right now, I see the snow is getting heavier. You should head home. I made you a container of food to take home."

By the time Kathleen had her coat on, he'd returned with the food. "It was an honor to have you."

Kathleen nodded her head and tried to smile, but it never materialized. She couldn't help but recognize how her story paled compared to his. *How is it he is so peaceful and... even happy?*

"Good evening, young friend. Merry Christmas, Kathleen." Owen said.

"Merry Christmas, Owen."

Chapter 14

*B*am! Kathleen's car leaped a few feet forward. She looked in her rearview mirror, horrified to see a red Mustang on her bumper. The driver whipped into the other lane, giving one long blast of his horn as he passed her.

Fear roared in Kathleen's head. She exited off the freeway at the first opportunity, then onto a side street. Her breath huffed in short bursts and she felt light-headed. She spotted a sign for Creekside Park and made a quick turn, following the narrow road until she came to a creek. Parking under some low-hanging branches of gigantic oaks, she fumbled with the door handle in her haste to be out of the car. Outside, cold air, heavy with moisture from the recent rain, hit her body. Kathleen pulled her coat closer but didn't return to the warmth of her car—her lungs were hungry for fresh air.

A few yards away from the oak trees, she spotted a bench along a hiking trail. Kathleen sat on the cold metal. She leaned over her body when dizziness threatened to shut out the light with darkness. Her heart beat against her chest.

"Miss, are you okay? Can I help?"

Kathleen raised up quickly when another flash of dizziness hit. She went down again with a loud moan, waving the man away.

"I'm not leaving. You look like you're in crisis," he said in a voice that said he meant business. "Are you injured, in pain, or sick?"

She lifted her head enough to get a look at the stranger. He was middle-aged, with soft, caring eyes. "No, but I can't... breathe."

"I want you to inhale through your nose, then let all the air out slowly through your mouth." He sat on the bench next to her. "We'll do it together," he said. "Remember to sit up straight."

She stared at him for a few moments, then joined in. The light-headiness and trembling stopped. Her heart slowed down, and she found her voice. "Thank you. I'm feeling better. Maybe I just need to sit here a while." Kathleen hoped the man would leave.

"I should stay with you for a bit." He put two fingers on her wrist, his eyes on his watch.

Kathleen opened her mouth to speak, but he shushed her until he finished.

"Pulse is good. I'd say the panic attack is over. But it might be a good idea for you to see your doctor next week." He stood and put out his right hand. "I'm a doctor, by the way."

"Thank you for helping me," she whispered in a small voice as she shook his hand.

"My pleasure. And don't forget about seeing your doctor." He gave her a smile and returned to the walking trail. When he was about fifteen feet away, he turned and said, "Don't sit there too long. You shouldn't be in the park after dark."

Kathleen nodded and remained on the bench, not ready to return to the boarding house yet. She watched the gurgling stream of water making its way around large rocks. It made her think of home and the creek her mother often let her play in as a child. A wave of homesickness washed over her.

Suddenly, Owen popped into her head. She returned to her car and made a short drive to his home. Now that she was here, she felt foolish. *Why would I share what had just happened with him?* Yet, something led her to leave her car and knock on his door.

"Kathleen. Come in." Owen said, beckoning her in. "You're shivering. Go stand by the fire while I get you some hot cider. It's been a cold February, yes?"

Kathleen did as he commanded, still in her coat. The warmth of the fire and the kindness in Owen's voice were too much. She didn't realize tears were tracking down her cheeks until Owen walked in, holding a cup of steaming cider.

"My dear," he said. "You're crying. Please give me your coat and sit down."

The phrase brought more tears. She removed her coat, handing it to Owen, who hung it on the coat rack in the foyer.

Returning, he sat in the chair near her. "Please tell me what has brought on this cascade of tears."

With broken speech, Kathleen explained what happened. "I'm sorry to come to your home uninvited. Something just pulled me here."

"We call this God's intervention," he remarked with a slight smile. "But that is a talk for another time." His face turned serious as he reached for Kathleen's hand. "My child, it is time for you to report this harassment to the police."

Terrified by the idea, she exclaimed, "I can't ever do that." She knew if her parents called the police in Charleston inquiring about her whereabouts, they'd have her report in the system.

Owen sighed, but didn't push the issue. He watched the fire for a short while before he spoke again. "Then let me pray for you. I will ask our Lord to protect you and to keep you safe."

Kathleen saw a light in his eyes that she couldn't understand. It was the same light she saw each time he mentioned God. How could she say no to the man who had been so kind to her? Nodding, he surprised her when he took her other hand. Holding firm, Owen lowered his head and began.

"Almighty God, please have mercy on your child, Kathleen. Protect her from the harassment by these young men. And I pray for them, Father, that they may turn from their evil ways and see the light of Jesus." Owen paused but didn't release Kathleen's hands. "And, dear Lord, lighten her heart from the burden she carries. Thank you for bringing her into my life. All glory, honor, and praise go to you. In the name of Jesus, our Savior, Amen."

How does he know about my burdens? And why would he pray for those awful boys? Yet, she felt a small sliver of peace make its way into her hardened heart. She mumbled a word of thanks and stood to leave.

"Wait for a moment, please. Will you come to church with me on Sunday? It would give me great pleasure to have you there."

Kathleen stiffened, wanting to flee. "I can't. I promised a coworker I'd take her shift. She's going to a baby shower for her sister." Relief raced through her, for she had told the truth. Enough lying had passed through her lips since she arrived in Charleston.

She grabbed her jacket and started for the door, then turned back to Owen. "Thank you for the warm fire and the hot cider." Leaving, practically at a run, she had a myriad of emotions. Why did Owen have to be so kind? And why did he always bring up God? She knew God wanted nothing to do with her after all the deceitfulness and the hurtful actions. There was no way back, no way to fix her offenses. But deep down, a quiet question lingered: What if?

Chapter 15

"Walt! Get in here." His editor called from the large office in the corner. Every reporter in the room either stopped typing or put a call on hold and stared at their coworker.

He rolled back his office chair and let his shoulders drop with a sigh. Whatever he'd done, it needed to wait until he finished his current story. If Walt didn't complete it and get the copy to the typesetters soon, he'd really hear Joe's wrath.

"Now, Johnson!" Joe Rickman bellowed even louder, causing the staff to stop work for a second time.

"Better get in there," Liam said from his desk that backed against Walt's. The two had been best friends since meeting in their first journalism class as sophomores. They often helped each other through the challenges of class assignments and had coauthored several stories for the newspaper.

Walt knew his friend was correct. Among the

many character traits of their editor, tenaciousness ranked at the top. It made him good at his job, but did little to gain a relationship with his staff.

Walt grabbed the first three pages of his current story to validate he'd been working hard and headed into Rickman's office.

"WAL—"

"I'm here, Joe." Walt spoke in a soft voice, hoping to defuse some of his editor's agitation.

"About time! Sit down." Joe growled the order, sounding like a pit bull when a stranger approached. His bushy eyebrows made a unibrow when he squinted at his reporter.

Walt groaned inwardly. If it's a "sit down" moment, it must be bad. Most requested visits to the editor's office were standing since Rickman was a man of few words

Walt glanced around the messy office. Every chair had paper, books, and files piled high in the seats. "Where should I—"

"For goodness' sake, Johnson, put the stuff on the floor."

He did as his boss ordered, dreading what might come. He needed this job to pay for the rest of his graduate work.

Rickman scrambled through the clutter on his desk and found his notepad. He stared at the scribbled notes. When he looked at Walt, his forehead wrinkled. "Where's your notepad?"

Walt cringed and put both hands on the chair arms, preparing to rush back to retrieve it. It was a rookie's error not to bring a pad into the editor's office—or anywhere, for that matter.

"Never mind," the editor grunted as he ripped his notes from the pad. "Take these. We don't have time to waste."

When Walt glanced at the hen-scratched notes, he pulled his ever-present pencil from behind one ear and flipped the piece of paper over. He hoped Joe planned to explain the notes.

"The newspaper's owner called me," Rickman said, shaking his head.

Walt's stomach dropped to his feet as he scooted to the edge of the chair. "Sir, I've done nothing to result in—"

"Reign your imagination back in. With your work record, he's more likely to fire me and give you my job."

Walt was tongue-tied. Never had this man given him a compliment.

"Don't start arranging your things in my office just yet. You've more years of being a reporter before becoming an editor. I need a story and you're the one I want to write it."

Walt forced himself to stop squirming and listened. He started shaking his head before his editor could finish his next sentence.

"You're headed to a mining town called Farrowlee first thing in the morning. It's about three hours south of here. Tom Cobalt wants us to run a story about a coal mine. It's one of the few actual coal-mining towns left in our state." Rickman pursed his lips. "Seems he knows the head guy, Henry Carter, at Farrowlee Mine."

"But I need to finish my article about fraternity hazing. We're holding ten inches for it." Walt pulled his hands through his dark hair and continued. "The

Marshall University Conduct Committee meets in a few days to complete its plans about the hazing process. This article could help influence their decision."

"I know about the story. Who do you think approved those ten inches? You have two options. Either pass it over to Liam or get in gear and finish it this afternoon."

No way Walt would give his work to Liam. He'd put too many hours into it. The article might stop a tradition that had escalated out of control at many colleges. At Marshall State alone, three pledges had been injured last September, and one student left when he became traumatized by the hazing practices.

"I'll finish it by the end of today," Walt responded quickly. "The library stays open late. I can do mining research and write my questions tonight."

Rickman reached into his desk drawer and tossed a credit card on the table. "This is for your gas. Don't even think about putting as much as a bag of chips on it."

"Yes, sir," Walt said as he slipped the card into his shirt pocket as he left the office. He hurried to his typewriter, rereading the last line he'd typed.

"Well, are you planning to tell me what's going on?" Liam asked, irritated when Walt didn't fill him in.

He never looked up from his typing. "Oh, Joe gave me a story. Nothing big. Would you grab me a burger when you go to lunch?"

By four o'clock, Walt had his editor's approval of the fraternity story and handed it to the copy runner. He headed out but stopped and turned back to Liam.

"I won't be here tomorrow," he said, hurrying out before his friend could ask questions.

By the library's closing time, Walt had enough information to write a decent set of questions for the interview. Weariness engulfed his body like a marathon runner at the finish line. Too tired to stop for something to eat, he headed to his apartment, hoping for enough bread to make a couple of bologna sandwiches.

Walt woke tired after a restless night. In his waking moments, which were many, he thought about the town of Farrowlee.

It wasn't until he had wolfed down a bowl of cereal before sunrise that he remembered. He'd heard the word when Kathleen and a group of her friends were leaving the classroom. Had she said it, or did it come from another classmate?

He put his cereal bowl and spoon in the sink, trying not to notice the pile of dirty dishes already sitting there. Maybe the dish fairy would come today while he was gone.

Walt shivered in the cold January dawn as he bounded down the front steps, thankful they weren't iced over. Once in his car, he consulted a West Virginia road map, then started the engine. Walt tapped on the gas gauge, and it barely moved off empty. Good. He'd fill it up now, then again later today when he headed home—all on the newspaper's credit card.

An hour later, Walt took the exit for University Highway 119. *If the map is correct, this is going to be a ride full of twists and turns.* It didn't lie. The road had many sharp curves and switchbacks. His car groaned on the steep inclines as it wound through some of the most beautiful mountains he'd ever seen. At places, deep evergreen hemlocks and cedars lined each side of the road like sentries. All that stood between him and an enormous drop in the terrain was a highway rail guard.

Around one curve, he spotted a store nestled next to a mountain and pulled into the parking lot for a restroom and a snack.

Walt went through the front door and saw an older man with a long gray beard. He had on a plaid flannel shirt and overalls; both had seen better days. A tattered *Korea War Veteran* cap sat tilted back on his head.

"Mornin'," the man said, not moving his eyes from a small TV sitting near the edge of the counter. A news reporter standing in front of a group of Vietnam War protesters spoke about the scene behind him and similar ones happening around the nation. "Crying shame. In my day, we didn't protest the war. We went because Uncle Sam asked us to."

Walt wasn't sure if he was talking to him or the TV. He nodded and headed to the men's room. When he came out, he grabbed a package of Snowballs, laying them on the counter. "How much farther is it to Farrowlee?"

"As the crow flies, it's about thirty minutes. By car, you can add another hour to that." He grinned, showing several missing teeth. "But if you're hoping for a job at the mine, word is they're not hiring."

"Why is that?" Walt asked, always the reporter.

"When coal production at the mine slowed down, families fled north to Akron and Cleveland to find industry jobs. And not just from Farrowlee Mine, but mines all over the south. Now, US 77 is called the Hillbilly Highway." The ancient cash register clacked when the man put Walt's coins in the drawer. "Exact change. Don't see that too often. Most travelers come in here with those credit cards. I tell them I don't give no credit!"

"I'm not searching for a job." Walt grabbed the Snowballs and hurried out before the man could ask questions about his business in Farrowlee.

Throughout the remainder of the trip, he tried to concentrate on the interview. But his mind kept going back to Kathleen. Since the crash, he'd not seen her back in class. Eventually, the professor told him to take her name off the class roster.

Kathleen had the same last name as the mine superintendent. Could she be in Farrowlee? A prayer came from his lips. "Lord, if she's there, direct me to her so I can ask for her forgiveness."

After an eternity of maneuvering his car around curves, steep rises, and falls in the road, Walt finally saw a sign saying Farrowlee.

He turned onto a crushed shell road and slowed his speed when the grade steepened, not sure how his old car would perform on this type of terrain.

Before what appeared to be the last downward slope, he stopped the car to get a better look. Farrowlee sat at the bottom of a narrow valley surrounded by tall, majestic mountains. Walt spotted a river winding its way through the valley. Next to the river were railroad tracks and a loading dock.

He thought the open cars of the train might be where the coal was loaded for transport. It made him even more eager to get answers to the questions he'd fashioned the night before, although his gut told him they barely touched the surface of what really happens in a mining operation.

Across from the tracks, Walt spotted a double row of houses facing each other. They were identical, though some had flowers and a garden while others didn't look lived in. Beyond the houses, he saw a small church, a store, and a post office.

How did anyone live in such an isolated place?

Chapter 16

Walt drove through the row of houses and followed the road to a bridge that spanned both the river and the railroad tracks. He rolled to a stop on the other side of the bridge and found himself in a large, open area.

Turning off the engine, he stepped out and examined the surroundings, spotting a building labeled main office. Walt glanced at his watch, noting he was right on time for his 11:00 meeting. He retrieved his bag from the back, pulled out the lanyard identifying he was with the press, and entered the building.

Inside, a grandmotherly woman with gray sprinkled hair smiled broadly. "Hello, you must be the young reporter from Huntington. Mr. Carter is waiting for you. Go right in," she said, pointing to the door across the room. "I'll put the kettle on for the tea."

Before Walt could ponder why she planned to bring tea, the door opened and a tall, slender man with an inviting smile stood before him.

"Hello, I'm Henry Carter. Welcome to Farrowlee Mining Company." He extended his hand for a shake, then gestured to the chair facing his desk.

"I'm Walt Johnson with the *Herald Dispatch*. Thank you for agreeing to this interview."

Before closing the door, the superintendent turned to the outer office. "Betty, would you bring us a cuppa?"

Now Walt knew the reason for the tea—the superintendent was British. This brought even more questions for his interview. He watched as Mr. Carter eased himself into the high-back chair behind a small desk. "So sorry we can't sit without this desk between us, but as you can see, my office isn't much larger than a postage stamp."

Walt had already noticed the small, almost bare office. He had visualized much larger and nicer surroundings for the head of a mining company. "I appreciate your time today. As superintendent, I'm sure you are a busy man."

"I'm more than happy to talk to you about Farrowlee Mine and the mining industry. Besides, I have a soft spot in my heart for the city of Huntington and Marshall University."

Walt noted a great sadness in Mr. Carter's eyes when he spoke of the college.

Exactly an hour later, he had more than enough for his story. The superintendent answered all his questions in a thoughtful and informed way. His information about the plight of mining in West Virginia validated the words spoken by the storekeeper.

"Thank you for your time this morning," Walt said as he stood to leave.

"Wait. I'd like to show you the loading cars and the tipple before you leave. Maybe find a miner you can visit with. Besides, my wife insisted I bring you home for lunch."

"I couldn't possibly intrude on your day any longer."

"No intrusion at all. There was a time when I would've barely given you ten minutes. It took a war and the Lord to change me. Besides, my wife would be very disappointed."

Walt's stomach gave a low growl at just that moment. The early-morning cereal and package of Snowballs had left his gut empty. And he liked the idea of a tour and the opportunity to speak with some miners. It would make his story richer.

"All right, I'll stay, but I'll need to leave soon to get back to Highway 119 before dark."

Mr. Carter agreed. "The mountain roads can intimidate those who have never traveled them. And there's always the danger of hitting a deer or a bear." He laughed when he saw the look on Walt's face. "Don't worry, just be on the lookout."

During a brief tour, Walt saw the cable cars carrying the miners up to the mine opening and the cars bringing the coal to the tipple for sorting and eventually loading onto a train. Walt's conversation with a miner gave him more perspective for his story.

"Now, follow me to my home, where I'm sure

Emily is watching for us out the front window," Mr. Carter said, as he headed to his truck.

Walt rushed to his own vehicle, relieved when it started without a fuss. He followed the superintendent back across the bridge and slightly beyond the town. They climbed a small hill to a house that sat above the town of Farrowlee. Surprised he hadn't seen the stately home on his drive in, he stared at the structure that was a world away from the row houses.

Henry met him in the yard. "I know it seems pretentious for us to live in a home like this one—"

Embarrassed, Walt interrupted. "I'm sorry, Mr. Carter. I didn't mean to stare."

"No problem. Emily felt the same thing when we moved here, although then I thought it was fitting. Not anymore. The Lord changed me many years ago. We've no other place to live, so I try to use what funds I can to make the miners' homes better. And call me Henry, please."

The door to the home opened, and Emily called out. "What are you two men doing standing there in the cold? Henry, bring our guest in where it's warm." As she spoke, tiny snowflakes made their way to the ground.

When Walt stepped onto the porch, Emily greeted him with a handshake and a smile. A sense of déjà vu sent goosebumps down both arms. *Why does she seem so familiar?*

Inside the foyer, the beautiful scents of food were heaven compared to his usual fare of burgers and junk food. *Don't embarrass yourself by gobbling down this food.* He took off his coat and the warm knit cap.

Henry reached out to hang them on the rack against the wall where he'd hung his own.

"Why don't we go straight to the dining room?" Emily said in a soft voice. "I kept everything warm in the oven and started setting things out when I heard Henry's truck coming up the drive." She pointed to a chair for Walt. "I'll get the rolls." She disappeared into the kitchen as Walt stared at the feast before him. Baked ham, green beans, creamed corn, and fluffy mashed potatoes. His salivary glands went into action and he had to swallow hard to keep from drooling.

After a quick blessing by Henry, Emily passed the food. "Please take a lot. I'm afraid I cooked for six instead of three." Emily chuckled and continued, "Although I'm sure Daisy, our dog, would be happy to scarf down any leftovers."

Walt did as requested and heaped large portions onto his plate. He wanted to take two rolls but decided against it. Refraining from pushing his food in as fast as a train goes through a tunnel, he ate slowly, answering questions and asking some of his own.

As they ate, the dining room grew darker as the snow came down harder. Soon the wind howled, driving the falling snow sideways. "Oh, dear. I think we may be in for a blizzard," Emily said softly, with a look at her husband.

"I'm afraid so, although the weather report only called for a slight snowfall." He turned to Walt with an apology. "I should have let you leave straight from my office. If this keeps up, the roads will be impassible."

"Maybe I should get on the road now." Walt pushed his chair back when the phone on a small table near the staircase rang.

"Excuse me. I need to get that." Henry rushed to the phone and lifted the receiver. "Hello. Superintendent Carter here." Henry listened for a moment, then responded, "I'll call my foreman to spread the word. Thank you for letting me know."

Back at the table, he remained standing while speaking to Walt. "That was the weather service of McDowell County. They always call me when the roads around here are impassable. I'm afraid you can't travel this afternoon. If fact, it may not be possible until around mid-morning tomorrow." Henry sat down and continued. "Looks like you're our guest for the night."

Impossible. He needed to be at his TA job and then at the newspaper tomorrow. Walt stood. "If I leave now, I should make it fine. It hasn't been snowing long."

"That's the problem. This blizzard is moving slowly from north to south. The road you came in on was shut down a couple of hours ago."

"But I can't impose on—"

"You're not an imposition," Emily interrupted. "Please sit and finish your meal. There's a slice of warm apple pie waiting for you."

Her kindness calmed his frazzled nerves and brought the memory of the many times his own mother had settled his feelings with a piece of pie. "Thank both of you. I'm sure you weren't expecting an overnight guest."

"We didn't expect this blizzard, either. The Lord has taught us to not fret over things we can't change." He faced his wife. "Did I hear something about an apple pie?"

The blizzard roared all afternoon. At dinner, they shared ham sandwiches and more apple pie by the warm fireplace. By bedtime, Walt felt as though he had known his hosts forever. Henry shared more on the history of mining while Emily interjected stories about life in Farrowlee, most of them humorous.

The logs in the fireplace had turned to glowing embers when Emily turned to Walt. "I'm afraid the only room I can offer you is that of our daughter. I confiscated the third bedroom for my sewing space long ago. It's the door to the right at the top of the stairs."

Walt waited, thinking they might offer more about their daughter, but both were silent. He noted the same shadow in both their eyes.

Chapter 17

*W*alt grabbed his satchel and headed upstairs. He hit the light switch and blinked at the barrage of pink walls, pink rug, and pink bedcover. He put his bag on the small desk and noticed a pair of Henry's pajamas on the bed, grateful for Emily's thoughtfulness.

As he unbuttoned his shirt, Walt walked around the room, gazing at stuffed animals, a megaphone with pompoms placed on top, and a clarinet case. He stopped in front of a vanity with an oval mirror and touched the Mardi Gras beads and a Hawaiian lei hanging off its frame.

What he saw next caused his hand to stop in midair—a photo of a young couple taped to the mirror. The boy had on football gear and the girl wore a cheerleader's outfit. He pulled the picture loose to get a better look. Walt's throat choked out his breath when he realized he was standing in Kathleen's bedroom.

Confusion filled his mind. How could it be that he came here to do a story and ended up as an overnight guest in the home of her parents? Then he remembered his prayer, asking God to lead him to her if she was in this town. Peace and clarity replaced his foggy brain.

He sat on the bed, staring at the picture. Being in her bedroom wasn't the same as finding her. The reporter in him wanted to rush back downstairs and get answers. Yet, Walt knew the Lord had sent him there and would keep leading him to find her at the right time. Still, he lay in bed, sleepless for a long time. When he finally slept, he dreamed about the crash and Kathleen's painful eyes.

The smell of coffee and the clang of pots and pans startled him awake. Walt rushed to get dressed, but not until he peered out the window, squinting at the sight. The sun sparkled on a deep accumulation of snow.

He grabbed a comb from his satchel and stood in front of the vanity, trying not to glance at the picture he'd replaced last night. Staring at his image in the mirror, he talked to himself. "Okay, mister. Don't go into reporter mode with Kathleen's parents. Leave it in God's hands."

When he walked through the dining room and into the kitchen, Emily was taking steaming biscuits from the oven. She looked up with a smile. "Oh good. Your timing is perfect. Everything is ready for breakfast."

Walt glanced at the table filled with scrambled eggs, sausage and bacon, biscuits, and several jars of jellies and jams. "Wow, I can't remember the last time I had a breakfast like this."

Henry laid down his newspaper and beckoned him to take a seat. "Being English, a hearty breakfast is part of my routine. Thankfully, my lovely American wife is faithful to the custom."

Emily joined them, and after grace, the three made short order of the delicious food. When they finished, Henry turned to Walt. "I've spoken to the weather station. The snowplows have been working since 3:00 a.m. I think you can safely head back to Huntington around noon."

"That's great news."

"I called my secretary to let her know I'll be late today. Emily and I would like to visit with you in the living room this morning."

"Of course," Walt agreed, though his mind swirled with curiosity.

"Thank you. It won't take long."

When the three settled before the fireplace, Walt saw a look between his hosts.

"Right-o. I'll start with why we're here." He inhaled deeply and stared at the fire he'd stoked when they entered the room and turned to Walt. "Emily and I felt bad last night when you went up to our daughter's room. We discussed so many things last evening but steered away from talking about our only child." Moisture formed in his eyes. "Kathleen was a student at Marshall. A tragic accident has changed her so much, we hardly know her any longer."

Emily spoke in an urgent voice. "Oh, she wasn't in an accident."

"That's correct," Henry interjected. "She lost someone she cared for in the airplane crash."

Before he could continue, Walt nodded. "Yes, I covered the accident for the newspaper. It was—horrific." He fully intended to reveal the entire story, but something stopped him. What if they blamed him for taking Kathleen to the crash? Would Kathleen want them to know she was there? The two thoughts warred against each other. His ego won the battle. He didn't want the Carters to change their opinion of him. He remained silent, ignoring the soft urging in his heart to be honest.

Emily leaned in toward Walt and uttered in a soft voice, "I was sure she'd want to attend Cody's funeral." Emily stopped, wiping her wet eyes. "Three hours later, she phoned to say she couldn't face coming home."

"Our world stopped." Henry said. "It's unlike our daughter." He paused and redirected his attention to the fire, then continued. "I have a war buddy, Homer Stillman, who is a private investigator in Charleston." Henry raised his shoulders and let them fall with a sigh. "I hired him on the chance she might be in the city."

The silence throughout the room was deafening. But he kept quiet.

"Homer found her the first night. She was in a motel," Emily murmured with a watery smile. "We were so relieved."

"He since reported to us she now lives in a boarding house and works in a diner," Henry said. "We're amazed by her resourcefulness. Not to mention how grateful we are to God for His providential care of our child."

Walt asked only one question. "Have you contacted her?"

"No, we're respecting her privacy. Emily and I are at a loss about why this tragedy has affected her in such a drastic way."

Hearing what Henry said made Walt regret his question. He could fill in the gaps and help Kathleen's parents, but he chose not to. "I'll pray for her," he said, feeling like a hypocrite.

By noon, Walt was in his car, traveling north. The roads were clear but required some driving skill on the bridges because of ice.

He tried to compose his notes for the article as he drove. Yet, he couldn't shake the undeniable fact that he had ignored his faith for his own benefit. He couldn't even pray about it. The web he'd spun put a tremendous burden on him—something he thought he deserved.

He drove in silence without the radio on. In the quiet, he heard a small voice. *Go find her.* He jerked the steering wheel and quickly realigned the wheels. Could it be God was communicating with him despite his recent behavior?

He spoke a prayer as he drove. *Lord, thank you for loving me even when I don't follow your commands. Your unfailing love humbles me. Forgive me for my dishonesty and lead me to her.*

When he finished, Walt realized his cheeks were moist with tears.

By the time he arrived at the newspaper building, Walt knew what he had to do. He'd finish the article by print time on Friday and drive to Charleston after work.

Chapter 18

"Man!" Kathleen groaned, flopped over, and pulled a pillow over her head. It didn't help. She could still hear the landlady's loud singing of gospel tunes while preparing breakfast.

She lay there for another minute before turning over and throwing back the bedcovers. With a loud sigh, Kathleen sat up just as the alarm went off. She hit the top button with more force than necessary to stop the buzzing. "All right! I'm up!" Kathleen grumbled, as though it were a person.

A thought moved from her brain to her heart, and she whispered, "How many times did I say those same words to Mom?"

Kathleen forced herself not to think about her mother. Homesickness was one of the many demons she wrangled with every day and long into the night. Last evening proved especially bad. The recurring nightmare about the crash disturbed her sleep.

In it, Kathleen stood nearby as the plane made its descent then collided into the mountain. She perceived the screams, the crushing of metal breaking up, and saw the craft burst into flames—screaming as the flames engulfed her as well. She woke up, sweating and breathing hard. As usual, the dream kept her awake until morning.

She stood, wincing when her feet hit the cold wooden floor. Walking to the armoire across the room, Kathleen grabbed a uniform, shoes, and a pair of socks. Within ten minutes, she walked into the kitchen, grimacing at Mary's singing. *How can anyone be that cheerful at five in the morning?*

"Oh, there you are. Perfect timing. Breakfast is ready," Mary said, with a joyful smile. "Have a seat, dear."

"Why do you sing those songs every morning?" The question popped off Kathleen's tongue, surprising her.

Mary laid down her fork and wiped her mouth with a napkin. "The psalmist David said, 'Weeping may tarry for the night, but joy comes in the morning.'"

Kathleen's forehead wrinkled downward, causing her eyebrows to form a straight line. "I don't understand. What does this have to do with your singing?"

"Joy's a choice. I choose to be joyful every morning by singing praises to God. The best part is, joy always brings peace." Mary retrieved her fork. "I find it stays with me throughout the day."

Baffled by the answer, Kathleen gave a slight nod and finished the meal. Mary's words were still in her head when she entered her vehicle. How could she find joy, let alone peace, when she hurt so badly? She sat there for a long time, holding the key in her hand.

The blast of a car horn on the street jolted Kathleen awake. She checked her wristwatch, then closed her eyes and moaned. Her unexpected nap in the car would make her almost an hour late for work! Thrusting the key into the ignition, she jerked the shift stick into drive, turned the heater full-blast, and squealed her tires leaving the driveway.

Kathleen went through the doorway and walked into a warm diner with a few customers already sipping coffee and waiting for their orders.

"Sorry I'm late. It was a terrible accident. Police were rerouting everyone, and I found myself lost," she lied to Jazzy.

"Fair's fair, honey. You covered for me when I couldn't get here because of the last bad rainstorm."

"Would you let Bella and Joe know what happened? I feel stupid telling them I couldn't find the diner."

"Sure, once I finish the refills." Jazzy said, flashing a smile.

Kathleen headed to her locker, blinking to stave off the tears crowding her eyes. *When did I become so deceitful?*

She deposited her coat and purse in her locker, then grabbed an apron and her order pad just as four young women entered. They were all laughing as if one of them had told a joke.

"Great, cheerful people. That's all I need today," Kathleen mumbled in a low voice before heading to their table. She laid four menus in a pile on the table without distributing them to the customers. "What can I get you to drink?" She felt her lips press into a straight line, which contrasted with their wide smiles.

After getting their drink orders, she walked toward the counter and overheard one of them speak in a distasteful tone. "Looks like someone woke up on the wrong side of the bed this morning." The same raucous laughter as when they entered rang throughout the diner.

Kathleen's bad mood stayed with her for the rest of her shift. She glanced often at the big wall clock, willing it to move faster so she could go back to her room. *I'll feign a headache so I won't have to eat dinner with Mary.* How easy it had become to tell lies!

When the clock's hands indicated 3:30, Kathleen sighed with relief. Half an hour and she'd be out of there. She stood at the counter with her back turned to the door when someone came through the front entrance. Kathleen heaved a shoulder-dropping sigh. "Take a seat. I'll be right there." Her monotone, unfriendly voice caused Bella to turn from her workstation with a frown. "I'm sorry," she whispered and picked up a menu before walking to the man sitting alone in the far back booth.

He had his head lowered, staring at his hands fastened on the table. When he looked up, Kathleen froze.

"Walt, what are you... how did you—?" She felt blood pulsing through her veins, terrified by his presence.

"Find you? I'm an investigative reporter. It's what I do." He interrupted snidely, then changed to a softer tone. "I'm hoping we might talk?"

A dozen responses ran through Kathleen's

head. Instead, she rushed from the booth without an utterance. Even though it wasn't quitting time, she retrieved her things and sprinted to the door without putting on the coat grasped tightly in one hand.

Pulling out of the parking lot, she stayed in the outside lane, planning to turn at the first right. The last thing she wanted was for Walt to follow her to the boarding house. She replayed the scene at the diner. Could it mean her parents might also sit in the booth one day? Kathleen's stomach soured. *I can't face them. Not now, maybe never.*

She saw a right turn, but traffic had slowed to a stop at the red light ahead. Drumming her fingers on the steering wheel, she uttered, "Come on, come on!"

She looked away from the light as a green truck in the inside lane slowed to a stop, catching her attention. A tall man with a long uncut beard sat in the driver's seat. Fear blew over her like a strong north wind.

From two car-lengths back, Walt rolled forward at a slow speed. He watched the truck change lanes and move behind the little yellow car when the light turned.

Chapter 19

The spring weather soon became an unusually hot June. Customers arrived at the diner sweating and grumpy. Kathleen and Jazzy stayed extra busy with everyone asking for refills on their water and tea. The calendar seemed to move extra slow during the days when temperatures rose near one hundred.

July brought even more heat and no rain. Kathleen was concerned about Owen, who continued to walk to the diner every day.

"Maybe you shouldn't walk in this heat. I can bring your order to your house when I get off work." Kathleen gave Owen a small smile and continued, "After all, I know what to bring every day of the week."

"Yes, you have learned my daily menu selection very well," Owen said, then shook his head. "No, I will keep walking here. Beata and I never complained about the weather."

A week later, Owen didn't come to the diner for

his Monday meal, nor did he come for the next two days. The staff all agreed it had to be the heat, but Kathleen was concerned. When it was time for her lunch break on Wednesday, she cut a slice of Bella's apple pie for Owen. "Even if he's cooking for himself, I doubt he's making pies."

Kathleen pulled to the curb, surprised to see uncut grass. "That's not like Owen," she mumbled to herself. Just as she raised her hand to knock, the door opened. She blinked when a young woman holding a large sign stood in the doorway. "I'm Cindy Evans, a Realtor for Maxwell Real Estate. The house isn't on the market yet. I'll give you my card and you can call in a few days to see if it's listed."

"On the market? Owen would never sell his house. He's lived here for years."

Cathy put down the *For Sale* sign. "I'm sorry. Mr. Levenson died of a heart attack two days ago. He visited me last spring to retain my services upon his death."

The container of apple pie hit the concrete porch.

Kathleen pushed on the handle of the diner door, then had to lean her body against it. Heaviness consumed her like a boulder laying deep in one's chest. She went to the storage room where Bella kept a stack of week-old newspapers for wrapping fish carcasses and bones. Kathleen grabbed yesterday's paper. Her hands trembled as she rifted through the pages until she came to the obituaries. There it was.

Owen Levenson died on July 15, 1971, at age 81. The funeral will be at 3:00 p.m. on Thursday, July 18 at the Shady Oaks Bible Church. Preceded in death by Beata, wife of 56 years, Mr. Levenson lived in

Warsaw, Poland until he and his wife immigrated here in 1946. He worked at Charleston National Bank until his retirement in 1955. Mr. Levenson was an active member of his church and a good neighbor, most known for his great wisdom and his kindness to everyone he met. A host of friends will miss him.

She turned and went to the front counter where Jazzy was pouring some coffee and silently handed her the paper, pointing to the obit. "He's gone, Jazzy."

Her friend reached out and pulled Kathleen into her arms. The act of kindness became a catalyst for a torrent of tears.

"How about you go outside for some air? I'll cover for you. Stay as long as you need," Jazzy said when Kathleen's sobbing came to a stop.

She drew a deep breath of fresh air when she thought of what her father always told her. *"Be strong, Daughter. God will give you the courage to face anything."* Her father had endured torture and starvation at a POW camp during the Korean War. Yet, he returned with a strong faith, claiming God was with him every moment he was there.

"Oh, Daddy. I don't think He's with me," she whispered.

A week later, the phone at the diner rang. "It's for you," Joe stated, as he frowned at Kathleen, never happy about personal calls at work.

"For me?" The only person who might call her would be Mary. But Kathleen knew she'd never call her at work.

"That's what I said." He laid the receiver on the counter and returned to the kitchen, shaking his head and grumbling in Italian.

Fear crawled up Kathleen's backside. Her hand trembled as she lifted the receiver. "Hello?"

"Hello, my name is Thomas Bartlett. I'm Mr. Owen Levenson's lawyer." He cleared his throat before continuing. "Am I speaking to Kathleen Carter?"

It took her a moment before she realized she was nodding her head, not using her voice.

"Yes, it's me." She cringed at how lame she sounded.

"Would it be possible for you to come to my office today at 4:30 p.m.?"

She grabbed hold of the counter's edge with her other hand. *Why have I been summoned to a lawyer's office?* Her mind ran in circles, wanting to hang up, yet she clenched the receiver.

"Can you tell me what this is about?" she inquired in a shaky voice.

"I'm sorry, but I thought you would know it's for the reading of Mr. Levenson's will."

Stunned by what he said, she froze. It was only when she heard the lawyer speaking in a louder voice that she came back to reality.

"Miss Carter, are you there? Have we lost connection?"

"I'm here and I'll come." If Owen had wanted her there, then she'd go.

"Good. My address is 1800 Capitol Street, Suite 204. It's the old Steiner Building."

Kathleen scribbled the address on her order pad and hung up without saying goodbye.

Chapter 20

*J*azzy threw a questioning look at Kathleen, which she ignored by grabbing the coffee pot. Her hand shook as she moved around the diner, offering refills.

"Wow, little lady. You almost filled my meatball sub with coffee," the construction worker commented with a wink.

Before she could respond, Jazzy appeared beside her. "Why don't you go take a couple of menus to the couple who just walked in?"

The day didn't improve for Kathleen. She struggled to focus long enough to take customers' orders correctly and had to return food to the kitchen when it came out wrong. Joe grew more irritated each time and mumbled words in Italian. Kathleen was grateful she didn't know what the words meant.

When the lunch rush ended, she hoped Jazzy wouldn't question her behavior. No such luck.

"I don't have a clue what's wrong with you today, but you look like you could use some fresh air. I promised the kids that I would take them to the park when my shift ends. Why don't you come with us?" Jazzy gave a quirky smile. "If nothing else, you can watch how long it takes before they fight with each other."

"I can't. I have to go somewhere."

Her friend's smile faded as she leaned closer to Kathleen. "Honey, I hope you're not in some kind of trouble. Maybe I can help

"No!" Kathleen interrupted in a loud voice, rapidly shaking her head. "I'm not in trouble. Why can't you leave me alone?"

Jazzy was silent for a moment, then turned to walk away.

Embarrassed by her outburst, she drew in a deep breath and lowered her voice. "I'm sorry. I have an appointment."

Jazzy turned back and squeezed Kathleen's arm. "I'm here if you need me."

Oh, man. It's hotter than blue blazes out there. If you weren't an inside person before this heat wave, you are now. And the weatherman says we can expect more high temperatures throughout the week.

Kathleen leaned in and turned off the car radio. She usually listened to this station, but not today. She needed to concentrate on finding this lawyer's office building. Ten minutes later, she spotted the Steiner Building. Finding a parking place under a shady tree, she rolled down her window to get some breeze, albeit a sultry breeze. Her thoughts went to the many encounters with Owen over the past eight months. Why had she been so drawn to the person who was so unlike her? Then she knew. Owen was like her father—kind, patient, and wise. Both men could settle her mind and calm her heart.

Her thoughts took an unwanted turn, and she pictured the fire and Cody's burned body. "Not today," she said to herself. Glancing at her wristwatch, she gasped. Four thirty on the dot.

She rushed from the car and headed to the Steiner Building. Once she was inside, she stopped for a moment to inhale the cool, air-conditioned air, then froze. What was the suite number? A sting hit her eyelids as she glanced around in a panic.

On the wall near the elevator hung a directory. Kathleen hurried to it, searching for the lawyer's name. Her finger stopped on Bartlett. Suite 204. She pressed the elevator button and drummed her fingers on the doors. After what seemed an eternity, the doors opened. She rushed in, thankful no one was getting off.

Moments later, she paused at the door stating Bartlett & Bartlett Law Firm. *I can't do this. I can't talk about another death in my life.* As she turned to leave, scenes of the times Owen patiently tried to teach her how to play chess flooded her mind. Kathleen knew she'd never learn the game, yet she enjoyed her time in the booth across from this kind old man. "You can do this," he encouraged each time she sat, not knowing her next move.

She turned around and pushed the door open

with a force. The two secretaries looked up from their desks, alarmed by her quick entrance.

"Can we help you?" asked the older of the two.

"I...uh...I have an appointment with Mr. Bartlett."

"Senior or Junior?"

"I...I don't know. He called and said he was Thomas Bartlett. I have an appointment with him."

"It's okay, Betty. I failed to add senior when I called her." Mr. Barlett walked from his office and put his hand out. "I apologize for confusing you. Would you like to come to my office, Miss Carter?"

Kathleen gave a small nod and shook his hand. She followed him into a large, well-furnished room with a vast desk and leather chairs. What amazed her were the bookshelves lining the walls on three sides. The only place she'd seen so many books was at the Marshall University library.

"Please sit down, Miss Carter." Mr. Bartlett said. He pointed to one of two small leather chairs facing his desk.

Her patience had run its course. Still standing, she asked, "Can you please tell me why Owen wanted me to see his lawyer?"

The lawyer blinked and set forward in his chair. "You're here today to hear the reading of Owen Levenson's will."

"His will?"

"Please take your seat and I'll explain."

Kathleen sat down and waited. Her breath hitched in her throat.

"Owen changed his will a few months ago. You'll understand when I read it. May I begin?"

She fought down the impulse to bolt and nodded to the lawyer, feeling trapped by the surroundings and the words being spoken.

"Good. Let's begin," Mr. Bartlett stated. He cleared his throat and started reading.

I, Owen Jan Levenson, being of sound mind, and full understanding of the nature of all my property, do bestow upon Kathleen Carter the sum of forty-five thousand dollars with one condition. She must use these funds for tuition, housing, and living expenses while attending West Virginia University.

Kathleen popped out of her chair and took two steps away from the desk. "No, I decline it. Surely, he had family, maybe some relatives in Poland."

"All his relatives died in concentration camps during WWII. Only he and Beata survived. This is what Owen wanted for you."

"But I can't take it. I don't deserve it." She blinked her moist eyes, hoping not to cry. "Give it to his church," she said and started to leave. She needed to be out of the room, away from the document laying on the lawyer's desk.

"I'm unable to do that. Besides, his home and all its contents are to be sold. The proceeds of the sale will go to the church. Take a few days to think about this." The lawyer opened his desk drawer and pulled out two items. "Mr. Levenson asked me to give you these."

Kathleen returned to the desk as her eyes filled with tears. She picked them up and left without a word.

Only when outside did she realize she'd run through the building in her need to be away from what she'd learned. The hot air hit her lungs, which begged for relief from her sprint.

The next day at work, Kathleen was quiet but managed not to be so anxious that she repeated yesterday's mistakes. Every time she thought of Owen's offer, she pushed it away, determined to concentrate on her job.

"Hey, kid. Why are you so quiet today?" Jazzy asked when the lunch crowd was over.

"I'm trying to prevent any mistakes. I'm afraid I'll be fired."

Jazzy hesitated before responding. "Please remember what I said yesterday. I'm here for you. Sweetheart, did you have a doctor's appointment yesterday? Are you—?"

"No... Oh, no!" Kathleen said, shaking her head.

The relief on Jazzy's face was evident, making Kathleen laugh. "All right, I'll tell you. I went to see Owen's lawyer. He read Owen's will to me, stating I was to have money for tuition and living expenses to attend West Virginia University. But I—"

Jazzy grabbed in a bear hug before she could finish. "Kathleen, that's wonderful. Such a kind man. Of course, we'll miss you around here, but what a great opportunity for you."

Kathleen waited for her friend to finish before saying, "I'm not going."

"Have you lost your mind? Even though I love having you here, there's no future in this place."

"I won't take Owen's money. It isn't right.'

"Honey, it's right if Owen wanted you to do this. My mama always told me to not let an opportunity get past you because it might be bobtailed."

Kathleen tilted her head and pulled her eyebrows into a question.

Jazzy sighed. "What I mean is, you may regret this later on but then it might be too late to say yes."

Kathleen reached around her friend and grabbed a wet cloth. "I'll bus those two booths." She knew her friend's eyes were on her back as she walked away.

Chapter 21

When Kathleen's shift was over, she hurried toward her car but stopped dead still when she spotted a green truck parked next to her little bug. Fear crawled up her spine and made its way through her body. She wanted to rush back to the diner, but her feet seemed to be glued to the asphalt.

When a tall man wearing a cowboy hat and boots exited the truck and walked toward her, the fear turned to anger. Kathleen quickly closed the distance between them.

"Why are you following me? I want you to stop. If you don't, I'm calling the police," she sputtered, hands coiled into tight fists.

The man put both hands in the air. "Whoa, I'm not stalking you, Miss Carter. I'm a private investigator hired by your parents. They asked me to find you and to watch over you. My name is Homer Stillman. Here's my card."

It took a moment for his words to sink in. When they did, Kathleen struggled to find enough air in her lungs to speak. Her heart beat against her chest. She stared at the asphalt, willing herself to calm down. Finally, she returned her gaze to the man.

"My parents know where I'm at? How can they possibly know?"

"They've known since the first night you were here. Your father thought you might come to Charleston, a city large enough to hide in." Homer smiled. "I think he was betting on your intelligence. Once they described you and your yellow car, it wasn't hard to find you." He paused, then continued, "Your father called this morning. He asked me to tell you how much they miss you and want you to come home."

Come home? Homesickness made her stomach coil, yet her mind told her she could never go home.

"Please let my parents know I can't come home." She bit her bottom lip hard, feeling it trembling against her teeth. "Tell... tell them I love them and I'm sorry."

Kathleen knew she couldn't stay in Charleston. In one swift moment, it became clear what to do—accept Owen's gift.

When Kathleen arrived at the boarding house, she barely remembered the drive there. Her mind swirled with the details of going to Morgantown. She sat in the car, not wanting to take the first steps toward leaving. She liked Charleston and hated to leave her job and her few friends at the diner. Even Mary's constant chatter and talking about faith no longer grated on her nerves.

"Dear, are you okay?" Mary called the porch.

"You've been sitting in your car for thirty minutes. I'm worried about you."

Kathleen leaned over and rolled down the passenger's window. "I'm fine. I was just thinking." Only then did she realize that the early August heat had the inside of her car sweltering. She wiped the sweat off her forehead with the back of her hand.

"Come inside. I have the attic fan on. It's much nicer in the house than in your car," Mary said. "Goodness, you could have a heat stroke. There's gingerbread just out of the oven. We can sit in the cool living room, eat a slice, and catch up."

The last thing Kathleen wanted was to visit with Mary. "I should accept the invitation," she whispered as she exited the car. She walked up the sidewalk between the rows of blooming roses of very color, surprised that she would miss them and Mary's boarding house.

Sneaking away from those who helped her added to Kathleen's list of guilts. A load of bricks pushed down on her body at the thought of what she must do next. Plastering on a fake smile, Kathleen walked into the house and attempted a cheery hello.

"I'm in the kitchen. But don't come in. It's hotter than chili peppers in here. Wait for me in the living room. I'll bring the gingerbread and a couple of cold Dr Peppers."

Kathleen's smile became genuine at the thoughtfulness of her hostess. She moved to the living room, reveling in the cool air from the attic fan. Sitting in one of Mary's overstuffed chairs covered with a rose-patterned fabric, she wondered why she ever thought this decor was ugly. Now she liked the coziness of the room. Some of the day's tension drained slowly from her, like a partially clogged sink.

"Here we go. How good God is to bring someone to share this bake with me."

Kathleen jerked at Mary's entrance. She didn't realize she'd laid back her head and closed her eyes.

"Poor thing, you look exhausted. Was it a busy day at the diner?" Mary asked as she put the tray holding the treats on the table between the two matching chairs.

Nodding her head, Kathleen reached for the Dr Pepper and took a long drink before turning to Mary. "Gingerbread is my favorite. My mother made it often when I came home from school." The memory squeezed at her gut.

"How nice. Tell me about your parents. Are they believers?"

Kathleen had a fluttering in her chest before she responded with a quiet, "Yes." Before Mary could ask the same question about her, she changed the subject.

"How was your day?" Kathleen asked as she leaned toward Mary.

"Oh, I had a wonderful day. Twice a month, several of the ladies from church meet for a Bible Study. Today's lesson blessed me. We talked about the need to spend time with the Lord every morning and how it brings peace and thanksgiving for the rest of the day."

Mary paused for a moment, then continued. "You know, there's a young people's group at my church. They get together every Friday evening at someone's home. You might enjoy joining them."

"I might do that." Kathleen hated herself—another lie. She'd be gone long before Friday.

After dinner that night, she asked Mary, "May I use your phone before I go up?"

"Of course. I'll do the dishes, so you'll have your privacy. I know how young girls like to speak to their special friend with no one listening." Mary raised one eyebrow and winked.

"Thank you," Kathleen said. Better to let her hostess think it was a boyfriend she was calling than her lawyer.

She pulled Mr. Barlett's card from her purse and called the home number listed under his office number.

When she shared her plans over the phone, he urged her to meet him at the office now to sign the transfer documents necessary for her inheritance to move to a bank in Morgantown.

Kathleen went by the kitchen door and informed Mary she was going out for a while.

Mary waved one hand in the air, dripping soapy water onto the floor. "You kids have fun."

"I'm so glad you're accepting this inheritance. Owen would be pleased," Mr. Barlett said, when she arrived fifteen minutes later.

"I'm doing it to honor his request." She smiled, hoping the statement didn't sound as insincere to him as it did to her.

Back inside her room, Kathleen quietly pulled the suitcase from under the bed to pack her clothes. Her parents gave it to her when she went away to college. How different her life was then.

Kathleen slammed the top of the suitcase so hard she was sure her landlady must have heard it. She tiptoed over and pressed her ear to the door, relieved at the sound of Mary's singing, no doubt while doing some final household chores before bed.

She'd wait until Mary was sleeping before retrieving her toiletries from their shared bathroom. Back in her room, Kathleen sat down and pulled out a sheet of rose imprinted stationery.

Dear Mary,
Thank you for being a friend over the past months. I enjoyed being in your home and appreciate all you did for me. My circumstances have changed, and I must leave now. Please don't worry, I'll be fine.
Kathleen
P.S. I love your roses.

Kathleen reread the letter, then folded the paper, inserted it into a matching envelope, and wrote Mary's name on the front. She tapped her pen on the desktop, then drew a happy face in the corner. She wanted Mary to think she was happy about leaving. When was the last time she felt truly happy?

She leaned back in her chair, exhausted from the turn of events the day had brought. When Kathleen heard Mary's footsteps coming up the stairs, she quickly snapped off the desk lamp.

Kathleen set her alarm for four a.m. and placed the clock under her pillow to muffle its sound, then fell into bed, sure sleep would never come. But it did, and with it came a dream of her running toward something but never arriving there. The farther she ran, the longer the road became. Worst were the dark smoke billows lining each side of the road from the ground to high above her head.

When the pillow vibrated under her head, Kathleen jolted straight up. Blinking hard to orient herself, she tried to shake off the bizarre dream. Dressing in the light from a full moon, she tried to not make any noise. Waking Mary might dissolve her determination to leave.

Kathleen grabbed her suitcase and overnight bag, the letter, and one of the fresh roses that appeared every few days in her room. She slipped into the hall and made her way slowly down the stairs, careful to make as little noise as possible. At the front door, she placed the letter and the rose on the entryway table and quietly opened the front door. Keeping her walking speed at a minimum, she made it past the rows of roses. But not before taking a deep smell, savoring the rose scent for the last time.

Kathleen stowed her luggage in her tiny backseat and settled into the driver's seat. Switching on the overhead light, she pulled the road map from under the seat and studied the route to Morgantown. After starting her car, she made a quick jerk from park to drive, pressed lightly on the gas petal and let the tires roll out of the driveway, then turned left and increased her speed.

Mary stood on the front porch, her head bowed in prayer.

Chapter 22

Friday afternoon, Walt pulled into a parking spot at the newspaper office, turned off his engine, and stared at the keys in his hand as though they would give him an answer. Kathleen was the first thing he thought of in the morning and the last thing at night.

He dropped his head and asked God to either show him how to make things right with Kathleen or take her from his thoughts. Then he listened. Nothing. Discouraged, he pulled his checkbook from his backpack and flipped it open. Dismal! And he didn't get paid from the newspaper for another week. His TA check wouldn't come until the end of the month.

Walt put the checkbook and keys in his backpack and exited the car, his brain not ready to say no to going back to Charleston after work today. But how? Gas, food, and lodging would likely put him in the red. Head down, he walked toward the building.

"Hey, Walt. Wait up."

Walt knew the voice without looking back. He halted and waited for Liam to make it to his side.

"You're in a rush this morning. You usually sweep in a few minutes late," his friend said. Walt started walking again but Liam grabbed his arm.

"Wait a minute, will you? I have something for you, and I'd rather not give it to you in inside."

He stopped, but not willingly. Walt was in no mood for Liam's lame jokes. He'd been bitten by them too many times. "What is it, Cleburne? It's already too hot to be standing in the parking lot."

"Remember the money you loaned me in April so I could go back home for my sister's wedding?"

"Yeah," Walt answered, haltingly. He hoped his friend wasn't about to hit him up for more, because his well was almost dry.

"I saved ten dollars a month until I had the fifty dollars to give back," Liam said with a silly grin. "I should have told you my plan, but I was afraid you'd ask for it sooner." He dug into his pocket and handed Walt five crumpled ten-dollar bills. "Thanks again, man. My sister would've killed me if I'd missed her big day." He slapped Walt on the shoulder and jogged toward the building.

Walt stared at the bills in his hand. Then, at the back of his friend. He knew what it meant for him to save this much money. Liam came from a family of miners, deep in the southern part of West Virginia. He came to college on a wing and a prayer, consuming a steady diet of peanut butter sandwiches.

The plan materialized as he took the elevator up to the newsroom. He'd leave before sunup tomorrow and go back to Charleston. If Kathleen would talk to him, he'd stay the night so he could buy her dinner. A smile spread across his face as he imaged this scenario.

After a long day at work and an even longer night, Walt finally headed his car toward Charleston. He'd intended to leave at six, but after staring at the bedside clock for over an hour, he gave up and headed for the shower. By five, he was on the road. In the quiet stillness of pre-dawn, he thought about yesterday's events—how he went from pauper to prince in a matter of minutes. Then he realized it was the Lord's provision. He immediately spoke to his Savior. "Thank you for this provision. And forgive me for thinking it was luck. Now let her be willing to speak with me."

A few hours later, Walt pulled up to the Lombardi Diner, searching the parking lot for a yellow VW bug. "Maybe she's parked around back, or someone gave her a ride," Walt whispered. He smoothed his hair before getting out of his car and walked into the diner.

Walt scanned the place, full of hungry customers, but didn't see Kathleen. His stomach plummeted. *Maybe she doesn't work on Saturday.* No, it was a Saturday the first time he came.

Then a familiar face came into view. He'd seen this waitress the last time he was here. He raised his hand to give her a little wave when he saw her sigh and close her eyes. Confused, he took a seat at the closest empty booth and waited.

After what seemed an eternity, a waitress came by and asked if he wanted coffee. He stared at the short, brown-haired lady old enough to be his mother. "What happened to the other one?"

"Don't know. I was just hired yesterday. You want a menu?"

"No, thank you. Coffee's fine for now," Walt said, while his eyes roamed the diner.

"How long are you going to milk that coffee? It's been nearly thirty minutes, and you haven't seen the bottom of the cup yet. If stares could kill, it would be exploded by now."

Walt jerked his head upward and saw the familiar waitress. He remembered hearing another customer calling her name. "Your Jazzy, right?"

"I am. And I'm wondering why you have been in this booth for so long without ordering food." She stood over Walt, both hands perched on her hips.

"Oh, sorry. I... uh... I was hoping Kathleen would be here today. Is she on break or... something?" Walt cringed. As a reporter, he rarely spoke in jumbled words.

Jazzy sat down across from him. "Look, Kathleen's not here. She called yesterday morning and told me she was leaving Charleston."

"Left? Was she going home? Did she leave a forwarding address? Surely someone knows where she went." His voice rose with panic.

"No one here knows where she went." Jazzy slid out of the booth. "I should get back to work."

Walt reached into his pocket and threw a crumpled dollar bill on the table before rushing from the diner. Outside, he forced his starved lungs to draw in air. "This can't be," he whispered.

Walking to his car, Walt knew his need to see Kathleen was much more than an attraction to her. He closed his eyes and let the truth come into his heart.

He was the reason she fled. Taking her to the crash site had been a mistake, something he selfishly did because he wanted to get to know her. Guilt spread through his body like a wildfire. He had to find her and make things right—but how?

The name Homer Stillman came into Walt's mind. Maybe he had some leads. He found the address of the PI in the phone book hanging in the phone booth outside the diner. Walt read the address twice, then drove to the location, hoping the man might be in his office on a Saturday.

After several knocks on Stillman's office door, Walt returned to the elevator, his mind deep in thought about his next move. He stared at the dated black-and-white tiles on the floor of the old building. When the elevator opened, he stepped in without lifting his eyes.

"Whoa there, partner. I need off this horse 'fore you can get on."

Lifting his gaze, Walt recognized the man he'd seen in the green truck. "I'm sorry… guess I wasn't looking. Are you Homer Stillman?"

"If you're here to ask me to take your case, you'll need to make an appointment for next week." Homer started for his office, digging a key from his jeans pocket.

"I won't be here next week. I just have a quick question."

"All right. Come on in. But you'll need to make it quick." He unlocked the office door and stood aside, waving Walt in. "I'm on a case and already late for a stake-out. I came by to get more film for my camera."

The reporter in him wanted to ask about the case, but he held his tongue. Instead, he blurted out, "Do you know Kathleen Carter left Charleston two days ago?"

Homer sighed and shook his head. "Son, I don't know how you are involved in this, but I don't talk about my cases with strangers. But I can tell you this: when someone flees, and the trail is forty-eight hours old, I doubt a coon dog could pick it up."

"You really don't know where she went?" Walt shot him a narrow-eyed look. As a reporter, he'd become adept at knowing when he was being lied to.

"I really don't, son. And if I did, I couldn't tell you." Homer grabbed a couple of rows of film from his desk drawer and stood up. "The part of my job I don't like is when I must give bad news to someone." He approached the door and held it open for Walt to leave. "I'll call my client tonight. It'll break their hearts."

Guilt flooded Walt's heart. He'd wronged them as well.

Walt hesitated for a split second, feeling as though he'd lost his last tie to Kathleen. Sighing, he followed Homer to the elevator, riding down with him. They were parting to go separate ways when Walt said, "I'm grateful for you giving me some time."

"You bet, partner." Homer threw up his hand without turning around.

He drove away and meandered around the city until he came to a park beside the river. Walt parked and trudged across the green thick grass, his shoes sinking into the thick turf.

A cool breeze wafted off the river, and Walt's tense muscles relaxed. He watched as a lone duck paddled by, leaving a V-shaped ribbon of water behind. A way down the river, a group of kids stood at the river's edge, skipping rocks.

Walt cleared his mind of all thoughts, but his heart kept speaking. He knew what he needed to do. Bowing his head, he whispered, "Lord, forgive me for what I've done. I'm ashamed of my actions. I've caused others to have pain. Please take care of Kathleen. Hold her hand wherever she is and direct her back to her family someday."

Chapter 23

A late August breeze rustled through the half-opened window near Kathleen's single bed. She lay there, reviewing the last two weeks since coming to Morgantown. Within three days of her arrival, she'd opened a bank account to transfer the inheritance money, enrolled in WVU, and moved into a dorm. She'd hoped for a single room, but her late registration limited her choices. However, her roommate, Ainsley Wallace, was fun, kind, and respectful.

She glanced at the bed opposite hers and sighed at the sight of a body wrapped in a tangle of bedsheets, emitting a series of whispery snores. "Ainsley, wake up. Classes start soon."

"Nooo!" Ainsley moaned as she flopped over and pulled the sheet farther over her head.

Kathleen moved to the bed opposite hers and leaned over Ainsley. "If you want those pancakes you can't get enough of, you need to get to the cafeteria before they're all gone."

Stepping back, she knew how her roommate would react. Ainsley came from a Scottish mining family with eight kids. Food had to be shared with many hungry mouths. The fact she could eat her fill was motivation enough to bounce out of bed.

"Well, let's get ourselves in high gear." She planted her hands on bony hips, her clear blue eyes shining with anticipation. "Like my pa says, 'Don't waste daylight, for night is comin'.'"

Thirty minutes later, the roommates were eating pancakes slathered in butter and dripping with maple syrup. Kathleen shook her fork at Ainsley. "You're a bad influence on me."

Ainsley pushed back her long, curls with her free hand while putting a forkful of pancake into her mouth. "Nothing could ever be bad about food."

Unable to take another bite, Kathleen watched her friend finish every morsel on her plate.

Leaving the cafeteria, they parted ways—Ainsley to the School of Education and Kathleen to the English department.

She found her classroom after a few wrong turns, inhaled deeply, and walked in. When the professor began his lecture, Kathleen's love of learning returned. Then she remembered the biology class she and Cody took together at Marshall University. She'd never have made it through the tough subject if Cody hadn't tutored her in the evenings. It was a bittersweet memory of the old Cody—the one she'd fallen for in high school. After that, she had a hard time focusing on the instructor.

She walked alone in the hallway, watching groups of friends and hearing snatches of conversations about their classes, their significant others, and parties planned for the coming weekend. Funny, she was their age but felt decades older. The night of the crash stole her youth.

Kathleen left the second class, composition, rhetoric and research, sure she'd die of boredom before the semester was over. The professor was dry as desert sand with a monotone voice that would put anyone to sleep. When the torturous forty-five minutes ended, she couldn't get out of the lecture room fast enough. Apparently, other students felt the same because there was a mad dash for the door.

After a quick lunch, Kathleen headed to her chemistry class, pleased to know this was the last science course needed for her degree since she and science had never gotten along well. She walked into a lab classroom and hurried to the only open stool. "May I take this spot?"

"I can dig it," responded the student. He wore a tie-dyed T-shirt, a pair of denim bell-bottoms, and a fringed leather vest with a red bandanna tied in the back around his forehead. His long, brown hair reached about six inches below his shoulders. A peace-sign necklace hung from his neck.

Kathleen took his answer as an affirmative. "My name is Kathleen Carter. Nice to meet you."

"I'm Russell Dunn. You can call me Rusty." He held up his first two fingers to form a V. "Peace, Kathleen," he added with a grin.

She suddenly realized she was staring at him and twisted back to find a syllabus someone had laid at each place around the room. Her chest fell to her feet when she realized her high school chemistry class would serve poorly for this course.

"Do you understand any of this?"

"Sure."

"How? It looks like hieroglyphics."

Rusty ducked his head toward her and whispered, "Not if your dad is a high school chemistry teacher. He made sure I was ready for college chemistry. His goal is to make me a science teacher like him." Rusty wiggled his eyebrows and flashed a silly grin. "Imagine his disappointment when I chose poly sci. I'll help you."

Relief swelled in Kathleen's body like the sea rising at high tide. She opened her mouth to reply when the professor entered the lab.

"Hello, everyone. I'm Professor Wells," he stated with a stern face. "First thing is to choose lab partners. Should you not want the person on the stool next to you, make your choice in the next sixty seconds."

She watched as a few students scrambled from their stools to new partners. Kathleen turned back to Rusty. "Are we good?"

"It's cool with me."

Professor Wells waited for the class to settle down and spent the rest of the time meticulously explaining the syllabus. It was all Greek to Kathleen. When the class ended, she threw Rusty a panicked look.

"Don't worry, you'll get through this."

Kathleen wished she felt as confident as her new lab partner. Determined to do as Rusty said, she focused on the beautiful WVU campus with tall trees and manicured lawns as she walked toward the library. She stopped to watch two chipmucks chasing each other in perfectly concentric circles up an ancient oak.

"Ugh!" Kathleen exclaimed as she went flying off the sidewalk on to the grassy knoll. Books, notepads, pencils, and pens spilled across the grass.

"Why did you stop so suddenly? That could have been dangerous."

Could have been? The nerve of him to blame it on her. She moved to a sitting position, ready to give this guy a piece of her mind. But at the sight of her assailant's face, the words never made it to her lips.

"Uh… that's okay. I shouldn't have stopped on a sidewalk full of walkers."

The student checked his watch. "I have to go." With that, he raced off, dodging walkers to his left and his right.

Kathleen watched his back from her place on the grass. Why had she apologized to him when he clearly was in the wrong? And why was he dressed in military fatigues? She searched for the reason for her behavior but found she could only think of the amazing brown eyes.

"Bummer. Looks like you may have had a collision. Can I help you up?" Rusty extended a hand and offered her a sympathetic smile.

Once on her feet, Kathleen dusted the grass off her pants. "I'm glad you came along. Someone ran right over me."

"Yeah, I saw it from a little way back. Totally wrong for the jerk not to help."

"Tell me about it." She bent to retrieve her things from the sidewalk before any more students came by.

With Rusty's help, they soon had everything back in the bag.

"Thanks again, Rusty. I'll see you in class on Wednesday."

"Wait. You look like you need to chill. Come with me to a great coffeehouse. Best java in town. It's just a one-block walk."

"I'm going to the library to get a start on my assignments. I'm overwhelmed at how much work there already is in all three of my classes—and it's the first day. With two more different classes tomorrow, I dread to see what they'll assign."

"All the more reason to get a cup of energy before starting the work. It's what I always do."

"Okay, but I have to make it quick."

"Cool. It's this way." He turned around and headed back to the way they'd come.

One block later, they crossed the street at the light and walked a short distance to Roasters. The words on the glass window said, Where the coffee is groovy. Inside, a collection of different tables and mismatched chairs filled the middle of the room. Against one wall, cubicles held small tables with two stools. Colorful beads hung from the ceiling to the floor for privacy. The employees wore tie-dyed T-shirts and navy reject pants.

Kathleen looked around at a sea of long-haired hippies wearing an assortment of anti-establishment clothing. She felt out of place in her blue pedal-pushers, sleeveless white blouse, and a pair of flats.

Rusty seemed to sense her thoughts. "Don't worry. This is a mellow crowd, unless a uniform walks in. Take a seat at an open table in one of the cubicles and I'll get our coffee."

She walked through the beads, surprised by the pleasant sensation of the beads melting apart as her body passed through. Some of the tightness in her anxious muscles relaxed.

"Sorry it took so long. I had to wait for the percolator to finish dripping." He sat a steaming mug of black coffee in front of her.

Kathleen took a sip of her coffee and pulled her face into a grimace.

"Too strong? There's sugar and cream on the counter. I can get—"

"No, this is fine. I need it strong." She studied her coffee for a moment, then shifted her eyes to Rusty. "Tell me what you meant when you said, 'unless a uniform walks in'."

"Simple. Most of the students in this place are anti-war. Several of the regulars here were a part of last May's demonstrations on our campus. Military students aren't exactly welcome here." Rusty leaned back in his chair. "Those three days of our demonstrations were statements against the killing of four students at the Kent State tragedy and the bombing of Cambodia by US forces."

"Our?" Kathleen asked as her eyebrows curved downward.

"I take part in all the anti-war protests on this campus. I hope this doesn't mean you want a new lab partner."

"No, not at all." Kathleen took another sip of coffee and reached for her bookbag. "Thanks for the coffee. Now I need to get to the library. By the way—I feel energized."

"Cool." Rusty threw her a peace sign before emptying his mug and headed to the counter for more.

Kathleen spent three hours in the library but got little done. Her thoughts kept returning to the brown-eyed guy in the Army fatigues.

Chapter 24

"Ainsley, last call. I'm about to leave," Kathleen called from her stance by the door.

"All right, I'm up!" Ainsley's feet hit the floor with a thud. She unfolded her thin frame, then raised her arms and yawned widely. "Wait, you're leaving now? What about breakfast?"

"I'm not hungry. I want to get to my first class early to ask my professor a question."

"It's a wonder to me that anyone would pass on food." Ainsley scratched her stomach and flopped back down on her bed.

"You're not going back to bed, are you?"

"Nope, just trying to remember which pair of my two jeans I wore yesterday."

"Look at the pair on the floor. That may give you a clue." Kathleen chuckled as she exited the room.

Outside, she rushed down eighty-five steps, the only way to or from Stalnaker Hall. At the bottom,

Kathleen rotated to gaze at the dorm she now called home. Built in 1918, the Classical Revival building stood on a hill in the middle of campus. Red brick contrasted with white trim around the many windows. It was reminiscent of the Old Main building at Marshall. If she'd enrolled at WVU earlier, this dorm would have been her last choice.

Once she hit the sidewalk, she breathed in the cool mountain air. The heat wave of the past two months was succumbing to the coolness of fall. "About time," she grumbled under her breath.

After a quick run to the student union for a to-go coffee, Kathleen walked to her first class, Intro to The Classics. She arrived early and chose a seat at the end of one of the many rows in the lecture-style classroom.

Sighing, she watched as the room quickly filled with students. Another large class, which made it more difficult to meet one-on-one with the professor if she struggled. Her mood went from tense to fearful. So different from the girl who loved adventure and challenges.

Kathleen scanned the large textbook in her lap, hoping it might calm her nerves, when she heard a low, tentative voice.

"Hello?"

She jerked her head to the right. The voice had come from a student sitting in the next seat. "Uh... hello. Sorry, I was leafing through this enormous book."

"I wasn't sure if I should interrupt you. You seemed so intense."

"It's daunting... the textbook, I mean." She was stunned by the beauty of the girl, who had gorgeous deep brown eyes and creamy skin. A single, long braid of jet-black hair lay across the front of one shoulder.

"I'm Kathleen Carter."

"It's nice to meet you. I'm Mahira Dasgupta."

Their discussion continued no further since a small, young professor in flared jeans and pink blouse entered from a side door and moved to the lectern on the stage. After adjusting the attached mic downward, she smiled and said, "I'm Dr. Willet. Please don't let my size bother you. As the great classical writer Dr. Seuss wrote in *Horton Hears a Who*, 'A person's a person, no matter how small.' My teaching assistant is giving copies of the syllabus to the first student in each row. Please take one and pass it down."

Kathleen almost laughed at the sight of the TA, who had to be well over six feet tall. He had hair the color of straw, which apparently had not seen a comb that morning. When he reached Kathleen's row, he flashed a big smile and paused briefly before moving on. "You'll like Dr. Willet. She's cool." Then he continued to the next row.

Mahira leaned over with a whisper. "I think you have an admirer."

Kathleen rolled her eyes, bringing a small giggle from Mahira.

The next hour and a half went by quickly as the professor reviewed the course outline with efficiency and humor, then moved into an interesting lecture about classical writers, offering bits of quirky facts about them. Surprised when the ninety minutes ended, Kathleen faced Mahira. "I don't think I should be frightened about this class. She's amazing."

"I agree. As a classical literature major, I'm sure

I'll have more classes with her. Maybe we can study together sometime."

Kathleen couldn't believe her luck—another study partner. "I'd like that. Thank you."

Her next class was creative writing. She loved to write and had always wanted to fine-tune her amateur attempts at the craft. When the professor gave the assignment to write about why they chose to attend WVU, Kathleen knew she'd write about Owen.

After a quick lunch and three grueling hours of study in the library, Kathleen returned to her dorm, tired but pleased with Tuesday/Thursday classes. Before reaching her room, she heard loud sobbing coming from inside. She picked up her speed and rushed into the room to find Ainsley in her bed facing the wall. Her sobs gained momentum with each passing moment. Hastily, Kathleen closed the door and went to her friend. "What's wrong?" Never would she have thought she'd see tears from her cheerful roommate.

Ainsley rolled over, took one glance at Kathleen, and pitched back to her original position, crying harder than before.

Alarmed, Kathleen put her hand on Ainsley's heaving shoulder. "Tell me what's happened. Did someone hurt you?" Her roommate shook her head. "Then nothing could be this bad." As soon as the words came out of her mouth, Kathleen thought of her own past. Many things could be bad enough for the pain she heard in Ainsley's sobs.

A sting hit Kathleen's eyes. She blinked rapidly before grabbing a box of tissues for the crying girl. "Please turn over and speak to me. Maybe I can help," she said, grimacing at the voice in her head saying she couldn't even help herself.

Ainsley slowly sat up and faced Kathleen. The sobbing ended, replaced by silent tears drifting their way down her face like a lazy river. She jerked several tissues from the box in Kathleen's extended hand, blew her nose, and looked at her friend. "I have a letter from my Joe." Her face crumbled at the mention of his name.

"No more crying. Just tell me what happened."

Ainsley continued in a shaky voice, punctuated by a series of hiccups. "He doesn't love me anymore. He says he wants to... to date Amy Withers." She looked down at the crumbled tissues in her hands. "Amy! Can you imagine?"

Kathleen couldn't but nodded her head anyway. Roomies stick together, right? "Go on," she whispered.

"We were getting married as soon as I graduated. I planned to teach at the local school back home, and he would keep working in the mine. And we were going to have lots of babies!" Ainsley dropped her head again, tears dropping off the end of her chin onto the bedcovers.

Kathleen said the first thing that came to her mind. "Life has a way of changing on a dime. Better get used to it." She cringed at her comment. *How can I be so hardhearted?* She knew the answer. A hardened heart can't fix a broken one.

After a night of sleep interrupted by the soft sobs coming from the other bed, Kathleen woke with a headache. When she stood up, her head felt like someone had kicked her with a blunt-toed boot. She gingerly went to the bathroom medicine cabinet and wolfed down a couple of aspirins, hoping they would lessen the pain.

After dressing for class, she stood beside her roommate's bed. "Ainsley, if you're going to class today, get up."

"I can't go. Please leave me alone."

She stared at the mangled bedding, only seeing a tuff of Ainsley's auburn hair. "Okay. Rest today. Maybe you'll feel better tomorrow." She tiptoed out of the room, worried about leaving her friend alone. Once in the hallway, she whispered, "I'll call her between classes."

That never happened.

Without her lab partner, who wasn't in class, Kathleen made several mistakes on the lab assignment—so many that the professor called her out in class. By the time the fiasco was over, her headache had doubled in size. She trudged out of the class, wondering if she should go to the infirmary. Before she could decide, someone stopped her on the sidewalk.

"Miss, my name is Jackson McBride. I'm the person who ran over you and left you stranded in the grass. I'm so sorry. I was rushing to catch a ride. It was rude of me to not stay and help you." His speech came rolling off his tongue at double-speed. "Oh, these are for you." He held out a bundle of flowers, which appeared to be on their last day.

Kathleen glanced at the sad flowers, then back at the guy who was no longer in soldier fatigues. Today he wore jeans with a dark green T-shirt.

"I bought them yesterday. Guess I should've put them in water."

She looked at his sheepish grin, thinking of several snide remarks until her glance moved to his eyes. They were full of kindness and something else she struggled to identify. Was it... hope? Her lungs tightened, stealing her breath for a moment, then she heard herself saying yes when he asked her to lunch.

"But it will need to be a quick one. I have a class in thirty minutes," she lied. Her class wasn't for another hour.

"Let's go to the student union. It's right here."

Ten minutes later, Kathleen sat in a booth across from the guy who had literally mowed her down the day before. She stared at her burger and wondered why she'd agreed to this. It was her second time in a week to be with a guy. Her brain went into hyper-mode. *What's wrong with me? I can't do this! I shouldn't be with men at all, not after—*

Suddenly, she realized he was talking to her. Kathleen felt heat hit her face. *He must think I'm nuts.* She swallowed her thoughts and spoke. "I'm sorry, Jackson. What did you say?"

"Please call me Jake. I asked where you're from."

She froze, then responded in a cold voice. "Why do you want to know?" Kathleen watched as his face went from peaceful to questioning.

He lifted one shoulder before answering. "I... I'm just making conversation."

"I can't do this." Kathleen grabbed her bookbag and scooted out of the booth without looking at her lunch partner. She rushed out of the student union as moisture collected in her eyes. The wilted flowers stayed on the table.

Chapter 25

"Why do you keep writing about the war?" The words spewed out of Liam's mouth like water from a faucet with air in the line.

"Same reason you write about anti-war protest. It's called news... and we're called reporters." Walt took a long draw of coffee, weary of the same argument his friend started each time they sat in a booth. He'd prefer to have his coffee with the early edition of the *Herald Dispatch*. "Don't call it a war. It's termed a 'conflict'."

"Yeah, by those warped heads in DC." Sarcasm dripped from Liam's voice. "A conflict is something between friends. This is war. Thousands of American soldiers are dead." Liam's voice broke with his next words. "What about those that are missing or in a POW camp?" His eyes grew glassy as he stared at a young man sitting across from him with only one arm and a T-shirt with an American flag and the word *Veteran* across the front.

"Give the Vietnamization policy a chance. The strategy is to train the Vietnam Army to fight the Viet Cong without us. Troops are being shipped home daily. Soon the South Vietnam Army will fight the communists alone."

Liam stared at Walt as if he'd grown a second head. "It's been three years since the policy was put in place and there are still troops on the ground, not to mention the helicopters and aircraft!"

Walt pushed his empty coffee cup to the outside edge of the table, hoping the waitress would come by with a refill. He glanced at the large clock on the wall opposite him. His teacher's assistant job would begin in fifteen minutes, followed by a graduate class and, finally, his work at the newspaper. It would be a long day, but he felt compelled to stay put.

Liam had been combative since his older brother re-upped for a second tour in Vietnam. Walt said a quick, silent prayer. *Lord, give me the right words for my friend. His fear for his brother is making him bitter and causing him to make poor decisions.*

"I understand your fear for your brother, but God says *fear not* so many times in His Word. Isaiah 41:10 has always been my go-to for fear. It might help if you tried reading these scriptures in your—"

"I quit reading my Bible and praying. Why doesn't God stop this atrocity, or does He agree with the warmongers in our government?" His voice raised in volume with each word.

"Lower it, man." Walt glanced at the other diners.

Leaning over the table, Liam whispered through

clenched teeth, "If this lunacy doesn't stop, we'll have another Kent State, and more college students will be killed!"

"You know those protests happened because of our invasion into Cambodia."

"Our invasion? Surely, you're aware Americans didn't back the invasion. It was the work of our president and his crony generals."

There seemed to be no way to settle his friend down. "I'm late for my TA job. And you have a journalism class you've cut too many times. You need to think about your GPA." *When did I become Liam's mother?*

"Tell Rickman I won't be back to the office. I'm going to a sit-in this afternoon." Liam stood and threw two crumpled dollar bills on the table. "Coffee's on me."

He watched his friend leave, head down, shoulders slumped. A new thought materialized, which made Walt grimace. Was Liam headed to the sit-in to cover it for the newspaper or to be a part of it?

Walking out of the diner, Walt barely noticed the drizzle coming from the low ceiling of gray clouds. By the time he entered the lecture room, his hair was wet and his windbreaker shined with moisture. The professor gave him a sour look. He mouthed a sorry and grabbed the seating chart to do a head count. When Walt came to the empty seat assigned to Kathleen, his gut tightened as it did every time he thought of her. Where was she? Was she safe? Was she happy?

A wet September floated into a dry October, resplendent with wild splashes of yellow, red, and gold. It adorned the mountains like a Jackson Pollock original.

As Walt drove south after work on Friday, he breathed the crisp, clean air through his open window and took in the beautiful array of fall colors until the sun set and darkness followed. His visits to see Henry and Emily always helped with the tension that had taken up residence in his neck and shoulders.

Added to this were Liam's irrational behaviors. Walt feared they may cost his friend the newspaper job. How many times had he covered for his coworker? After a while, he feared losing his own position for being deceitful with Rickman. The lies weighed down his spirit. Something needed to change.

His thoughts became popcorn in hot grease, popping from one to the next. Should he leave graduate school? Would it lessen his chances of becoming editor of a large city paper—a goal since he took his first journalism class in high school?

Another pop of corn put him back to age five. His mother unhappy being the wife of a miner left when he was four. His father died in a mining accident within a few months. With no living relatives, he bounced from one foster home to another.

Walt finally had a break at age fourteen by being placed with the Cushmans. As strong Christians, they felt led to open their home to children who needed care. Through their faith, he came to accept the salvation offered by Jesus.

Before Walt made the last turn of his journey, he pulled his foot from the accelerator and took in the night view of Farrowlee. A full moon and cloudless sky created a shimmer on the town as if it were a magical kingdom. The corners of his lips turned upward when he thought about the Carters' friendship. His continued correspondence and occasional visits filled a hole in Walt's heart he hadn't known existed. Yet another hole needed to be filled—the one caused by his lie of omission about the part he played in Kathleen's disappearance. "This time, Lord. This time I'll do it."

"Hello, Walt. You made good time," Henry said from the front porch when Walt exited his vehicle.

"It's always a miracle when my old car gets me here. This time, her motor purred like a kitten the entire trip. I think she wanted out of the city as well."

Henry chuckled. "Someday you're going to have to put her out to pasture."

"Someday, but not yet," Walt announced as he proceeded up the sidewalk, carrying his overnight bag.

He followed Henry through the big wooden door and immediately heard Emily's soft, distinctive voice.

"I'm just taking the roast from the oven. I'll be right out."

When Emily emerged from the kitchen, Walt looked into her eyes and saw the familiar pain and the slight shake of her head. Disappointment and shame surged through him.

After they ate a meal of roast, potatoes, and fall vegetables, Walt excused himself. "I'm sorry. I had a busy morning, then spent my afternoon chasing down a story about two candidates running for mayor. If it's not too rude, I'd like to hit the sack."

"Of course, we understand. We're pleased you came for our Fall Festival. It's always a fun time, though this year may..." Henry's voice trailed off without finishing the sentence.

Emily came to her husband's rescue. "Walt, your bedroom is to the left now. I've cleaned out my sewing stuff. I never seem to get the time to sew. It's made up and ready for you."

Walt headed up the stairs, noting that his hosts appeared relieved when he left early for bed. Both Emily and Henry seemed off their game. Something was amiss.

Chapter 26

The morning sun coming through the bedroom window woke Walt with a start. He shook his head, trying to dispel the dream where he was chasing a yellow bug through mountain roads and city streets. Every time he drove close to the little car, it disappeared, only to show up at a different place. It wasn't the first time the dream had tortured him in his sleep.

He rose and moved to the window, trying to clear his muddled head. Pulling back the curtain, he saw men milling around in the meadow across from the miner's homes. Their voices carried up the hill to the home of their superintendent.

"Pete, you get some men to help set up the tables for eating. The rest of you help with the vendor booths." Walt widened his view to where men were constructing what appeared to be a football field.

One knock and Henry's voice came through the

door. "Emily has breakfast prepared. She says to come have some, though it's lite. We'll fill ourselves with festival food later today."

"I'll be down in five minutes. Thank you."

"No problem. We knew you needed some rest."

Downstairs, he hurried to the breakfast table, feeling guilty when he saw both his hosts already seated.

"Sorry." He sat down quickly. "I guess I really was tired last night." He wished the visions of last night's dream would leave this mind. More than this, he wanted to know the reason for Henry and Emily's forced smiles.

"It's not a problem, Walt. You've given me time to get the food ready for the festival. I've made scones with sausages this morning so we can save some space for the delicious food we'll have later today," Emily said as she faced Henry, her signal for blessing the food.

After downing a tasty cinnamon scone, Walt asked, "What's the story behind the Fall Festival?"

Emily spoke first. "It's a wonderful story. Most of our miners have lived here for generations. Their ancestors came here as immigrants to work a new mine. The first year brought difficulties and tragedies. Many died from mine accidents and others lost their lives to diphtheria, whooping cough, and other diseases. The next year was better with fewer accidents and illnesses. The town council had a festival to celebrate. It's held every year since then."

"With one exception," Henry interjected. "In the past years, we stopped work for the entire day. We can't shut down the mine for twenty-four hours now.

Too much is at risk. A skeletal crew will work the day shift and there'll be full crew tonight."

Walt wondered why he used the word "risk." He tucked it away, determined to ask later.

The festival was as much fun as the Carters promised. The food, though simple, was a tasty combination of savory dishes and sweet desserts. After filling his belly into overload, Walt meandered around the booths, purchasing homemade jam and local honey for Liam's peanut butter sandwiches.

In the late afternoon, flag football turned into a hard-hitting game by the end of the first quarter, something the crowd appeared to accept as the norm.

Walt turned to Henry at half-time. "Has anyone ever been hurt?"

"A few over the years, but nothing major. Miners are as conditioned as pro players. Pulling coal out of a mountain is hard physical work."

The night crew won by a touchdown. When the cheering died down, Walt asked Henry how they could work their shift in just a few hours after such a brutal workout.

"On pure adrenaline. It's a big deal to be the winning team. Gives them bragging rights for the entire year." Henry glanced at the mine entrance before continuing. "They'll need something this coming year, for sure."

Once again, Walt wanted to ask why, but the appearance of Emily kept his question inside his mouth.

"Let's go, you two. It's been a pleasant but long day. My feet are begging for my ottoman. Tonight's dinner will be ham sandwiches." She pointed to a basket that held the remains of a large ham.

After the meal, they sat in the parlor before the fireplace, drinking hot cider. Emily stood. "I'll let you two continue to visit. I'm tired—too much festival. Goodnight." She smiled at them, her gaze lingering a moment on her husband. At the foot of the stairs, she stopped and turned back to Walt. "I'm so glad you came, especially on this day."

Walt shifted his gaze to Henry. His eyes registered a question.

"Kathleen loved the festival. I knew it would be a hard day for Emily. It's the reason I invited you to come. I thought it would help." Henry gave a half smile. "Guess I needed you here as well."

Walt stared at the dying embers, then went into reporter mode. "Why did you use the word 'risk' when you referred to the mine earlier today?"

"I guess there's no harm in sharing this. The company that owns Farrowlee Mine isn't happy with the decrease in our coal production. They think the vein is running out."

"Can't you search for another vein?"

"We have power augers for drilling dynamite holes, but the only reasonable and safe way to find another vein is to bring in big machines like a bolter, which places steel rods into the earth to hold the ceilings, eliminating the need for wooden poles that can give way easily. There's also the long-ball cutter, with blades pulled by a power chain along the vein of coal that can dig deeper into the mine walls than men with picks and explosives can."

"Will the company get these for your mine?"

"Not if they think the current vein in Farrowlee Mine is running out—which they do."

"And what do you think?

"Honestly, I think they're right. Our production is down. She's not giving us as much as she did in the last decade."

Walt smiled at Henry's personification of Farrowlee Mine. "Do the miners know?"

"Not officially, but I suspect they might. If we're shut down, I fear there'll be a massive exit to cities in Pennsylvania for industry jobs there. Many of the families here are fourth and fifth generations now. Mining is all they know." Henry returned his gaze to the fire. "If the mine is closed, the town will die."

Walt's gut rolled at the thought of Farrowlee becoming a ghost town. What if Kathleen came home? He opened his mouth to voice the thought, then closed it, sure Henry and Emily had the same fear.

"Something must be done. Maybe I can —"

"Son, short of a miracle, it's a company decision." Henry raised from his overstuffed chair and stoked out the fire. "Best to call it a night. Emily will shake us out early for breakfast before church in the morning."

Walt lay sleepless until late into the night. His brain churned with ways to help save Farrowlee. Slowly, a plan came together. He'd talk his editor into allowing him to write a story about the plight of the mining families. It was a Hail Mary, but if APS picked it up, it might be enough for the company to back down.

Eager to begin his research on the mining company, Walt announced he was leaving after breakfast.

"Probably best. Weatherman says rain and sleet may move in later today," Henry said, between bites of sizzling sausages.

"Really, Henry. That's your sixth sausage. Leave some for our guest." Emily softened her reprimand with a smile.

Walt smiled. He'd never seen a man who loved sausages as much as his host. Henry could out eat him three to one.

The Carters followed Walt to the car when he was leaving. Henry shook Walt's hand. "Drive safe. Those tires look a bit worn."

Walt nodded and climbed into the driver's seat. He rolled down his creaking window. "I'll be careful. Thank you for your invitation. I enjoyed the weekend."

Emily stepped closer to the window. "Come for Thanksgiving, if you're free."

Walt smiled and watched in his mirror as the couple hugged each other, then walked back to their home hand-in-hand. A few miles down the road, he thought of the day he'd seen their daughter speaking to the student next to her. She suddenly burst into laughter; her face illuminated in beauty. Remorse filled the cavity of his chest. Once again, he left without telling Kathleen's parents all that happened the night of the crash.

So deep in his thoughts, he hadn't realized rain was pelting his front window. Walt turned on his wipers, which squeaked and groaned. Another thing among many that needed to be replaced on his vehicle.

He groaned when the rain turned to sleet. *Didn't Henry say this weather would be later in the day?*

The condition of the road went from passable to dangerous.

Walt tried to think of his options, which were few until he remembered the store was only a few miles back. He'd go there and wait out the storm. He slowed and started making a U-turn when his left front tire blew. Walt tried to straighten the swerving car, but he proved no match against the icy road. The last thing he knew, the car was heading for an enormous oak tree.

Chapter 27

Walt's eyes popped open, his breath coming in ragged, short bursts. Then the pain hit—a gnawing, hungry beast. He heard a loud scream. *Was that me?* When he tried to raise up, a searing hot poker plunged into his chest. The torment ended as he slipped back into unconsciousness.

Loud voices and bright lights assaulted Walt's senses. He blinked and moaned as agonizing pain racked his body. Someone was talking to him. Swallowing a scream, he tried to focus.

"Mr. Johnson, listen to me, please. We've given you something for pain."

He knew the person was saying more, but he could no longer focus. He closed his eyes, willing the drug to work.

The beep of machines pulled Walt from a deep sleep. He stared at the IV in his right hand, trying to process the reason for it, but nothing came. His mind was in a lockbox with no key. He broadened his sight and saw a large arched contraption covering his left leg. *What's that for?* Walt tried to move his leg when a stabbing pain caused him to yell.

"Mr. Johnson, you're in the ICU at Charleston General Hospital." A middle-aged nurse appeared from nowhere. She patted his shoulder. "Try not to move."

In his fog-filled mind, he thought she was his foster mother, who often patted his shoulder, especially after she dressed him down for some infraction of the house rules.

"What… what happened?" Walt asked, his voice raspy and low.

"The doctor will be in soon to speak with you," the nurse replied, and busied herself checking the IV bags and recording Walt's vitals.

"But I need…" He stopped when a doctor the size of a boxer dog, with jowls to match, walked into the room.

"Hello, I'm Dr. Abrams. I performed surgery on you yesterday."

Yesterday? Walt blinked and tried to focus on the doctor, who had continued to talk.

"…sustained several injuries. We had to operate immediately because of blood loss. Your left leg and foot were crushed when the front of your car hit the tree. The damage to the bones and the tissue was extensive. I'm sorry. We had to remove it just below the knee."

The doctor looked at his chart before continuing. "You have a chest tube because your right lung collapsed in the ER from a couple of cracked ribs.

And a severe concussion from your head hitting the windshield." Dr. Abrams smiled at Walt and squeezed his right foot. "I'd say you're a very fortunate man."

"You took off my leg? That's not possible because I feel it. It's hurting badly right now. It must be there." Walt's voice became stronger and more desperate with each word. The news had dispelled the fogginess. His thoughts came a mile a minute. Broken ribs will heal, and so will a concussion. But life without two legs made his heart rate accelerate.

"What you're feeling is called phantom pain. The brain still thinks your leg is there and is sending pain messages to it. It usually lasts only a few months." Dr. Abrams wrote some notes in his chart, then looked at Walt again. "I know this is a lot to hear, but we'll take good care of you. You're looking at weeks of healing and rehab, so try to take all this one day at a time."

He was gone before Walt could ask anything more. It took a moment for his brain to catch up with his emotions. *How can I survive this... and do I want to?* It was his last thought before the morphine plunged him into a deep sleep.

Walt's eyes fluttered open, and he wondered how long he'd been asleep this time. He suddenly realized he wasn't alone. Emily and Henry were sitting in the only two chairs in the room. "What are you doing here? I can't believe you came all this way."

Emily spoke first. "Of course we came. You're family to us." Her eyes brimmed with tears.

"How... how did you know?" His head throbbed with each word.

"Sully found you. It was a miracle because after closing the store, he usually goes home on a small dirt road through the woods. But he took the highway last night because of the weather. When he rounded a curve, his lights reflected on your taillights." Henry cleared his throat, blinking rapidly. "He went back to his store to call for help, then came back and stayed with you until the ambulance arrived. Sully called us from the hospital."

"From the hospital? He was here?"

"Yes, he rode in the ambulance with you."

"And now you're here." Walt wrinkled his brow, taking in what Henry had shared. "And you know?"

The tears filling Emily's eyes made silent streaks down her cheeks as she nodded.

Henry murmured. "Yes, we know, and we're very sorry." He leaned closer to the bed. "I saw many limbs removed during the Korean War. And I know it's difficult to accept and that you're probably stunned and angry by the loss."

Walt nodded. This was exactly how he felt. It helped to know Henry understood.

"Is there anything you need? Anyone you need us to call?" Emily's kind voice caused Walt's eyes to sting.

"No, I can't think... wait. Please call Liam Cleburne at the *Herald Dispatch* newspaper in Huntington. Tell him what happened. Ask him to tell our editor and the professor I work for. Their numbers are in my—" Walt panicked. "Where's my backpack?" He tried to scan the room, but the chainsaw buzzing in his head prevented the slightest movement.

"It's right here," Henry said, retrieving it from the floor beside his chair. "Sully grabbed it from your car and left it with the hospital staff. An aide brought it in while you were sleeping."

Relief and gratitude surged through Walt when he realized the fullness of what Henry said. "You were here while I was sleeping?"

"Yes, we didn't want to disturb you," Emily said in a soft voice. Walt stared at his friends, amazed by their kindness.

"We can't stay long in the ICU, but I want you to hear this before we leave." Henry moved closer to the bed, lowered his head, and clasped his hands together.

He was silent for so long, Walt wondered if he was praying.

Henry's voice wavered when he continued. "God says in Joshua 1:5, *I will never fail you or forsake you.* Remember this, Walt, in the tough days ahead. I know you'll feel a loss of control, but God always has a purpose during times like this. Don't ask why you lost a leg. Ask what you can learn from this."

Before Walt could respond, a phantom pain struck. Walt bit his lip and tried not to react, but he couldn't hold back a deep moan.

Walt watched as Emily's face paled as if it were her pain. Henry turned to his wife. "Let's go, dear. He needs his rest, and it's a long way back home." Standing, he said, "We'll get those phone calls made before we leave Charleston."

Walt could only manage a quick nod. After they left, he called for the nurse. "I need some pain meds."

"I'm sorry, Mr. Johnson. You can't have any for another hour." When she'd left the room, tears drained down his face as agony consumed him. He couldn't wait another minute, much less an hour.

Chapter 28

Despite Henry's words, later that night, when sleep failed to come despite the narcotics, Walt railed at God. "Where are you? Why have you allowed this to happen?" The vengeance in his voice caused spittle to project from Walt's lips. "I've believed in you since I was fifteen years old. Is this what you do to one of your believers?" He'd partially raised up from his bed, then fell back down, out of breath. "How could you do this?" he whispered.

A week later, Walt moved from the ICU to a private room on another floor. The pain was better, but his emotions were still at the edge of despair. He wanted his life back and his anger was a steady, low flame that frequently ignited into a fire. He fussed at the nurses and refused to eat or to be cleaned up. Walt questioned his doctor endlessly, wanting to know why they did the surgery without his consent and the exact extent of his leg injury. He couldn't understand why they didn't wait to see if his leg would heal before removing it.

Dr. Abrams patiently answered his questions, but it always came back to the threat of him bleeding to death. Since he was unconscious and unable to understand what was happening, the doctors made the life-saving call.

He heard the same answer every time, but still couldn't accept it. Even though in his heart he knew it was futile, his mind told him things could change.

One day, when Dr. Abrams arrived, a young woman with long blond hair wearing a white doctor's coat accompanied him. The doctor held up a hand when Walt started talking.

"No, Mr. Johnson. Today you will listen. I've consulted with Dr. Everley. We believe you have post-traumatic stress disorder, or PTSD. She's the hospital psychologist and would like to help you move from your current state of mind to one more healthy."

Walt gazed at the woman and saw a world of compassion in her eyes. He couldn't muster his usual bad temper. Tired of the man he'd become, he gave a simple nod.

"Good! Now we'll get somewhere." Dr. Abrams looked as proud as if Walt had been his own son. "It's time for me to stop being your doctor. I've seen you through the surgical part. Dr. Everley, Dr. Smith, and a PT will take over your case." He gave Walt a devilish smile. "I hear the PT is even more stubborn than you."

He saw Dr. Everley daily after that. She slowly helped him see that his life could be good, albeit different.

Then, one day, he remembered the scripture Henry had shared. *I will not fail you or forsake you.* He sat still a moment, then asked in a whisper, "God, is this part of your plan? Heal the mind, heal the body?" He waited. Nothing.

Then it came, a feeling of complete peace. He understood he needed to stop striving and to trust God. Before he could form another thought, a large man with long brown hair tied in the back and a bushy mustache burst into his room.

"Hello, Walt. I'm Pete. Can I call you Walt? Hope so, because we're about to spend a lot of time together. When I say a lot, I mean every day and often twice a day."

Walt blinked. "And you are?"

Pete snapped his fingers and offered a wide grin. "I always forget that part. I'm your physical therapist. And as your PT, the first order of business is a bath. Eventually, we'll move on to more fun stuff like weight training, sit-ups, and push-ups. But until the ribs are better, we'll work on balance and using crutches. You're gonna love it."

"O—kay." Walt doubted any of it would be fun. "How can I take a shower if I can't stand?"

"Easy, dude. We get you into a wheelchair, then move you onto the shower chair."

Walt didn't think it sounded easy, but something told him it would be futile to disagree. An hour later, with multiple grunts and groans, Walt had showered and was back in bed, exhausted but cleaner than any time during the past few weeks.

"Thanks, Pete."

"Don't thank me yet, man. The road ahead will

be tough, and I doubt you'll be thanking me on most days."

Walt didn't let the PT's last words bother him. He felt a clean body and a clean spirit. "Okay, God, you have this."

The week had been grueling. Late Friday afternoon, Walt finished his last PT session until the weekend was over. He lay on the covers of his bed, exhausted from his last workout, his eyes closed.

"Looks like a life of leisure, Buddy."

Walt raised his head and found Liam standing nearby. He noted his friend's smile didn't match his eyes. "Liam, it's good to see you. How are things in Huntington?"

"I haven't been there for the past two weeks."

The sadness Walt saw in his eyes prompted him to ask, "What's wrong, buddy?"

"I've been back home. My father was injured in a mine accident. The section of the mine where he worked had a minor explosion. He has a broken leg and some broken ribs. Two other miners weren't so fortunate." Liam paused, glanced at the floor, then back to Walt. "My father has black lung, so his coughing isn't good for those broken ribs. Not being home for the past two years, I didn't know his lungs had become so bad."

"I'm so sorry. Unfortunately, it's impossible not to breathe in the coal dust while working in the mines. It's a shame so many miners get the disease." In his recent research about mining, he learned the disease was often fatal.

"But, hey man, how are you?" Liam asked. He stared down at Walt's stump, then quickly moved his eyes to Walt's face.

"It's okay, Liam. Most people look there first. I'm good."

Realizing Liam deserved more, he added, "Don't get me wrong. I wasn't always like this." Walt shook his head. "I was a real pistol. Angry, uncompliant with the doctors and the medical staff, constantly demanding answers as if any of them would change the fact. My leg is gone, and I'll always be one-legged. I'm surprised they didn't load me into a wheelchair and dump me at the curb."

"Really, Walt. How bad has it been?"

"At first it was excruciating. The pain was like being hunted by a villain waiting around every corner. Just when I thought I had it licked, it would come back with a vengeance." Walt glanced down at his missing leg. "Even the missing part of my leg hurt."

"How—"

"Weird, right? As if the actual pain of losing a limb isn't enough, you get phantom pains in the missing part." Walt chuckled. "Seems my brain's not convinced the leg is gone."

When he saw the horrified look on his friend's face, he quickly added, "Don't worry, they're almost gone." When Walt sensed Liam couldn't come up with a response, he changed the subject. "Aren't you going to ask about my workout clothes?"

"Uh... uh, sure. Why the workouts?"

"I'm training for the Boston Marathon." He burst into laughter at the look on Liam's face. "Gone too far? I've just returned from physical therapy. It's grueling, but I can tell I'm getting stronger with each session. And my balance is improving. Soon I'll be ready to be fit for a prosthetic. Enough about me. How's things at the newspaper? Is Ed still trying to steal bylines? How about Rickman, still yelling his lungs out?"

He watched Liam's lips pull into a tight line. "What's wrong?"

"The boss hired someone for your job, Walt."

Disappointment crawled up his spine. *Then why am I working so hard in this place?*

Chapter 29

In the bright, early-morning sun, the campus was ablaze with every color of autumn. Thankful for her jacket, Kathleen pulled it tight around her chest. When had September passed into October? Between classes, studying, and group projects, she barely had time to notice her surroundings.

When she woke this morning, something had changed. It took a moment to identify the reason. Her chest, usually a hard rock, weighed less. Some of the tightness had relented. Most of all, Cody wasn't her first thought.

"Ainsley, wake up. It's a beautiful day."

Her roommate pulled herself up from the waist, forearms supporting her in the bed. "Someone woke up in a good mood."

"I guess I did," she responded, as surprised as her friend.

"Well, at least one of us is in a good mood." Ainsley released her arms and fell back on the bed. She jerked the pillow from under her head and laid it across her face. "I understand it's difficult for you to face each day right now, but staying busy helps." Kathleen couldn't believe she was giving advice to anyone. Thoughts of her past tried to worm their way into her mind, but she dispelled them. *No. Today I won't let my past drive me.*

"Being busy won't help. All I think about is Joe... and Amy Withers." The pillow muffled Ainsley's voice.

Kathleen stepped closer and removed the pillow. "Then think about your scholarship. If your grades drop any lower, you'll lose it. What would that do to your parents, who are so proud of you?"

Ainsley was silent for a moment, then sat on the side of the bed. "You're right. I can't lose Joe and my scholarship." Her voice had a hardness—like steel against steel—that Kathleen recognized.

Loud shouting pulled her attention from her thoughts. Ahead of her stood a group of protesters in front of the ROTC building, waving signs and demanding freedom of speech and freedom of assembly, led by a young man who stood on an apple crate with a megaphone. The crowd parroted everything he was saying. His long hair, held down by a bandanna tied around his head, hung on each side of his shoulders, almost hiding the peace sign on his tie-dyed T-shirt.

Kathleen stopped at the edge of the protesters; her jaw dropped. The man with the megaphone was Rusty. She glanced at her wristwatch. Their chemistry class started in fifteen minutes. Would her lab partner miss class again? When she moved her eyes back to Rusty, he'd changed his chant to "Stop the war. Stop Nixon's lies!" As if on cue, the protesters laid their signs on the pavement ground and picked up new signs, each heralding anti-war statements. Kathleen read the ones she could see from where she stood— *Stop the Killing; Make Love, not War; Stop Bombing Cambodia.*

She watched as a peaceable demonstration escalate when a student picked up a rock and hurled it through a window of the ROTC building. The urge for flight kicked in and she rushed back to the sidewalk. The number of student protesters had grown, jamming her path. She pushed her way through the crowd, twisting and turning her body to get past those who crowded together, linking arms as a sign of solidarity.

Sirens blared as she tried to force her way forward. A jab in the stomach by the elbow of a protester sent her to her knees on the pavement. Another push by the crowd pummeled her body downward, causing her head to strike hard on the concrete. She lay dazed, unable to get up.

"I have you."

Kathleen struggled to identify the voice. Was it familiar? Before she recognized it, a powerful arm scooped her up and moved through the crowd. He carried her to a bench and sat her down.

"Keep your head down until the dizziness stops."

Dizzy and nauseated, she did as the man asked.

"Look at me now. I want to check you out. That was a nasty fall."

She lifted her head and stared into brown eyes. "Jake! How did you know—"

"I started for breakfast at the student union when the crowd escalated. I saw you pushing through them and then fall." He squatted to eye level and continued. "When you think you can stand, we need to head over to the medical clinic. That's a big knot on your forehead. You need to be observed overnight for a concussion."

Moving her head, she intended to say no, but came out with, "Ouch!" Holding still, she continued. "I'm already late for chemistry and I can't miss my other classes."

"Let's take it a step at a time. First, try to stand."

Kathleen placed her palms on the bench and pushed up, then plopped back down. "Oh," she murmured as she put her hand to her head. Dizziness assaulted her, as did the severe ache in her head.

"I'm officially diagnosing a concussion. Let me help you up so we can get you to the clinic. You need an ice bag for that bump, and I used all my ice last night when I stumped my toe on the coffee table."

Kathleen wondered what made him think she'd go to his apartment. "All right. I'll go to the clinic, but I'm not staying." She lifted a hand to let Jake help her up. This time she felt a little better, especially when he grabbed her around her waist for support. If her head didn't hurt so badly, she might have shrugged away. Feeling defenseless, she leaned into him, surprised by how good it felt.

An hour later, Kathleen lay on a bed with an ice bag on her forehead. Her headache was better from the aspirin the nurse gave her. She'd resigned herself to staying, knowing she couldn't sit through her classes. Without moving her head, she slid her eyes to the corner of the sockets, surprised to see Jake sitting in a chair.

"Hi," he said in almost a whisper.

"Hi. Why are you still here?" she said without turning her head.

"Where else should I be?"

"Anywhere… at class, or the library, or wherever you go during your day." She flapped her hands to motion him to leave.

"You're not getting rid of me that easy," he said in a low voice that pleased Kathleen's headache. "I'm here to make sure you stay awake, at least for a while until we know how serious this concussion really is." He gave a lopsided grin before continuing. "And to hold the trash can if you barf."

How does he know about my headache? She slowly turned her body to the side, so she had a better view of this man who kept showing up in her life. His enormous frame seemed out of place in the small, hard clinic chair. How had she not already noticed how tall and muscular he was and how his black hair curled just slightly—enough to make it seem unkept?

When she realized she was staring at him, she rushed to say something. "If you must stay, tell me how you know so much about concussions. You correctly diagnosed me while I was still on that bench."

Jake studied his lap briefly, then leaned forward. "I'm a combat medic. I've done two tours in Vietnam and still serve in the Army Reserve. When I left you sprawled on the grass, I was late to catch my ride for weekend duty. As you can attest to, being a Vietnam vet isn't the most popular thing in our country."

Kathleen watched his eyes, which she sensed were begging her not to berate him. *Why does he care what I think?* The moment the thought entered her brain, a second one came so fast it almost rear-ended the first. *I care what he thinks of me.* She blinked, wondering if she'd said this out loud. Could a concussion cause confusion?

Kathleen realized she'd been silent for several moments. "I... uh..." Still not knowing what to say, she asked a question. "Why are you at WVU? Why aren't you still active military?"

"Being a combat medic means transporting wounded soldiers from a combat zone to a field hospital." Jake glanced at the IV drip before he continued. "Time is critical for a wounded soldier. I served on a medevac team known as a dust-off crew. There were three of us on a Huey—a pilot, a crew chief, and a combat medic. Our mission was a rapid evacuation of the wounded... at any cost."

"Wasn't it dangerous, flying into a battle?" The aspirin had eased her headache, and she found herself genuinely interested in Jake's past.

"Sometimes, but not as dangerous as it was for the ground troops. I'm here because the experience made me want to become a doctor. Hopefully, I'll get into medica—"

The curtain around the cubicle swung up. "Oh, bless your heart. How awful for you! And here I am, moaning and whining about my problems when you were in the throngs of attackers. I'm ashamed of myself—truly!" Ainsley put a grocery bag on the floor and placed her hands on her hips. "Now, what can I do for you? Do you need water, or your pillow fluffed?" Without waiting for Kathleen's response, she bent and opened the bag. "I brought you a few things. Here's a gown because those things they call hospital gowns aren't anything but misery, not to mention how impossible it is to cover everything."

When she started rummaging in the bag again, Kathleen turned to Jake, who was working hard not to laugh. "Jake, meet my roommate, Ainsley."

Ainsley straightened, holding a hairbrush in one hand and face cream in the other. "Oh, my gracious. I didn't know you had company, and here I'm rattling on like my ol' granny."

"Nice to meet you." Jake said. "Kathleen is fortunate to have a roommate like you. Looks like you thought of everything."

Kathleen found his kindness to Ainsley impressive. But hadn't he shown her that same kindness? She suddenly felt gratitude, a feeling she'd almost forgotten. In only a few months, she'd made friends who seemed to care about her.

"I searched through your desk, hoping to find a phone number so I could call your parents. I couldn't find a thing. If you give me their number, I'll call them for you. They said a news crew was at the protest. I know you wouldn't want them to worry." Ainsley waited for her response.

Gratitude evaporated like fog lifting over a pond. The hard rock returned to the pit of her stomach. "My parents live in London, where my father works. They won't see any news of this. And shouldn't you be in class?" Her voice held a harshness that spoke volumes.

"But I thought I'd stay and keep you company."

She watched Ainsley's eyes grow glassy. Ashamed of her bluntness, Kathleen softened her voice. "Remember our discussion this morning? Right now, your job is to be in class... all of them."

"Well, in case you need something else, just call."

Kathleen watched her friend leave the cubicle with less energy than when she entered. Turning to Jake, she said the same thing. "I think you need to go as well. You must be missing your classes."

"Whatever you say, Kathleen. I hope you feel better soon."

Kathleen knew she'd hurt both her friends. Tears flooded her eyes. She'd become a vessel of lies and deceit.

Chapter 30

The clang of metal on tile startled Kathleen awake. Disoriented, the cubicle took shape as her foggy mind came into focus. The crowds, her injury, the clinic, and Jake materialized in her mind with the speed of a swarm of bees. She touched the bump on her head to make sure she hadn't dreamed it.

The urge to relieve herself came strong. She raised from the bed, then fell back on her pillow when she became dizzy. "Nurse... someone?" Her call brought no one. Trying again, Kathleen gingerly sat up on the bed and waited, feet dangling off the side. Gradually, the dizziness abated. She stood, closing the back of her hospital gown with a death grip, and made her way down the hall to the restroom. Job accomplished, she started back to her cubicle when a nurse spotted her.

"Miss Carter, it's not good to be out here alone," the nurse chastised.

"I called. No one came and I couldn't wait. Most of the dizziness is gone."

"I'll let the doctor know. He'll probably release you."

Back in her cubicle, Kathleen stared dismally at the breakfast tray on her bedstand, noting a box of cornflakes, a carton of milk, and a cup of weak coffee.

"I don't blame you for that grimace. That's not much of a breakfast." Marhira laughed.

She spun around, surprised to see her friend. "What are you doing here?"

"Jake McBride told me. I saw him getting coffee this morning. He's in my poly sci class." Marhira tilted her head and continued in a soft voice, "I'm so sorry this happened. It must have been very frightening."

"I can't believe you came."

"Of course, I came."

"But. .. I didn't think you'd ditch class to come see me."

"We're friends, Kathleen. It's what friends do. I'd be disappointing God if I didn't come to a friend in need."

"I don't need anything." *Or anyone.* Dislike of herself ripped through her body. Kathleen knew nothing could remove her self-loathing. Yesterday her world seemed bright. The old feelings had turned off the light.

The doctor walked through the curtain, head down, reading her chart. "I'm Dr. Jai Kumar. My nurse tells me you're feeling better. She'll be by soon to take your blood pressure. If it's good, you may leave. You'll still have concussion symptoms, so take it easy for the rest of this week."

"Can I attend classes?" The doctor looked up from the chart and saw Marhira. His eyes locked onto hers. Kathleen asked again, "Doctor, what about my classes?"

"Yes, of course. But no night life until next week," he answered without taking his eyes from the young woman standing across the bed from him.

When Marhira lowered her eyes, the doctor looked down at his charts again. "Uh... I think that's all." He hurried from the cubicle after a quick glance at her friend.

"What just happened?" Kathleen almost laughed, observing the redness on Mahira's face.

"Nothing." Marhira raised her hands to her flaming cheeks.

"Oh, I think something happened. He's handsome, isn't he?"

Her friend glanced at the curtain still moving from the doctor's quick exit. "And very Indian," she whispered.

"I simply don't understand, Miss Carter, why you can't do this test properly when any third grader could manage it," Professor Wells said in a loud, critical voice.

"I'm sorry," Kathleen mumbled. Her slight headache, left over from the concussion, grew exponentially. Another low grade on her in-class lab work would put her already pitiful average in danger. To make it worse, Rusty hadn't returned since the protest. She left the class thinking of all the things she would have preferred to say to her professor other than a meek, "I'm sorry."

"You must have a bee in your bonnet," Ainsley said when she joined Kathleen.

Kathleen stopped and faced her roommate. "Excuse me?"

Ainsley regarded her as if she'd been born yesterday. "You really don't know that expression, do you? It means you're highly irritated with someone or something."

Kathleen resumed walking. "Someone—my chemistry professor. He doesn't like me and it's a mystery to me why."

"My mum taught me that a person's actions always have a reason. Figure out the reason, and you can solve the problem. Until then, all you can do is give the person grace."

"Give him grace?"

"Yeah, like the grace God gives us."

Kathleen stared at her feet. Where was God's grace when all those people died in the plane crash? "You want me to give Wells grace for *his* actions?"

Ainsley held her hands open in front of her chest. "Grace is when God gives us something we don't deserve. Professor Wells doesn't deserve grace from you, but giving it will ease your feelings about him."

"Thanks, but I don't think I can do what you're saying."

"Just think about it. Hey, I'm heading to the student union. Joe and I always had a milkshake on Friday when high school released for the weekend. I'm keeping our tradition alone. Wanna come?"

"No, I'm exhausted. All I want is a nap before dinner."

She watched Ainsley walk away. Her body posture made it clear she still hurt from her boyfriend's rejection. Kathleen remembered what Mahira said about being there for a friend in need. *Maybe I should have gone with her.*

After the promised nap, she joined Ainsley at the cafeteria for some dinner. For over an hour, she listened to her roommate reminisce about things she and Joe had done in high school. Kathleen tried to be attentive to make up for not joining her earlier, but when she sneaked a peek at her wristwatch, Ainsley picked up on the action.

"I'm sorry. I'm hoggin' the conversation with all my talk about Joe and me. Tell me about your high school days."

Kathleen froze. *What do I say? I had a boyfriend and he burned to death right after I broke up with him?* The chicken tetrazzini she'd eaten soured in her stomach. "Let's go back to the room and watch *My Fair Lady.* The *TV Guide* shows it's coming on at eight o'clock." She hoped this was correct, since she'd only skimmed the guide before her nap.

Sleep was a long time coming that night. Her thoughts swung back and forth like a yard swing in the wind. Finally, her eyelids became heavy, and she drifted into a light sleep.

Find Jake. Kathleen's eyes flew open. "Ainsley, did you say something?" She opened her mouth to ask again, but heard soft snoring coming from the second bed. Confused, she lay back down, shut her eyes, and tried to force sleep. But the phrase became a conveyor belt in her mind. "Find Jake for what?" she asked the surrounding darkness. The moment she said it, she knew—to apologize for her behavior at the clinic. But how would she find him? They'd met three times, each time on a sidewalk.

Monday morning, Kathleen left her room twenty minutes early and headed for the student union. She'd spent the weekend trying to figure out a way to find Jake. She didn't know if he lived in a dorm or an apartment. Nor did she know any of his friends. But the need to apologize remained strong.

Late Sunday night while preparing for bed, Ainsley said something that sparked her memory.

"You know, when I heard you'd been in an accident, I rushed to the clinic afraid of what I'd see. I'm still thanking God that He spared you from serious harm."

Surprised that anyone prayed for her, Kathleen offered a meek 'thank you' when she thought of something Jake had said when he rescued her. He was going for breakfast at the student union. *Maybe that's where I can find him.*

"Why have you been leaving so early for class the past couple of weeks?" Ainsley asked. "I miss having breakfast with you." She wrinkled her forehead, causing her green eyes to squint. "I'll bet you're meeting someone, right?"

Kathleen bristled, trying to think of a lie. But she was tired of lying. "Actually, I'm looking for someone."

"I bet it's the brown-eyed fellow. What's his

name?" Before Kathleen could respond, her roommate blurted out, "Jake, the guy who rescued you!"

"I want to apologize to him for the way I treated him at the clinic." She realized she'd never done the same with Ainsley. "I should've asked for your forgiveness for the way I treated you long before now." Kathleen took a long breath. "Please forgive me."

"Psst, I never hold on to an offense. It takes too much energy. But if you need it said, then I forgive you, girlfriend." She closed the few steps between them and grabbed Kathleen in a bear hug.

Surprised by her response, Kathleen hurried out of the room and exited the dorm building. Halfway down the many steps, she stopped. Had Ainsley shown her grace?

Kathleen followed the same routine as the past nine weekdays. After checking the post office, the bank, and the WVU info center, she bought a cup of coffee. Taking it to a strategic location where she could see the coffee station and the front door, she sat down on a bench and watched. A disappointing thirty minutes later, she left for class with her mind made up. She'd stop her morning stake-out.

After a dismal weekend of drizzling rain and excruciating study for a chemistry test, she walked to class Monday morning, dreading the week ahead. Two tests and an essay about a life-changing event held the promise of many hours of study. She tried self-talk to lift her spirits. "Come on, Kathleen, at least the sun is shining."

Writing the essay in her mind, she almost missed seeing Jake walking ahead of her. Heart racing, she called out, "Jake. Jake, wait up." She sped up her walk and soon closed the space between them. When he turned around, she cringed when she realized he was minus his usual smile. Apprehension pushed her rehearsed speech into the hidden corners of her mind.

"Hello, Kathleen." Jake said, still not smiling. "I only have a moment, or I'll be late for class."

Did I really treat him that badly? She knew she had, and the desire to make amends grew. "Jake, that day at the clinic, I... uh, I was rude to you. After all you'd done to help me, I should've never spoken to you in that way." Kathleen stared into his eyes, afraid she couldn't make things right between them and surprised by how much she wanted this. "I'm so sorry. Please forgive me."

She held her breath and watched as his face went from stoic to compassionate.

"I'm happy you stopped me. My feelings were more confused than hurt, but I'd like to talk it over with you. Will you have dinner with me tonight?" With a grin, he continued. "Besides, we have to stop meeting on sidewalks."

Kathleen astonished herself when she said yes.

Chapter 31

*A*insley stood from the chair at the study desk and pointed one finger at Kathleen. "All right, roommate. You're going to tell me about this frown and all the mumbling... right now. Tomorrow I will teach my first lesson to real kids in a real elementary school, and I need to prepare. This won't happen if you don't stop your behavior."

Kathleen looked up from the boot she was trying to zip closed. "Mumbling?"

"Yes, mumbling." Ainsley rolled her eyes. "I thought you were pleased Jake asked you to dinner. Didn't you spend two weeks looking for him?"

"Well, yes. But after what hap..." Kathleen snapped her mouth closed as her eyes grew large.

"Look, whatever happened in your past, then let it be your past, not your present," Ainsley's harsh voice became soft. "Hope for the best."

Stinging hit Kathleen's eyelids. "I've forgotten what hope feels like."

"Well, honey, ask God for some. He's full of it!" Ainsley gave her a wink and returned to her desk.

Kathleen stared at her roommate's back leaning over the large textbook. Gratitude for Ainsley fixed another shard in her damaged heart. Was it true hope could move her to the present? Could she ever leave her past? She mulled it over, the second boot still in her hand. Somewhere in the deep recesses of her soul, she almost believed it might be so.

A stunning, yellow harvest moon put on a spectacle as it rose above the campus on its way west. Kathleen stuffed her hands into the coat's pockets and stopped to stare. It looked close enough to touch. Somehow, the sight calmed the queasiness sitting in her stomach.

When a burst of cold wind hit Kathleen's face, she resumed her walk, berating herself for not letting Jake pick her up at the dorm. Just another way to keep a distance.

The walk to the restaurant, located a few blocks from campus, should've been easy, but the powerful winds made it a struggle. Kathleen pulled up the hood of her coat and lowered her head against the oncoming gusts. Her pace slowed as she tried to navigate the powerful force.

The wind pelted Kathrine's face, drowning her hearing with its loud swishing sound. She thought of turning around and going back to the dorm when she felt a hand on her shoulder. Fear shot through her. She tried to wiggle out of the hold when she recognized Jake's voice.

"I honked twice. Didn't you hear it?"

"Jake! Why are you here? We're meeting at the restaurant," she said, her freezing lips trembled. And to her horror, her nose chose this moment to drip.

"Let's get in the car and I'll explain."

Kathleen didn't resist. Her bones screamed for warmth.

Sitting in the car, she held her hands close to the vent. Warm air flowed from her hands, up her arms, and finally to her face.

After a few discreet wipes at her nose, she turned to Jake. "So, why did you drive here? I thought we agreed we'd meet at the restaurant."

"Unlike others, I check the weather report. I knew a cold front was coming—one with high gusts of wind and lower-than-usual temperatures for this time of year. Rain with sleet is predicted later tonight. I thought your walk might be uncomfortable."

"Uncomfortable? I felt like I was in a wind tunnel. I'm glad you came along."

Jake's smile spread wide. "Can we get to the restaurant? Our reservation is in five minutes."

Kathleen couldn't imagine getting out in the windy cold again. She nodded and rubbed her numb hands together. Within moments, they were parked in front of the restaurant, near the door.

"I guess I wasn't the only one to check the weather. Seems almost deserted." He turned to Kathleen. "Stay put. I'll come around to you. Small as you are, you'll be swept all the way to Oz," Jake said, chuckling.

Why was his silly grin so disarming? It was like a secret weapon, making anyone who saw it follow his commands. Jake opened her door and said, "Let's go, Little Bit."

She stiffened at his use of a nickname. It brought back the memory of what Cody called her. Then Ainsley's words occurred to her. *Live not the past.* She forced a smile when Jake offered his arm and escorted her inside.

Inside, the hostess seated them at a table next to a roaring fireplace. A large window allowed them to see the wind blowing tree limbs and scattering fall leaves. A stereo played the crooning of Tom Jones. After they placed their orders—steak for Jake and chicken for Kathleen—silence fell across the table.

Jake finally broke the uncomfortable moment. "Right, you wanted to know why you couldn't find me on campus."

Relieved to have the conversation started, Kathleen replied, "Yes. I waited for you at Mountain Liar every weekday for two weeks, thinking I'd find you there getting your morning coffee."

"I was at Fort Sam Houston in San Antonio."

"Why?" Kathleen asked, then cringed. It was a personal question, not the sort of familiar relationship she wanted.

"I was doing my two-week Army Reserve duty. I go once a year. Fort Sam Houston is where I did sixteen weeks of combat medevac training before I went on my first tour of duty."

"Why did you choose WVU?"

Jake smiled. "My mother's sister and her husband, Bill and Mary Thornhill, raised me on a farm near Beckley. My father died in Korea and my mom died shortly after with cancer."

"I'm sorry."

"It's okay. I was young when they passed. Bill and Mary are strong believers and pointed me to become a Christian myself. Plus, I had two boy cousins close to my age. As an only child, this was a bonus. I go to see them as often as I can. But enough about me. Tell me about yourself."

Kathleen refolded her napkin and placed it back into her lap. She lifted her eyes and saw Jake staring at her expectedly.

"Not much to tell. I lived in a small town in South Carolina, near the outer banks. I was an only child, like you. My father was the president of a bank, on the city council and the school board. He spent his remaining hours on the golf course and in the country club lounge. I never saw him. When I was sixteen, he became president of a branch from the same bank in London and my parents moved there. I stayed because I was in boarding school." Kathleen paused, then asked, "So tell me, Jake, why the Army Reserve?"

Jack tilted his head and waited a moment before responding. "The Reserve is helping put me through college. I became a combat medic because I've always liked medicine and hope to get a medical degree."

Kathleen knew by his flat tone he wasn't buying any of what she told him. Her heart plunged in despair. Yet, she couldn't be truthful because she never wanted her past to find her.

The rest of the evening raced by, though most of their conversation was generic. Do you go to the Volunteers' football games? What's your favorite movie, favorite music, favorite thing to eat? Despite the rough beginning, Kathleen enjoyed the time they spent at the restaurant, maybe more than any evening spent with Cody.

When they ordered a cup of coffee at the end of their meal, Jack spoke candidly. "I've enjoyed the evening, and I'd like to see you again. But, for us to be friends, I'd like you to be truthful."

Kathleen stood and grabbed her coat from the back of the chair. "I must get back. I have a test in chemistry in two days... need to study." At the conclusion of the sentence, her lips trembled. "I'll meet you in the lobby." She turned away from Jake before he could see her tears.

A fine mist of rain had begun when they walked to Jake's car. "Looks like your weatherman was correct." Kathleen said brightly—a little too brightly.

The ride back to the dorm was quiet, but when Jake pulled in front of the dorm, he turned his body to face hers. "I haven't known you long, Kathleen. but in this short time, I've learned you can change in a moment. I sense you have been deeply hurt. That hurt has put a hardness in you that shuts out the light in your soul. I'd like to help you relight it because I believe it's there."

A harsh reply almost came to Kathleen's lips, but she pushed it away. She heard the sincerity in his voice—and something else she couldn't name, though her mind searched hard for it.

"Thank you for a nice evening and for rescuing me from being blown away." She exited the car and hurried toward the steps to her dorm.

As Kathleen made her way, she heard Jake's yell from an open window. "Kathleen, wait! Let me go up the steps with you. They may be icy!" She pretended not to hear and continued walking.

Exhausted from navigating the multiple icy steps, Kathleen hoped Ainsley wouldn't still be up. She didn't want a barrage of questions about her time with Jake.

Relieved to hear the soft snoring of her roommate, she put on her warmest pajamas and crawled under the covers, still shivering from the bitter cold. Sleep didn't come quickly as she replayed the entire evening.

Could she trust this man with her past? Something in her heart seemed to confirm she could. *Is this what Ainsley calls hope?*

Chapter 32

Kathleen woke early and rushed to the window. The morning sun cast a glistening glow on the thick layer of ice covering everything from the tiniest leaf to the rooftops, resplendent with long icicles hanging beneath the eaves. Far prettier than snow, and far more dangerous.

The sun disappeared slowly, like curtains closing at the end of a movie. A heavy layer of clouds now hovered over the ice. Kathleen knew from living in Farrowlee there would be no going out today.

She raced back to her warm bed, her feet tingling from the cold floors, but a surprising smile on her lips. Jake was right! Somehow, it pleased her.

Kathleen turned on her bedside radio, twisting the channel to the weather report.

"Thick ice covers most of Preston County. Residents are advised to remain inside. WVU will—"

Heavy static drowned out the rest of the report.

She grabbed the knob, searching for another weather channel. A cacophony of sounds filled the room.

"What *is* all that racket? I have to teach in a couple of hours," Ainsley muttered from under her pile of covers. "Let a girl get her rest."

"Shh! I'm trying to get a weather report."

"Why on earth would you—"

"Shh. Listen." Kathleen landed on a different channel and heard a repeat of the previous message.

Ainsley sat up and listened.

"County schools and WVU in Morgantown will be closed until further notice." Ainsley flew to the window and gasped. "It can't be closed! I have my first mock lesson."

"Not today." Kathleen chuckled, amused at how the tide had turned. It was usually her that grumbled, not Ainsley. "Now, you'll have all day to study."

"Not until I sleep more. Please, stop that noise!"

Radio off, Kathleen sat under her covers with bent knees, hands latched together around them. She listened as the radiator hissed and iced limbs scratched against each other in the wind. *Maybe I should call Jake to congratulate him for his correct prediction about the steps last night. Wait, why do I want to do that? It was the weatherman, not him.* She refused to listen to the hint of apologizing for her behavior last night. Besides, she didn't have his phone number. Their conversation never went that far.

It was a long, quiet day. They cooked noodles in their electric corn popper for lunch, the only appliance allowed in the room. By mid-afternoon, Kathleen wanted Ainsley's grumbling to stop. She put away the essay she was drafting for her writing class and said,

"We've been at this for hours. How about we put our studies away and play cards?"

Ainsley jumped at the idea. Next to food, card playing was her favorite pastime. Halfway through a hilarious game of hearts, both girls moaned when they heard the sleet on the window. Kathleen dove to the radio, hoping the sound would be short-lived.

"More sleet for the next hour, then a possibility of four to six inches of snow."

Kathleen smiled. Snow wouldn't halt everything like ice.

When a knock came from the door, Ainsley moved that way. "If that's a dorm mate, I hope she comes with chips and dip." At the sight of the dorm counselor, she moaned. "Miss Shafer, you know everybody cooks in their corn popper."

"I'll ignore that statement. But only this time."

"Kathleen, you have a delivery, though how the crazy delivery boy made it here without breaking his neck is beyond me." She handed her a small square box and gave Ainsley I'm-watching-you stare before leaving.

Ainsley turned to Kate and spoke in a low voice. "I think I'll go find someone with food other than noodles." She closed the door with a soft click.

Kathrine held the box close to her ear and then gave it a quick shake. Curious, she opened it and removed a beautiful dome with a crystal city inside covered in glittering ice. With a soft gasp, she turned it over, causing sparkling silver glitter to fall lightly. She looked in the box and found what she hoped for—a card. Kathleen grabbed it and read the words.

If you'll see me again, here's my number.

Tears filled her eyes as the layer of ice in her heart melted.

They were married in early December, just two months after meeting each other. It was an intimate wedding at the campus chapel. The only guests were Ainsley, Mahira and her doctor friend, and two of Jake's Army Reserve buddies. Kathleen wore a white flowing maxi peasant dress and a circle of white flowers in her hair. After a quick round of congratulations from their few friends in attendance, they left in Jake's blue 1970 Monte Carlo. They'd packed food and warm items for a stay in a mountain cabin.

The night before the wedding, Kathleen told Jake about Cody and the crash that took his life. "I couldn't marry you without telling you about my past." She cringed, knowing she'd not told him about fleeing from her parents and friends. She'd done so much without her parents' knowledge. The guilt weighed her down. What would Jake think of her if he knew the lie about leaving her family?

She held back her tears until she saw Jake's eyes were swimming in moisture.

"Oh, baby, I'm so sorry." He held her close and whispered, "It's okay," over and over until her sobs dried out.

Inhaling deeply, she stepped back and said, "I know now that I didn't love Cody. It was a youthful courtship, one that grew out of expectations from everyone we knew. I never truly loved until I met you."

"I plan to make you Mrs. McBride tomorrow.

Together, our future will write new pasts for both of us."

Their last night at the cabin, Jake asked Kathleen to join him on the couch near a roaring fire. His serious face lit a small ember of dread in the pit of her stomach.

"What's wrong? Too much canned spam?" she teased, a lame effort to stop the fear coiling around her body.

"No, sweetheart. There's something you need to know." He took one of her hands and rubbed it with his thumb. "I didn't want to tell you until tonight. On the morning of our wedding, I received a call from the commander of my unit. I've been called up."

"What do you mean by called up?" She desperately wanted to not have this conversation.

He grabbed her other hand and clasped them under his enormous ones. "I'm being sent to Vietnam. I leave in three weeks. The day after Christmas."

"No, that can't be. What about the Vietnamization policy? We're moving troops out of Vietnam." She fought a tide of panic with false hope. "We're not sending soldiers over there. We're bringing them home!"

"I know, sweetheart. President Nixon's intention is to train the South Vietnamese to fight the Viet Cong without our help. But even after three years, our ally is not ready to push back communism from their country on their own. And if any troops are still there, they need combat medics."

Jake's voice was kind, yet firm. "I won't be gone

for the usual one-year tour. My orders are only for six months. I'll be home by the Fourth of July." He squeezed her hands harder. "We'll watch the fireworks together."

"But…"

"I know this is difficult. I don't want to leave you. God knows I don't, but this can't change." He took her in his arms and whispered, "I'll come back, I promise."

Jake pushed back from her and smoothed her rumpled hair. "We need to plan, Little Bit." Hearing the nickname proved her undoing. She raced to the bedroom, locking the door behind her. Her sobs, racked with pain, filled the small cabin.

When the crying turned to hiccups, Jake came to the door. "Please let me in. We have more to talk about."

He waited and gave a heaving sigh when she opened the door. "There's much we need to do before I leave."

"I can't talk about this now." She grabbed several tissues from the nightstand and walked to the floor mirror in the corner of the room. She hardly recognized herself as she wiped the mascara from her red, puffy eyes.

"I know you're upset, but I need you to understand what will take place when we get back to Morgantown." He led her to the couch and gently sat her down, taking a seat on the coffee table, facing her.

"First, we can't move into the married couple's housing like we planned. We need to find an apartment for you near the campus." He stopped, raising one eyebrow. "Unless you want to stay at the dorm with Ainsley."

"No, I don't want that." Her pain was too big for a small room.

"Okay, apartment it is."

Kathleen knew he was trying to make things sound normal, but she'd only been a military wife for three days. All of it horrified her.

"We'll both need to sign papers for you to receive a portion of my pay and my… and other benefits."

She was aware he'd stopped short of saying what frightened her the most. Tears swelled up in her eyes.

"Hold on, sweetheart." Jake squeezed her hands. "I'm almost finished. My pay won't be much, so the apartment may not be what you're used to, and money may be tight."

"I have money, Jake." She responded, her voice suddenly filled with anger. "Besides, I'll live anywhere if it brings you home. It's the last of my worries."

"I'm sorry," Jake said. "But I need to know you'll be okay while I'm away."

She heard the pleading in his voice, and her anger dissipated. "I'll be okay. Just come back to me."

The next three weeks flew by. They moved into a one-bedroom apartment near campus, signed what seemed to Kathleen to be endless military papers, and spent as much time together as possible.

Relieved when school closed for Christmas break, she knew she'd have to repeat at least two classes, one of them chemistry. She couldn't concentrate on her work and had missed several classes.

They spent Christmas Eve and Christmas Day in Beckley with Jake's aunt and uncle, who greeted her with such kindness she was ashamed of her unwillingness to come. Christmas day, all the extended family gathered at the farm. The sheer number of relatives overwhelmed Kathleen.

His family's love for Jake was touching, but it reminded her of what she'd lost when she left her parents.

"Please let us know if you need anything while Jake is gone," Jake's aunt told her, pushing leftover fruitcake into her hand. "Jake's favorite."

Kathleen whispered a thank you and waited by the car as everyone hugged Jake and gave him well-wishes. She struggled not to scream out her desire to not be a part of the entire scene. It made things too real.

The morning of Jake's departure cast an atmosphere of unspoken tension in their small apartment. Jake, dressed in his newly pressed uniform, a duffle bag at his feet, stood near the door.

"Promise me you'll write." Kathleen squeezed the words from a dry mouth.

"I promise."

"Promise me you'll come back."

"I'll come back. I swear it."

Kathleen saw the determination in his eyes and felt some of the tension leave the small of her tightly wound back. She watched him leave through the front door, tears rolling off her cheeks.

Six weeks later, a doctor confirmed her pregnancy.

Chapter 33

Walt reached over and turned on the bedside lamp, lifted his head off the thin hospital pillow, and groaned. Only ten minutes until physical therapy, followed by occupational therapy and gait training.

He glanced at the cold, over-scrambled eggs and the hard, dry toast. He grabbed the most salvageable item on the tray, a single piece of bacon. Walt pushed the entire slice into his mouth. Greasy and cold, it was the only thing he'd have time for.

A hospital aide walked in while he was still chewing. "Time to get dressed for PT."

With what had become his trademark sound, Walt glared at the young girl. "Why didn't you wake me up? My breakfast is petrified." His glare was worse than the growl.

"I tried to wake you up. You refused," Cindy said.

Her syrupy voice grated on his ears, and the pink pin-striped uniform made him slightly nauseous.

Too sweet and too early! Walt envisioned jumping from his bed and escorting her out the door, then walking swiftly away from this hospital on two legs. Not going to happen. He plopped back on his pillow and chewed the hard bacon, one arm thrown over his eyes.

"Pete will be here any minute. He won't be happy with you or me if you're not ready for training." She walked over to the bedside and ordered in a surprisingly no-nonsense voice, "Sit, please."

Walt rolled his eyes and grabbed the bar above his head with both hands. It was easier than the day before, and he begrudgingly admitted to himself that Pete was correct. It got a little easier each day. Two weeks of therapy had made some progress, although he doubted he'd ever master gait training. Pete had caught him more times than he could count when he tried to walk with only one leg. Even with the parallel rails to hold on to, it seemed an impossible task.

With quick and efficient speed, Cindy removed his pajamas and replaced them with a T-shirt and a pair of warm-ups. Walt stared at the outfit, wishing it were his corduroy flared pants and flannel shirt—his usual clothes for class and work in the winter.

"Good morning, Bear," Pete said as he walked into the room, earning him a growl from Walt.

"Enjoy the sunshine. It's short-lived. Three inches of snow predicted by late afternoon. Everything is closed tight as a drum because of the ice storm from last night."

"Everything except this hospital." Walt spit out

the words, even though he knew they weren't true. The *Herald Dispatch* in Huntington would be open for work. Newspapers never stopped working, regardless of the weather.

"You're correct, my friend. We can't let the weary rest for a single minute." Pete smiled and pushed a wheelchair close to the bed. "Now, let's see how your transfer goes today."

Walt gritted his teeth. The only thing worse than lifting himself up from his bed was getting into the chair. After more than a few tries, he finally plopped into the seat with a thump. "You could have helped after the first... oh, dozen tries." Sarcasm laced Walt's voice.

"My rule is to never offer a hand until two dozen tries."

"That's such a comfort." Walt's voice wore a sharp contrast to his therapist's.

"Let's go, Cinderella. This carriage turns to mush at midnight."

Walt put his head in his hands and mumbled, "Whoopee."

Three hours later, Walt was back in his bed, exhausted but not displeased with the morning. He finally made it through the parallel bar without falling back into the wheelchair Pete pushed behind him.

Pain engulfed his body, and he wished the pain meds he received after his therapy would kick in. He tried the deep breathing technique taught to him early on, producing only a slight relief. "Whoever thought this would help?" Walt grumbled, then slipped into the blessed relief of painless sleep.

When he woke, his pain was better and his lunch

sat the bedside table. He touched his mashed potatoes, relieved they were still warm, and made a mental note to thank Cindy for holding lunch an hour late. He ate as though the food had a sign saying, *Will disintegrate in ten minutes.*

The day wore on as he worked with an occupational therapist for bathing and dressing. When his psychologist walked into his room, Walt closed his eyes with a sigh.

"Not happy to see me today?"

Looking at his covers instead of the doctor, he wished it was Dr. Everly from the hospital. She had more sympathy for her patients. The rehab psychologist was the opposite. He grated on Walt's nerves in every session.

Walt mumbled. "I'm happy to see you, but not happy with your questions. Let's save us both some time. No, I don't plan to harm myself. Yes, I'm unhappy. Who in their right mind wouldn't be? And, no, I'm not up for meditation today... just like all the other days."

Dr. Schneider sat in the chair farthest from the bed. "That's fine, Walt. I'll wait a while, if you don't mind." His accent was so heavy, Walt's ears had to perk up. Whoever thought he was a good match for a position here? Walt heard in a drawl, not in the clipped words of this doctor.

"Would it matter if I minded?"

"No, but the last thing I want is to make you uncomfortable."

Too late for that! A five-minute stare-down followed. Walt folded first. "All right, let's get it over with. How does this mediation thing work?"

When he finished, he had to admit he felt better. His pain, both physically and emotionally, had lessened.

"Goot," Dr. Schneider said. He stood and started for the door, before swinging back. "Oh, I'm supposed to let you know your prosthetist will see you tomorrow."

"Prosthetist?"

"The specialist who will help you learn about your artificial limb. He'll measure you for one that will fit you, but you'll start practicing with a loaner."

A loaner, like a loaner car? It still seemed surreal to Walt. He dreaded seeing the thing.

Walt woke and squinted at the sunshine flooding through his window. A candy-striper or nurse must have opened the windows while he was still asleep. As it did every day, this irritated him. Just one more piece of evidence of the loss of control in his life.

After his physical therapy, he was eating a lukewarm plate of spaghetti and meatballs from his wheelchair when Liam walked into his room.

"Man! I didn't expect you today. How'd you get here from Huntington in your car? It's almost as old as mine. Correction… as old as mine was."

"Rickman loaned me his Jeep. Four-wheel drive."

Walt's mouth hung open, not believing what he heard. "His Jeep. Seriously? The interstate must be a mess with last night's ice and snow."

"It is, but the Jeep handled it well."

"I can't believe the boss loaned you his vehicle."

"I think he misses you, or at least your reporting,"

Liam teased. "He sent me to tell you to hurry and get well. He's saving your old desk for you."

"I thought he replaced me with another reporter." Walt had a dozen questions, but his throat had tightened so much, they had to stay inside. He still had the job he loved, but would he be mobile enough to handle the movement required for being a reporter?

"Rickman did, but then he fired him. Told the poor guy he couldn't write his way out of a paper sack." Liam chuckled, then became serious. "I'll be glad to have you back."

Suddenly, a large grin trailed slowly across his friend's face.

Walt tilted his head. "Give it up, Buddy. You look like a cheshire cat."

Blushing, Liam heaved a breath and began. "I've met someone. Her name is Tiffany. She's a junior pre-med student... really smart. She likes me." His blush morphed into a dark crimson. "Actually, we love each other. We're getting married and I'm here to ask you to be my best man."

Unable to speak for a moment, Walt finally pulled it together enough to reach out his hand. "That's great, man. And I'm honored, but word is, I'll be here a long time." He hoped this would deter Liam's invitation. He didn't relish the idea of standing next to his friend, leaning on a walker.

"It's okay. Tiffany and I talked it over. We'll wait until you're out. She understands what it means to me."

Walt tried another way. "What about your brother? Isn't he coming home with the return of our troops?"

Liam's happy eyes darkened. "He volunteered to stay and help train the South Vietnam Army until the Vietnamization policy is completed. Knowing Donny, he'll be the last US soldier to come home."

Walt couldn't think of another excuse about the best man offer, but didn't plan to give up yet. No way would he be a part of a wedding party. "So, what else is going on Huntington, besides my best friend getting married?" he asked, wanting to change the subject.

Liam hesitated long enough for Walt to prompt him. "Come on, let me hear what else is on your mind."

His friend smiled. "Tiffany's a Christian. She shared the gospel with me on our third date. It's all about how God, in His mercy and grace, sent his only son to die for our sins. Belief in Jesus is our way to eternal life and to a righteous life here on earth." Liam paused, producing a huge smile. "Tiffany explained it much better than I can. But I'm a believer now. I don't worry about my brother or my parents any longer. I pray for them."

It was the most words at one time Walt had ever heard from Liam. Somewhere deep in his soul, a small flame emerged. He leaned toward Liam, suddenly not wanting to miss a word.

"Tiffany says we are a people trying to find our way through a wasteland of confusion and chaos, striving to navigate through pain and suffering around us and in us. She says we need to find our anchor in Jesus, not in the shifting sands of our own lives and of society."

"Your fiancé sounds like a smart woman."

"She knows a lot about the Bible, but more than

that, she understands how to have a personal walk with God."

Liam looked down at his hands before continuing. "I know you're a Christian. I've heard you talk about praying. You're in a tough position right now, one of the toughest, but I want you to know God is with you in all circumstances."

"Are you ready for a stationary bike ride today?" The occupational therapist asked as he walked in the room.

Walt shrugged his shoulders at Liam. "Guess I have to go."

"Sure. I understand." He grabbed his coat and beanie laying in a chair and held them against his chest. "Just one more thing. Tiffany made me promise to ask you to read the book of John."

"Thank you, and congratulations again. She sounds like a treasure." Walt hoped he sounded sincere, but his thoughts were on what Liam had said. He had left God out of his circumstances. After railing at God when the accident first happened, he simply stopped thinking about Him.

That night he reached for the Gideon's Bible from the drawer of his bedside table and turned to the book of John.

Chapter 34

A letter arrived on a Saturday morning, three weeks after Jake's departure. Kathleen had walked to the post office building near her apartment every day since her husband's departure, only to be disappointed. Her eyes fixated on her husband's handwriting, wondering what she was holding. Didn't he just run out for some milk? Then, her mind caught up with reality. "A letter," she mumbled, clutching it to her chest. Her heart skipped a nickel's worth of beats.

At home, she settled on the couch, turned the envelope over and opened the seal, careful not to tear the letter. She wanted—needed—every word. Kathleen blinked away the moisture in her eyes until Jake's handwriting came into came into focus. She searched for the date written military style at the beginning of the sheet.

09/Jan/72. A small hurt grew within. He promised to write daily.

Dearest wife of mine,

She read the opening a second time. So like what he would say. One of the many things she missed.

First, forgive me for not keeping my promise to write every day. The cargo plane, our Army's choice of airlines, bumped around so much none of us aboard could write. We were too busy trying to fit into a seat the size of a toilet lid.
Second,

Kathleen smiled. Jake loved to make lists.

When we arrived, a major battle was underway. Every medevac team loaded in a Huey and spent the next three days rescuing the wounded. Thank goodness my team's pilot and crew chief had experience. I felt like a fox without a hole.
Then we bugged out to…

A wide strip of black ink hid the rest of the sentence. Kathleen scratched at it with her nail, holding her mouth in a tight squeeze. Unsuccessful, she moved on to the sentence below.

It was quite an orientation. Everyone says I'll get used to this job. I doubt I'll ever get used to the bone-aching tiredness. Sometimes, I can't scratch two words together in a letter. Please be patient and know I'll write when I can.
Every night, when I finally hit my bunk, I stare at our wedding picture and miss you terribly. Would

you send me some pictures of our honeymoon and others we snapped during our short courtship?

When the mail came today, I had four letters from you. I cheered! Mail delivery when someone new arrives can be slow at first. I read two of them before getting a duty called, and I was off in the chopper again. I'll read the others after chow tonight. It's wonderful to hear from you, but it upsets me to hear your chemistry prof. is still unkind to you. I'm praying it will improve. You are going to class, right? I want you to keep a normal routine, so anytime I think of you, I'll know what you're doing. I must remind myself I need to rewind back thirteen hours. It blows my mind, darling, knowing your night is my next day.

I'm getting to know my medevac team.

Sweetheart, I must close now. Word just came that we're ordered to a meeting with our caption. Must be something big.

I love you, Kathleen McBride. I can't wait to look into your lovely eyes again.

Jake

Kathleen immediately went to the start of the letter to read it again. She would have read it a third time if she hadn't heard a knock. She returned it to the envelope and slipped it under the cushion on the couch. Kathleen moved to the window and pulled back the curtain with a groan. Ainsley and Mahira were at her door.

"I saw you, Kathleen. You're not avoiding us today," Ainsley yelled. "This is an intervention. So you might as well open the door, because we're not leaving."

She desperately sought an excuse but came up with none. Kathleen had no choice but to let them in. When she opened the door, Ainsley swooshed by her.

"Well, she let us in. At least her brain hasn't turned to mush with all this isolation."

Still holding the doorknob, she motioned for Mahira. "You might as well come too."

"Thank you," Mahira said softly. "Please forgive us for intruding. We're trying to be a good friend for you."

Kathleen sighed at how different these friends were. Yet, somehow, the word *friend* warmed her heart. Whatever might happen, she found herself glad they were in her living room. "Okay, tell me the plan for this intervention, though I'm not sure it's needed."

Ainsley snorted. "Oh, it's needed, best friend. My old granny—"

"We agreed to no 'my old granny' stories. Did you already forget?" Mahira chastised.

"Am I so pathetic now that I need old granny stories?"

"Well, I just wanted to tell you what my—"

"What Ainsley means to say is that you need a girls' day out." Mahira's eyes roved from head to toe over Kathleen. "Please go shower, wash your hair, and put on something less... crumbled."

Kathleen looked down at Jake's plaid shirt and her oldest pair of warm-ups, hoping her three-day-old socks didn't stink. She had the decency to feel embarrassed. She nodded in compliance and started for the bathroom.

"And you'd better return as beautiful as the Kathleen we know and love!" Ainsley said, before plopping herself down on the sofa with a magazine. She dropped it back on the coffee table. "And make it snappy. Where's a copy of *True Romance*? Nobody subscribes to *The New Yorker*."

In record time, Kathleen returned to the living room wearing a pair of jeans, a blue sweater, and boots. She'd blow-dried her hair and forced its curls into a braid that lay over one shoulder. Around her neck, she wore a tied blue and yellow scarf Jake had given her before he left. She smiled at the memory. Almost every day prior to his departure, he came home with a small gift. "Something to help you think of me," he'd say.

"Okay, the way to end an intervention is to get it started." Kathleen motioned to the door. "So, start intervening." She tried to keep her face and voice stern but was unsuccessful. *Maybe this is what she needed.*

Ten minutes later, Mahari parallel parked her blue Saab near downtown. "Everyone out. We're about a block from our destination," she said, struggling to get the car's shift stick into park.

Kathleen exited the car and pulled the back of her seat forward so Ainsley could exit the small, two-door car. She fought a chuckle, watching her roommate's effort to squeeze through the small opening. It was like pushing a square peg through a round hole.

Finally out, Ainsley gave Mahira a glare. "Whatever possessed you to buy this tin can? It's no bigger than my... than a chicken hutch."

"It's not tin. The body is fiberglass. Now let's

move. Our appointment time is in ten minutes," Mahira said, clearly today's leader.

Appointment? Kathleen halted as panic tightened her back muscles. "Surely, you're not taking me to a shrink because if you are, we can just—"

"Of course not, silly." Mahira hooked her arm around Kathleen's elbow. "We're going to a spa for a massage and time in the sauna. Then, after lunch, we'll do some reckless shopping."

An hour later, Kathleen was seated on the side of the massage table. "Thank you. It's incredible how much better I feel."

"You should, honey. Your muscles were wound up tighter than a corkscrew," Ulma, the masseuse, tilted her head and folded her hands on her large girth. "Child, whatever burdens you might carry should be laid at the foot of the cross. Our Lord takes that which weights us down and gives us peace."

"I'll get dressed and join my friends. Thank you again." Her speech was gracious, but her mind screamed, *I'll lay down my burdens the day Jake walks back through our door.*

Kathleen was in the sauna for only a short time when she felt the familiar queasiness. "Sorry, guys. I'm hotter than a chili pepper. I'm going to relax with a magazine in the lounge." She made it to the ladies' room before throwing up.

When spa time ended, Mahira took charge again. "There's an Indian restaurant within walking distance. They have great tandoori chicken, and the naan bread is the best around."

Ainsley wagged a finger and replied, "Oh, no. No Indian food today. If I must ride back in that clown car, I want some good, tasty West Virginia food. Follow me. It's not far either."

Kathleen smiled at the takeover. Clearly, a new leader had arrived.

When the three were settled at the Appalachian House restaurant, Kathleen scanned the menu and suddenly felt ravenous. She surveyed the menu as though she planned to buy stock in it.

Chicken and dumplings, country-fried steak, cheese grits, and biscuits with gravy all had her name on it. She settled on the dumplings and a side of collard greens and fried okra. "Oh, and bring me two slices of cornbread. Later, I'll have a fried apple pie." She looked up from the menu to see two pairs of round eyes staring at her. Kathleen shrugged her shoulders. "Must be the massage. It makes a girl hungry."

After eating her every bite of the food at record speed, she sat back and hoped she wouldn't regret it later when the heartburn started.

When the meal was over, Mahira announced, "Time for shopping."

Kathrine cringed. After the enormous meal, she was exhausted and feared she might go to sleep in one of JC Penny's dressing rooms. "Oh, let's sit here and visit some more. We can shop next Saturday," she said with the hope her friends would forget the suggestion by next Saturday.

"I agree. We don't want to take away the effects of the spa. I feel as relaxed as a coon dog sleeping on the porch." Ainsley finished her iced sweet tea and motioned for the server to bring another.

"All right. I'll start the conversation. I think Dr. Jai Kumar may want to marry me."

This brought squeals from both Kathleen and Ainsley. "Has he asked you?" they said in unison.

"Not yet, but soon, I think."

"And you'll say yes, right?" Kathleen smiled when Mahira gave her a nod.

"Well, I have nothing that tops that," Ainsley said. "Unless I get the news that Joe's new girlfriend has joined a nunnery."

After a chuckle, Kathleen said in a small voice, "I have a question. What if Jake gets killed and I'm pregnant?"

This brought silence to the table.

That night, she wrote to Jake, sharing her girl's day out—minus the lunch conversation.

Chapter 35

The overcast February day sky, with a continuous drizzle, matched Kathleen's mood. She pulled up the hood on her heavy coat and went around the corner of her apartment building to the post office, heading straight to their mail cubicle. When the key clicked, she held her breath before peering inside. Nothing. It had been empty for the last three weeks. Her disappointment followed with a fear so strong it felt like a bolt of lightning. What if...?

After finishing her last classes, Kathleen retraced her steps to the post office. Her heart squeezed when no letter lay in the opening. She closed the small door and leaned her forehead on the outside of the cubicle. "Jake, what's wrong? Please let me know you're okay," her voice wobbled as she spoke.

She entered her apartment after a teary walk home and went straight to the kitchen, where she woofed down a package of Twinkies and a large glass of milk. This had also become a routine. Before the pregnancy, she never touched anything loaded with so much sugar. Now she devoured Twinkies and Dong Dongs daily.

"At least I'm drinking milk," she breathed, putting her hand to her stomach. Whispering to the new life growing within her helped with the loneliness. "One day, I'm going to have to tell your daddy about you." Kathleen sighed. "Not yet, sweet baby. I'm sure he'd worry too much about us. We want him to focus on staying alive."

She leaned against the counter, deep in thought as her mind switched back and forth between Jake, the baby, and the war that separated them. The radiator gurgled with a hiss of steam, reminding Kathleen she was still in her coat and scarf. After hanging her things on the rack near the door, her glance moved to the couch where she'd left Jake's last letter. Sitting down, she reread his words, hoping to find a clue as to why he hadn't written.

30/Jan/72
Dear Wife,

Things have been intense here, hence the reason I can't write to you more often. We're short medics, so we're all working eighteen-hour shifts until replacements arrive. When I finally make it back to my bunk, all I can do is fall into it and sleep.

On the good side, I'll get twenty-four hours off at the end of this week. I promise, sweetheart, to write you a long newsy letter.

Until then, remember how much I love you.
Jake

Kathleen sat straight up and focused on the word *replacements*. What happened to those medics who were being replaced? Had they gone home, or were they killed? Anger consumed her like an angry beast as her mind vented frustration. What country would send their soldiers to a place eight thousand miles away to be maimed or killed fighting a war they couldn't win? It began in 1965, and soldiers were still there almost six years later. Rusty, her old lab partner, popped into her head. She finally understood why he left school to join the protests. For a moment, she wanted to find a sign and hit the streets as well.

When the room spun, she realized she'd been holding her breath. She bent down from her waist, hoping not to faint. Tears spilled onto the floor as she tried to fight against the panic attack. A knock at the door caused her to call out, "Who is it?"

"It's Mahira. May I come in?"

"The door's unlocked." Kathleen tried to sit but more spinning lowered her head again.

Mahira was at her side instantly. "Kathleen, what's wrong? Is the baby all right? Are you okay?"

The kindness of her friend hit the fire inside of her like a shower of water. She sat up and looked at Mahira with flooded eyes.

"I can't do this. It's too hard knowing Jake is in a war zone. And the baby... I don't know how to be pregnant, much less being a mom." She drew in big clumps of air. "What if Jake doesn't come home?"

Mahira grabbed her in a big hug. "Sweetheart, Jake will come home. He flies in a helicopter with a big red cross on its nose. He's not in a rice paddy or in the jungle."

She reached into her bag and pulled out two books. "As for being pregnant, I brought you a book called *"Nine Months' Reading: A Medical Guide for Pregnant Women"* and Dr. Spock's book about raising children from newborns to toddlers. You're not alone in this. Ainsley and I are here."

She took Kathleen's chin and raised her friend's eyes to her own. "Jake will be back before this baby is born. He'll be here to see this beautiful child come into the world. You must focus on that."

Mahira stood and put her hands on her hips. "Now, when is the last time you ate something besides Twinkies?" When Kathleen didn't reply, she said, "Come on. We're going grocery shopping and then come back here where I can make you a decent meal."

Mahira stayed long enough to make buttered chicken with rice and waited while Kathleen showered and put on her pajamas. She held back the covers so her friend could climb into bed.

"Promise me you'll sleep. Don't let those demons in your head rob you of rest. Our God says to cast our fears on Him. He'll take away your anxiety." She offered her signature wide smile before continuing. "Besides, it's not good for the baby. I read that in your pregnancy book."

The next morning, sunshine flooded her bedroom. "Good morning, baby. Let's see if we can do better today." For several weeks now, she had made it a morning ritual to say hello to the baby. As she dressed for class, Kathleen thought of reasons to explain to her chemistry teacher why she hadn't finished her homework. *The dog ate it.* No, she had an aversion to lying. She'd done enough if that to last a lifetime. *I had a panic attack and my friend made me buttered chicken.* This was the truth, but it sounded lame. She squeezed her eyes together. "Please don't let him even ask for it." She wondered if this qualified as a prayer.

By the end of the week, Kathleen still hadn't received any letters from Jake. On Friday afternoon, she unlocked the cubicle and jerked it open. She stood there looking at the white envelope with red and blue strips along the edges. Her hand couldn't reach for it. *He wrote* was all she could muster. Finally, she grabbed the letter and tucked it inside her coat pocket, then quietly closed the cubicle door. She resisted the urge to rip it open standing there, opting for the quietness of her living room.

At home, she slid out of her coat and pulled off her knitted cap with a single motion. Foregoing her usual milk and Twinkies, she moved to the couch and ripped open the letter.

30/Jan/72
Dear Kathleen,
I know it's been weeks since I've written. Sweetheart, I can't think of anything to write that's not morbid or worrisome. We had a long major offense called (blacked out) that took many lives and injured many others. I thought this battle would never end. The promise of twenty-fours off duty never happened.

Kathleen paused. Had she seen this on the news? She couldn't remember and moved her eyes back to the letter.

The offensive is over now, and our rescue effort prevented many more casualties. But this thought doesn't erase the sights we saw. This is a hellish war that no one can fully understand except those that are living it. I never want children if they'll be in such a place as this.

Kathleen stopped reading to wipe the wetness off her chin, blinking until she could focus on Jake's words.

On another note. I hope you won't be disappointed to hear I've started smoking. I apologize because I've broken a promise I made to you before we married. But, sweetheart, everyone here smokes. It really takes the edge off at the end of a medic run. I've tried them all because the Army supplies a large quantity in a wide variety. I go back and forth between Camels and Lucky Strikes, though my buddy, Leo, prefers Chesterfields. He says they put hair on a man's chest. Leo is a good friend who gets me through many tough times.
I think of you so often and of our little apartment. In my mind's eye, I can see you washing dishes at our tiny sink or sitting on the couch with your books and notepad, studying until midnight. The urge to return home can be so powerful it leaves me breathless.
I love you, Little Bit.
Jake

Kathleen didn't stop the tears this time. Never once had she thought about how Jake must feel. She'd only thought of herself. Guilt wound itself around her like a tight rubber band. She didn't read through this letter a second time. Moving to her little desk in the bedroom, she wrote asking her husband's forgiveness for not thinking of how he might feel.

Chapter 36

The next several weeks went past in a whirlwind of midsemester exams and spending time with Ainsley and Mahira, who treated Kathleen like a piece of china.

By March, she had a baby bump and had felt fluttering in the belly a few times. Suddenly, the baby became a reality as opposed to a little creature far away.

She still pushed back on any thoughts of preparing for the baby, but she read every word of the two books Mahira had given her. At her March monthly appointment, her doctor said everything was on track except for her weight. "Are you eating enough?" Dr. Coban asked.

Her mind said, *Sure, lots of Twinkies and Ding Dongs*, but her mouth opened with "Yes, I have a ravenous appetite." She hoped this would satisfy her doctor.

"At the five-month checkup, I'd like to see at least four more pounds on you. You've hardly put any weight on."

Kathleen nodded her head, picturing her pantry well-stocked with sugary items.

Over the next weeks, letters went back and forth between herself and her husband, albeit the ratio was one-to-three. Jake's were on the low side.

Then one day a letter came that shocked Kathleen.

19/Feb/72

Dearest Kathleen,

I have wonderful news. Something has happened that I must share. Being here in this sea of chaos, fear, and death is like being on a deserted island and using your last match to light a fire that the wind immediately blows out. Then there's only darkness with no hope left. This is where I've been—hopeless with nowhere to turn.

In desperation, I went to a guy in our bunker who seems at peace all the time. I asked Hank about it, and what he shared has changed my life. Remember when I told you my foster family were Christians and led me to the Lord as a teenager? That part is true, but what didn't happen was the spiritual walk God wants to be a part of every Christian's life. I simply hung my salvation on a rack, waiting to redeem it when I die. I know now that Jesus offers hope on this side of eternity along with eternal life when we pass.

Sweetheart, I hope you'll embrace what I've shared and come to understand the only thing we can trust in this life is the faithfulness of our Lord now.

Even our trust in each other pales in the true light of Jesus Christ.

Love and blessings,

Jake

P.S. Will you send me my Bible? I think it's on the top shelf of my closet, behind my gym bag. But first, please read the book of John. It will explain what I'm talking about.

Kathleen sat for a long time staring at the letter. *Why do I feel he's even farther away from me now?*

At her April monthly obstetrician's appointment, both Ainsley and Mahira insisted on going with her. When the nurse called her name in the waiting room, both friends stood up.

"I'm going back with her." Ainsley stated in a no-nonsense voice.

"So am I," Mahira replied. "After all, we're *both* her aunties."

Kathleen appealed to the nurse, who smiled and nodded. "Sure, the more the merrier."

Dr. Cohan praised Kathleen when he read her chart. "You've gained the four pounds, plus one. Very good, indeed."

"It's my buttered chicken," Mahira interjected.

"And the homemade chicken and dumplings from The Appalachian Restaurant." Ainsley had no intention of being outdone by Mahira.

Kathleen nodded her head toward her friends. "They're my food cops."

"Good. I say they keep it up. Now, let's measure that baby belly," Dr. Cohan responded as he patted on the exam table.

It was noon when the appointment was over and the trio arrived back to Kathleen's yellow bug. She listened to the banter back and forth about whether to eat home-style or Indian.

"Stop!" she insisted. "The three of us have already missed our morning classes. We're going to the student union to eat cheeseburgers so we have enough time to get to class. And honestly, there's a vast array of food out there besides curries and collard greens!"

Both friends had the grace to look contrite as they let their driver plan their meal destination.

Kathleen had never felt heavier. Not just from her growing belly, but also from her actions—or nonactions—in her marriage. When Jake received the Bible, he immediately wrote her a thank you and asked how she liked the book of John. Before answering his question, she went to the library and pulled a Bible off a shelf. But she couldn't make herself open it. She'd lied too much, hurt too many. How could she walk with Christ? In the end, she told Jake she had read it and was thinking about what it said. This lie and her failure to tell him about their baby plagued most of her waking hours and sometimes invaded her dreams.

Near the end of the semester, Kathleen glared at the grade on her latest lab project. Furious, she charged the podium before the instructor left.

"How can this be a D+? I worked for hours on this project, and I must pass this course this time."

Only then did she realize Professor Wells had his hand in the air. She stopped, confused by the gesture.

"I'm glad you came to me. There's a confession I need to make." He looked around to see if all the students had left, then turned back to Kathleen. "I've done you a terrible injustice. When you first entered my class back in September, I could barely stand to look at you."

"Why? You didn't even know me."

"I've recently realized how badly I've treated you. I know... knew someone who was your age and the picture of you. It was just too soon after..."

Kathleen's voice lowered by several degrees. "After what?"

Tears flooded his eyes before he continued, "My daughter died last July. It was an overdose of LSD. I tried to make her stop and when she didn't, I turned my back on her." A single sob interrupted his sentence.

"I'm sorry for what happened." Kathleen waited a few moments before asking, "And you think it's been okay to harass me all these months?"

"No, of course not. After Kelly's death, I became a hard, bitter man. It's only been my daughter and myself since my wife passed when she was ten. I not only lost my only child, but I also lost my faith. Now, through Christian counseling, I'm ready to give her death to God—and try to make right what I done to others these past months. The worst thing is what I've done to you. I've never had a student work as hard as you, yet I berated your every effort. Please forgive me."

Kathleen looked into his pleading eyes and saw a broken man who was trying to set things straight. *Will I ever get there in my brokenness?*

"I should have offered you this last semester, as I did with others who were struggling. Will you let me tutor you? I have an open slot at four p.m. every Friday from now until the end of the semester."

Kathleen couldn't believe what she heard. Her

enemy wanted to help her. She took a moment, then said, "Yes, I will."

"Trust me, Kathleen, the pleasure will be all mine. You'll still have to work hard to salvage this semester, but together, I think we can reach that goal."

Walking to the post office after this class, she couldn't wait to write to Jake about what happened. It'd been almost three weeks since she'd received a letter from Vietnam, but today, two letters were in the box.

She gripped the letters tightly with one hand as though they might evaporate and found a bench in the small park near the post office. Fluffy pure-white clouds drifted across a brilliant blue sky. The warm temperatures had burst open the blossoms on the redbud and dogwood trees, creating a stunning red and white scene.

Kathleen lifted her face upward to soak in the spring sun but dropped it quickly. How can she enjoy the beautiful day and these letters, when she carried so many lies between her and her husband? She laid the letters on her lap and sat in quietness. A thought materialized, yet it was more like a soft voice speaking to her heart. "Hang on, I will right your ship and draw you safely to my harbor." Her skin filled with chill bumps from head to toe. She didn't know where it came from, but she immediately had a peace—far from her usual stance of fear and guilt.

Opening the first letter, she read it softly out loud, somehow finding comfort that their baby could hear her father's words.

21/Mar/72
Dear Kathleen.
The fighting has finally slowed down here, which I thank God for—not just because we can all get a rest, but because God has given this time of respite by saving lives of soldiers on both sides. I've been spending a lot of time with Hank. We've finished reading the book of John and moved to the Old Testament to read the book of Isaiah. Kathleen, it's full of what Hank calls the 'fear not' verses. Boy, do we need these here in this jungle. This awful place is making me trust God more and more.

It's rained every day, sometimes all day, for the past two weeks and it's not yet monsoon season. I'm told this is even worse because it rains daily from May to September. Mud is everywhere. I struggle to keep my fatigues and socks dry. The first thing I plan to do when I get home, after giving you a kiss and a hug, is to buy one of those electric clothes dryers.

I must close now. It's time for a muddy trip to the mess tent. Thank goodness it's near my bunker because it's raining again. Tonight, the menu is ham and lima beans—not my favorite. What I wouldn't give for a cheeseburger and fries from Lynn's Drive -in. But I'm grateful for the food we're served here, especially whenI think of the c-rations soldiers eat when they're in the field—canned meat, canned vegetables, canned everything.

I'm glad your chemistry teacher is treating you better. Hank and I are praying for him.

I'm counting the days until I'm back with you.
Love, Jake

Kathleen smiled and whispered, "I'm counting them too." She was counting other days also—the days until her due date. Maybe it was time to tell him.

She opened the next letter, surprised by the two brief paragraphs.

15/Apr/72
Dearest Kathleen.
It's no longer quiet. A large counter-offensive started on March 30 called (blacked out). It's huge and keeps the medevac teams busy. I'm weary of the blood and the death. Yesterday, we evacuated a young soldier who was seriously hurt and calling for his mother. He stopped breathing while I was putting an IV in his arm during the chopper ride. I did CPR until we landed, but couldn't revive him. It hit me hard.

Sweetheart, I need to remind you again of what to do if I don't come home. All the papers for my death benefits and our life insurance documents are in the locked drawer of my desk. I put the key under the desk lamp. I have a small savings account. The details about it are in the same place as the military papers.

I love you with all my heart,
Jake

Kathleen put her hand over her mouth to suppress a sob. She wiped tears from her face and walked home. The beauty of the spring day had spun into darkness.

Chapter 37

"Ouch." Kathleen stopped and grabbed her lower back as she rubbed the knotted muscles. The multitude of students hurrying to class parted around her like the dividing of the Red Sea.

Fear made her fingers tingle. She'd pushed back the pain since it started three days ago. Could this be the baby? *It can't be. It's way too soon.*

She made her way to a bench just outside Woodburn Hall and sat breathing in through her nose and out from her mouth until her back muscles released. Any movement of her body now made the tightness return, though waiting meant she'd be late for class.

She rubbed the pit of her back, wondering again what was causing this pain. The answer came to her immediately—it started the day she read Jake's last letter. The one about death benefits.

Kathleen picked up her bookbag from the bench,

preparing to continue her walk, when she spotted a copy of a Morgantown's *Dominion Post* laying under her books. She glanced at the headline in the bottom right column on the first page. The words caused the squeezing in her back to return. *Easter Offensive Continues—see page three.* When did this war become third page news?

She forced herself to turn to the page and read the short column. Nothing new there. Kathleen already knew the North Vietnam Army had launched a major offensive strike against South Vietnam on March 30th when most of the US troops stationed there were being sent home.

She closed the paper and searched for the top front-page story. The headline read *War Protesters in Common Plaza at WVU.* Jake hated the protest rallies. He thought they were unpatriotic and dangerous. She hoped the protests would end before her husband returned to the States.

By the time she arrived at the apartment later in the afternoon, her back was so tight she found it difficult to walk. She dropped her bookbag on the floor and struggled to the sofa.

When the muscles finally released, she dropped off to sleep. Hard, repeating knocks on the door forced her awake.

"Oh, what now?" Kathleen grumbled as she struggled off the sofa and her coveted heating pad. She walked gingerly to the door, finding Mahira standing there holding a basket.

"Hello, little mama. I've brought some food." When Kathleen protested, Mahira dismissed her. "Don't worry, it's not buttered chicken. I've brought some hummus and naan bread. I thought you might have time for a visit."

Kathleen reluctantly swung the door open to let her friend pass. "Okay."

Mahira placed the basket on the coffee table and removed her light jacket. Only then did she see the heating pad. She spun around to Kathleen and gasped at her friend's stiff walk toward the sofa. "What's wrong?" Her eyes bore a hole into Kathleen's.

"Nothing, just a little back pain. I must have turned wrong."

"Back pain? How long have you had it?"?

"Three days," Kathleen answered as she eased herself onto the heating pad.

Mahira threw her hands into the air. "Has it occurred to you it might be the pregnancy? You should go to the emergency room," she said, reaching for her jacket. "I'll drive."

When Kathleen protested, Mahira shook a finger in her direction. "No buts. I'll call Ainsley to meet us there while you get dressed."

Kathleen sighed but followed the command. If she was wrong about the cause of the pain and something happened to the baby, how could she live with herself—or with Jake?

When she finally made it to an examination room, with two mother hens fussing over her, she was past exhaustion. All three pairs of eyes were on her belly as the doctor listened with his stethoscope and pushed on her stomach. The eyes moved to him when he stepped back from the examination table.

"The good news is the baby is fine. But I think you're under great stress, Mrs. McBride. You need to reduce some of what is troubling you. The nerves in our bodies can't stand up to acute stress."

Ainsley spoke first. "And how is she supposed to help her nerves when her husband is deployed to Vietnam?" She looked as though the doctor had grown horns. "Not to mention the pregnancy."

The doctor was gracious enough to look apologetic. "Forgive me, Mrs. McBride. I didn't mean to sound callus. I can give you something to relax so those muscles will stop spasming."

Kathleen gestured a no with her head before the doctor finished his sentence. "I won't take any drugs that might harm the baby."

"Then I suggest you talk with someone who can help you with your fear."

Kathleen held back a harsh reply. *Which fear is he talking about?* Instead, she meekly agreed with his suggestion—anything to get back home to her heating pad.

On a wet, late April day, Kathleen walked into Professor Wells' office holding a lab report in a brown file folder. "I finished it. Thank you for giving me extra time."

"No problem. How are you feeling?"

"Better, thank you."

Professor Wells opened the folder and scanned down the pages. "Central question... methods used... results... conclusion." He gave Kathleen a crisp nod, then smiled. "It looks as though you may have a strong report here. Of course, I'll have to look closer, but I expect you'll be pleased with your grade."

"I appreciate the tutoring sessions. You helped me see chemistry in a whole new light. One less thing to fear."

"I'm glad to help. Seeing a student's improvement touches my teacher's heart." He paused, growing serious before continuing. "Kathleen, you said "one less thing to fear" a few moments ago. Do you have other fears in your life?"

Kathleen saw the compassion written in his eyes and her mind whispered, N*ot again. No more lies.* "Yes, I do." Just those three words lifted her heart. She'd told the truth.

"When Kelly died, after I came back to my faith, I found many scriptures about not fearing, not being anxious. Those words brought me peace." He swiveled his chair to a bookcase and pull out a small book. "I want you to have this book. It's called *God's Promises*. In it, there are scriptures for every situation in our lives. It's organized by things like fear, anxiety, disappointment, loneliness, and more."

Kathleen's eyes brimmed with moisture as she reached for the book, not sure what to say.

"I'm always here if you need to talk," he said. "Kelly often came by my office when she was troubled… until the drugs…"

She identified with his pain but wasn't ready to unload her past to anyone. She gave him a quick nod and mumbled a thank you before leaving.

A week later, there were still no letters from Jake. Kathleen's emotions were scattered like corn in a chicken pen. She went from justifying—*He's just very busy. They're probably short on medics again,* to her greatest fear—*He's never coming home.*

Eager to not be alone with her thoughts, she called Mahira and Ainsley on Friday after her last class, inviting them to dinner and a movie at her apartment.

"I'm in. I'll ditch the guy who's taking me to dinner," Ainsley said. "Dating is so hard, and it only makes me miss Joe even more."

Mahira accepted as well. "Jai has a double shift at the hospital. I'd love to come."

Kathleen immediately scrounged her pantry and fridge for something to make. The search was futile. By the time she finished, she was talking to herself. "Really, Kathleen, you should shop more often." She glanced at the kitchen wall clock—too late to make a grocery run and cook dinner. "Pizza it is." Opening the refrigerator, she pulled out enough fresh vegetables to make a decent salad.

Pleased to have her friends over, she moved about the kitchen and living room, picking up and lighting some candles. Her back had improved from the breathing techniques Mahira had taught her. "But the greatest healer is God. Give these fears to Him," she'd said at the end of their lesson.

Ainsley arrived first. "You saved me, Kathleen. When I called this guy to reschedule our date, he became ugly and said a few choice words." Her eyes became glassy when she added, "My Joe would never have spoken to me like that." She stopped talking and gasped. "Honey, I'm so sorry. Here I am complaining like an old grouch when you don't know if your husband is alive or..." Ainsley slapped her palm to her forehead. "Oh, I've put my foot in my mouth... again!"

"It's okay. You're only stating the truth," Kathleen said and reached out to hug her.

"Any letters this week?" Ainsley asked, with a contrite look on her face.

"No, not in the last three weeks." Thankfully, the doorbell rang before Ainsley could ask more. "That's Mahira."

"My mother thinks I'm too skinny. She keeps me supplied with these by the dozen." Mahira handed her a box filled with peanut ladoo, an Indian sweet made from roasted peanuts, cardamon, and sweet jaggery.

Soon, the three friends settled in the living room, drinking sweet tea and catching up. Ainsley looked out the window. "Someone's here."

"That would be the pizza man." Kathleen stood, removed cash from her pocket, and started to the front door.

Ainsley peeked through the front window. She looked at Kathleen with wide eyes. "It's not the pizza delivery." She turned away and mouthed something to Mahira.

"Wait, let me open it," Mahira said, rushing to Kathleen's side while Ainsley sprang to her other side.

Kathleen ignored their words. Panic rose in her body, squeezing her air flow, while heartbeats drummed in her ears. With a trembling hand she opened the door and gasped at who stood before her.

Before she could speak, one of the military men said, "Mrs. McBride?"

Kathleen nodded, not trusting her voice.

"Ma'am, we regret to inform you…"

Mahira and Ainsley caught her as she went down. A visceral scream filled the apartment.

Chapter 38

Sunlight and an array of pink and white azaleas dotted the path to the gravesite. The brightness of the day assaulted Kathleen's senses. How could there be beauty when her world felt gray and forbidding? She had a myriad of feelings, from deep despair to denial. Surely, she was in a dream from which she needed to awaken. Then the unrelenting pain would stop.

The limousine pulled to a stop. The Thornhills exited first, then stood beside the door waiting for her to get out. But she couldn't move. Her muscles had stopped working.

The church service had been unbearable as she sat between Jake's aunt and uncle in the front row. She would rather have been in the back of the church, past all the rows of relatives to the pew where Ainsley and Mahira sat.

One or the other or both of her friends had been at her side since the two soldiers stood at her door.

They cooked for her, reminded her to bathe, and held her through long times of sobbing. The only time they penetrated her grief was when they reminded her of the child she carried and her need to eat and sleep for the baby. Now they sat far from her, and Kathleen felt alone and vulnerable.

"Kathleen, dear." Aunt Mary leaned into the open limo door. "It's time to get out."

She jerked. "Sorry," she said in a gravelly voice. Would nothing, even her speech, ever be the same?

Uncle Bill guided Kathleen to the tent over the gravesite. Again, she sat in the front row. But this time, the casket draped in the US flag sat much closer. Kathleen lowered her head, unable to view the reality of it. She only raised her head when the pastor came and stood at the head of the casket. Or was it Jake's feet? To her horror, she almost giggled.

She heard little of what the pastor said until he read Psalm 23. The verses brought a slight flash of hope. The words shepherd, green pastures, and quiet waters were a balm to her ravaged heart. *Is there really someone who understands this dark valley?*

Before she could process this thought, two uniformed soldiers marched to each end of the casket. Their white-gloved hands folded the flag over the casket into a triangle with impressive precision.

To Kathleen's dismay, one of them approached her, kneeled, and offered her the flag with the words, "On behalf of the president of the United States, and a grateful nation, please accept this flag as a symbol of our appreciation for your loved one's honorable and faithful service."

The words stunned her as she reached for the

flag. In appreciation? Grateful? Kathleen's mind recalled all the anti-war riots. She hoped what the honor guard said would become the sentiment of the nation. It's what Jake had wanted, and now she as well. Otherwise, Jake's death would be futile.

She dug her nails into her palms as three soldiers gave the twenty-one-gun salute. Each shot hammered into her bones. The notes of a lone soldier playing taps from a distance pained her ears. She tried to shut out the music, having no desire to hear the mournful song.

Back at the Thorndales' home, what seemed like hundreds of people approached her with their condolences. She said "thank you" so many times her saliva dried up, and her sweat-filled hand became numb from endless handshakes. Thankfully, Ainsley and Mahira stood on each side of her chair like sentinels guarding her heart.

When there was a lull in the number of guests, Ainsley would lean over and say something funny. "Uncle Rubert is sporting a toupee," or "Mrs. Curtis needs to lay off the Twinkies." Each time, Mahira sent her an exasperated look, but Kathleen was glad. It made the situation almost bearable.

The drive back to Morgantown was quiet. Kathleen sat in the backseat, listening to her friend's conversation but lacking the energy to let them know she could hear them.

Ainsley whispered to Mahira. "Do you think she'll be okay? My granny never got over her first husband's death and always said so, even in front of her next two husbands."

Mahira smiled. "We need to pray that she will be, for her sake and the baby's."

"Amen to that."

Kathleen's last thought before falling into an exhausted sleep was, *"I'll never be okay, prayer or not."*

Kathleen stumbled through her daily routine, shrouded in a cloak of grief. It angered her to see the other students carrying out their lives seemly without a care in the world. Don't they know how quickly life can change? It only takes a telegram or a phone call or a messenger at the door.

She stumbled through her classes half-hearing what the professors said and often had to ask the student sitting next to her about the assigned homework.

Kathleen spent her evenings working on the assignments for each of her classes. In the past, she'd put far less effort on her homework, preferring to spend time with friends or watch a movie curled up on the sofa with a bowl of popcorn nearby. Now, she worked until far past midnight, then fell into her bed for a few hours of fitful sleep filled with horrific dreams about fires, dead bodies, gunfire, and jungles.

Absorbed in her classwork, she barely thought of the baby and rarely went to the post office. What was the use? There would be no letters from Jake. But one day, she was surprised to see the telltale red and blue stripes on the envelope. She stuffed the letter in her pocket and went to her apartment to open it in the sheltered walls that had become a private refuge for her grief.

After dumping her bookbag and purse on the floor

near the door, she took the letter to the sofa—a place she and Jake had spent many hours contemplating their future. Her breath rose high in her chest, squeezing the air from her body. She held the letter and forced her eyes to the return address.

Unit Private Hank Cothmen
8th Field Hospital Box 3544
APO, AP 96667-1

Kathleen opened the envelope and stared at the folded letter, fearful of what kind of new grief this might bring. She finally unfolded the one-paged sheet, forcing her eyes to focus on the writing.

20/May/72
Dear Mrs. McBride,
The reason for writing this letter brings me deep sadness. Your husband was a close buddy, and I will miss him. In war, an intense camaraderie is forged in the face of constant danger and the challenge of doing our job. The number of casualties and wounded is daunting for all of us. Our shared experiences create a unique bond in this hostile environment.

Jake and I also shared our belief in Jesus Christ. Many strenuous days and nights were healed by God's Word. When the Army collected Jake's belongings, they neglected to include his Bible. I've mailed it to you, although this letter and the package will most likely not arrive at the same time.

When you receive your husband's Bible, you'll find underlined verses that spoke to him—verses bringing him peace in this awful war.

Jake spoke of you so many times, often about the life the two of you would have when he returned home. Now he is in his eternal home, and for this I praise God. Jake talked often about his prayer for you to see the life Jesus offers as he did.

It's a great blessing to know my friend is home with Jesus where there is no pain or suffering as he witnessed here in Vietnam.

In closing, please accept my condolences over the loss of your husband. He was a great man and respected by many here at the field hospital.
Sincerely,
Hank

That night, sleep evaded Kathleen. The letter from Hank kept her mind swirling, and she felt a grief so deep she feared her heart would burst. Then she remembered the *God's Promises* book Professor Wells had given her. After thirty minutes of searching, she found it stuck behind her canisters of flour and sugar in the pantry. When Kathleen received the gift, she didn't want it but resisted tossing it into the trash can.

Back in a chair near an open window, Kathleen let the late May breezes flow over her until she felt brave enough to open the book. From the table of contents, she found the page number of the section on grief.

Overwhelmed by the many scriptures listed under grief, she almost gave up her search. The words didn't resonate with her personal pain until she landed on Isaiah 43:2.

"When you pass through the waters, I will be with you; and when you pass through the rivers, they will not sweep over you. When you walk through the

fires, you will not be burned; the flames will not set you ablaze."

Her breath hitched, and she wondered if this could be true.

Kathleen sat at a table with Mahira and Ainsley eating a quick lunch before their next class.

"Slow down there." Ainsley gave her friend a

cheeky grin. "You're eating that burger like it might dissolve before you finish it."

"I need to visit the registrar's office before class to sign up for both summer sessions. I'm taking three classes each session."

Mahira spoke in a concerned voice. "Are you sure you want to take summer courses with the baby due at the end of August? The heat and the walking will be hard on you. Especially during the second session."

Kathleen finished the last bite and stood, grabbing her bookbag. "It means I can graduate in December. My plan is to get a master's degree in library science."

"Jiminy Cricket!" Ainsley said in a loud voice. "Do you want your water to break while you're in class? Because that's what's going to happen!"

She had to admit the possibility scared her, but not enough for her to spend long summer days at home with her loneliness.

By mid-August, Kathleen's feet were so swollen she had to borrow Ainsley's larger shoes to wear to class. The heat and her size brought such fatigue, she struggled to make the walk to and from campus.

Paisley Rose McBride was born two weeks late on Saturday, September the ninth, at two o'clock in the afternoon. Kathleen labored for eighteen hours before her daughter finally made her appearance into the world. She had a head of fuzzy blond hair and Jake's brown eyes.

Chapter 39

Kathleen groaned as she stood up from her bed and moved to the bassinet where Paisley screamed at the top of her lungs. How such a tiny baby could make such a loud noise was beyond her. "Okay, I'm here." She picked her up and felt her diaper. "Oh, you're soaking wet."

How many times had it been the same nightly ritual—change her diaper, give her a bottle, rock her asleep, return her to the crib and fall into bed, only to repeat it all again three hours later?

Her days were filled with washing bottles and diapers, rocking Paisley when she was fussy, and sleeping when she slept. Sometimes, in the early-morning hours, she watched her daughter sleep and felt an abundance of love for this new child in her life. But always in the front of her mind was Paisley's father, who would never hold his beautiful daughter. Kathleen took four-day-old Paisley home with the help of her friends. Mahira drove while Ainsley gave orders. "Be careful going over that speed bump," and "Don't take the turns too fast. You'll frighten the baby."

Seventy-two exhausting hours later, Kathleen fought against the thoughts bouncing in her head. She ricocheted between *I can do this* and *I can't do this.* At those moments, her grief rose and a speck of doubt stirred within her.

The days blurred into weeks and weeks into months as Kathleen struggled to take care of her daughter. The few minutes she had to herself were spent in doubt that she could ever give her daughter what the child needed.

Kathleen had just put Paisley down for a nap after a fussy morning when a knock at the door threatened to wake her. She hurried to the door and opened it with her index finger over her mouth. Ainsley stood there with a balloon and a small stuffed tiger.

"Hi," she said in a hushed voice—as hushed as Ainsley could be. "Where's that little angel? Her aunt is here to celebrate with her."

"Celebrate what?" Kathleen asked, as she waved her friend in with another signal to be quiet.

Ainsley rolled her eyes. "Her third-month birthday, of course."

A spear of guilt shot through Kathleen's heart. What kind of mother was she? She barely knew what day it was, much less remembering her daughter's age. Did three months mean a milestone, and should she have known this?

"And why aren't you in class?" She spit out her

words, jealous of her friend who went to classes and slept through the nights. Another stab of guilt. Thankfully, Ainsley couldn't hear her thoughts.

"My morning class was canceled. Something about the professor getting sick. Personally, I think she just partied too much this weekend." Ainsley's loud voice had returned.

Before she could shush her friend, Kathleen heard Paisley's cry.

"Cool, she's awake. I'll just go get the little angel."

She quietly spoke to Ainsley's back. "Yeah, please do that and then leave me with a cranky baby." Still, she knew how much both her friends loved her daughter. They helped as much as they could, but each had their own lives. Mahira was involved with her doctor friend and Ainsley had developed her own circle, many who embraced the hippie lifestyle. Today, her friend wore a long peasant dress, moccasins, and a jacket with long fringe.

Ainsley left an hour later spouting words about getting her Paisley fix. "I'll see you soon," she said to Kathleen after a quick hug. She turned around at the door with a sweeping look at Kathleen. "Really, little mama, you need to clean up. You look like something the cat drug up."

Kathleen bit back a response, shut the door, and stared at the baby in her arms. "How about you, little one? Do you think your mama looks that bad?" Sighing, Kathleen knew she probably did.

By early afternoon, she understood why her daughter had been so fussy. She developed a cough that steadily grew worse, racking her little body each time she emitted the sound. Scared, Kathleen called

Mahira. She panicked when her friend didn't answer. She thought of calling Ainsley, but feared she'd race over with some weird concoction from her granny.

Another spasm of coughing propelled Kathleen into action. She grabbed a blanket and rushed to her car, not stopping to get her coat. At the hospital's ER entrance, she left her vehicle at the door, ignoring the security guard's shouts not to park there.

Once inside, she found the first nurse who walked past and clasped her arm. "My... my baby. Something's wrong. Please help her."

The nurse glanced at Paisley and smiled at the sleeping child. "Just take her to the desk and sign in. We'll call you back soon."

Kathleen looked at her daughter and felt betrayed. Where was the cough? She quietly registered on the form a receptionist handed her.

Sitting in a hard chair in the waiting room, she glanced down at her fleece pajamas she wore most days. Now she sat in a chilly waiting room without a coat and only slippers on her feet. *What's wrong with me?*

Twenty agonizing minutes later, her name was finally called. When she stood up, Paisley woke with the return of the hacking cough. Kathleen followed the nurse to an exam room, only to be told to wait for the doctor.

"My baby needs to see the doctor right now," she said in a no-nonsense voice.

The nurse smiled and asked, "First baby?"

She glared at the nurse and spewed out her frustration. "And what does that have to do with the price of eggs?" Her eyes brimmed with moisture.

"I'm sorry," the nurse replied. "I'll see if I can hurry the doctor along."

Kathleen didn't trust her voice to respond. She repositioned the coughing baby to one shoulder, patting her back and watching the big clock on the wall.

When the doctor finally walked in, Kathleen tightened her grip on the baby. Was this the doctor? He looked all of twenty. She'd expected a grandfatherly type who would be full of knowledge and take away her fears.

"I'm Dr. Ivanston. Please put your daughter on the examination table and we'll have a look."

We? Who are we? Am I supposed to stand by, sit back down, or what? Chiding herself for her lack of knowledge, she stood near the table as the doctor did the exam. He was silent for so long, Kathleen's mind went into a frenzy. *Is this good or bad? Why doesn't he speak to me?*

Finally, the doctor turned to her with a smile. "Your daughter has the croup. It's not uncommon for children and it's not dangerous. You'll need a humidifier near her crib and to put VapoRub on her chest for a few days. If she has trouble breathing, bring her back. But I don't think she will. It seems to be a mild case." He paused and looked down at his clipboard. "How was she at her two-month checkup?"

Kathleen's stomach dropped to her feet. She'd forgotten about the appointment. She lowered her head and raised it back to the doctor. "Umm... I... uh." She could say no more.

"Mrs. McBride, these monthly check-ups are important. Your daughter needs her immunizations."

Reproach rushed through Kathleen's body. She wasn't fit to raise her child. An already full bag of remorse added one more stone, the weight threatening to crumble her to the floor.

Somehow, she made it out of the exam room, paid her bill and left—a plan already forming in her mind. But first, she needed to get Paisley well. Back at the apartment, she held the baby close as she dialed the pharmacy to order the humidifier and VapoRub.

"Deliver it to 206 University Dr., Apartment 124. Put it on my tab. And please rush it. My baby is sick."

Kathleen held her daughter close as she walked the floor, watching out the front window for the delivery man. She cringed at each cough and sighed with relief when the delivery truck arrived.

The smell of VapoRub permeated the bedroom, while mist rose from the humidifier. Before long, Paisley fell into an exhausted sleep. Kathleen stayed in the rocker near the baby's crib, her cheeks moist. She bit her lips to keep from crying out loud. With her mind made up, she tiptoed out of the room to call the bus station from the wall phone in the kitchen. "I'd like to buy a bus ticket to Welsh for a week from next Monday." Her next call was to her doctor to make her daughter's three-month checkup.

Within a few days, Paisley's croup cleared up, and she returned to the cheery baby she'd been before. When her two aunties visited, Kathleen said nothing of her plans for fear they'd try to talk her out of it. Three days before she planned to leave, she called her mother at a time when her father would be at the mine.

Kathleen rushed into a practiced speech the moment her mother picked up. "Mom, it's me. I need you to be at the Welsh bus station the day after tomorrow at three p.m. Please don't ask why, and don't bring Dad."

"Kathleen, darling, it's wonderful to hear your voice." She could hear her mother's soft sobs through the phone.

She pressed her forehead against the wall as she fought to compose her voice. "I'll tell you why when I see you. Bye for now." Kathleen pressed the button to end the call and held the phone receiver in her hand. A small part of her wondered if she could take the message back.

Shame churned in her mind. Yet fear told her this was the only decision. Her body trembled when she spotted the picture of Jake on the bookcase. Beside it was the picture Owen had left her, the black-and-white one of him and his wife. What would Owen have said about her decision? Worse, what would Jake think?

The evening before she left, she asked Ainsley and Mahira to come over before the baby's bedtime. She watched as they each held Paisley, laughing when she cooed or kicked her feet in delight over all the attention.

"I declare, Kathleen. She might be the prettiest baby I've ever seen," Ainsley said. "And where I come from, there're more babies than coal trucks."

"I agree," Mahira added. "And she's as sweet as honey."

Their words stabbed her heart. *I can't tell them this is the last time they'll see her.* When Paisley went to sleep, Kathleen made three cups of hot cocoa and asked them to sit at her small table. She stared into her cup, mindlessly stirring it.

Mahira finally spoke. "Kathleen, is there something you want to tell us?"

"Yes, there is," she responded, still looking at her cocoa. When she lifted her eyes, she conjured up a fake smile. "Tomorrow Paisley and I are taking the bus to see my parents."

Chapter 40

*T*he Greyhound bus pulled away from the terminal at 5:00 a.m. on the dot. Kathleen barely had time to find a seat and settle Paisley in her lap. When the bus rolled forward with a jolt, Paisley woke with a loud scream. Several passengers turned to the back of the bus where she was sitting—a few with smiles, most with scowls. *How will I make it alone with a baby for the next thirty hours?*

Before long, the purr of the bus motor put Paisley to sleep. Kathleen was grateful for the quiet.

When Paisley woke with a whine which escalated into a wail, Kathleen struggled to hold her and pour powdered Similac into a bottle. She silently scolded herself for not fixing the bottle while the baby was sleeping. As she added water from a green thermos, it spilled on herself and the baby.

"Can I help?"

She looked up to see a young, dark-haired woman, with the kind eyes and a sweet smile. "Umm…"

"I don't have any kids yet, but I've plenty of nieces and nephews, so I know how to hold a fussy baby." She sat down in the empty seat next to Kathleen and held out her arms.

Paisley stopped fussing when the exchange was made and then stared at the new person's face. Both women chuckled. "I guess she's looking me over to see if she approves."

"It seems she does since the crying stopped." Kathleen returned to her task of filling the bottle with water, then shaking it to mix it up.

"My name is Dana. I'm headed to Beckley to meet my fiancé's family. I'm as nervous as a mouse hiding from a cat." Dana reached for the bottle. "May I feed her? Might help settle my nerves."

"Sure. Just make sure she doesn't suck so fast she gets air in her tummy." Kathleen couldn't believe she had advice on how to feed a baby. Who was she to give instructions on anything baby-related? "I'm Kathleen, by the way."

Kathleen watched as her daughter sucked the bottle, her velvety brown eyes locked on the face of the one feeding her. She reached over and stroked the blond curls. *How can I do what I'm about to do?* She glanced over, hoping she'd not said the thought out loud. But Dana was watching the baby. She grinned when Paisley stopped sucking to smile at her new friend.

After burping the baby, who rewarded her with a sound loud enough to make the gentleman across the aisle smile, Dana handed the baby back to her mother.

When she stood to leave, Kathleen thanked her for the help. "No problem. I'm right up front if you need me."

At noon, the bus pulled into a diner parking lot just outside the town of Lost Creek and the driver announced, "Thirty minutes for a meal. Best meatloaf and cheese grits you'll find anywhere in West Virginia."

"Thirty minutes! That's not enough time to finish a cup of coffee, much less a full meal. I intend to talk to Greyhound corporate about this," grumbled the man in a rumpled suit with a scraggly beard. "And about the noise in this bus, especially that wailing kid in the back."

"If you don't have time to finish your meal, the waitress will be happy to wrap it up to carry out," the driver said with a big smile.

How dare he talk about my child! But Paisley wouldn't be her child for long. She had no right to her motherly feelings. How the bus driver could be so pleasant when he had to drive for thirty hours straight and deal with unhappy customers was a mystery to her.

For the rest of the day, Paisley accepted the bus ride like a trouper, happy when she was awake, and took long naps, lulled by the gentle movement of the bus.

The sun was just slipping under the horizon when Paisley decided she'd had enough of the bus ride. Her fussiness became full-scale screaming. Nothing Kathleen tried quietened the tired baby. Finally, her daughter fell into an exhausted sleep. Her small hiccups and wet eyelashes ripped slashes in Kathleen's chest. How could she subject her child to this long bus ride? Yet, she couldn't drive her car and take care of Paisley alone.

"I'm sorry, little one. Soon everything will be right," she whispered, lying to herself. How could it be? Would she miss not having a mother? Would her child hate her?

Around ten p.m., most of the other passengers turned off their overhead lights and settled in for sleep. Paisley woke twice in the night for a change and a bottle. Each time she only whimpered while she waited to be fed. Kathleen was grateful, knowing her cries would wake the sleeping passengers.

She tried to sleep while the baby slept, but her mind was too full. She finally drifted off in the late hours of the night, only to be jerked awake a few hours later when the bus driver announced they were twenty minutes from Beckley. A glance at her watch informed her it was 5:30 a.m.

Several passengers disembarked at Beckley, including Dana, whose eyes sought the back seat before exiting the bus. Kathleen gave her a thumbs up and watched as she mouthed a thank you.

In all the commotion, Paisley woke up but, to Kathleen's amazement, she didn't fuss. After blinking the sleep from her eyes, she gave her mother a big smile. Kathleen's heart squeezed as she whispered, "Thank you, precious, for knowing what I needed to see." The sweet moment dispelled like morning mist over a valley. In a few hours, Paisley would no longer be hers.

Kathleen occupied herself with changing Paisley's diaper and feeding her. Then she pulled out her daughter's prettiest outfit. Once dressed, she added a bib. Paisley drooled like a bulldog since turning three months old. Ainsley called it teething. Was this why she often pushed her fist into her mouth? For the hundredth time, Kathleen wished she knew more about babies.

Far too quickly, the driver announced they were arriving in Welsh. Kathleen steeled her herself against the coming scene by not looking into her daughter's eyes—Jake's eyes. If she had, she could never step off the bus.

She waited until all the passengers exited, then made her way down the aisle, holding her daughter tightly in her arms, a bag over each shoulder. Her heart broke a piece at a time with each step.

When she reached the door, the bus driver stood. "End of the line for me as well. If the Lord wills, I'll have a good night's sleep in the terminal before I drive again." His smile disarmed Kathleen. How could anyone be so cheerful when her world was crashing around her?

She stepped off the bus and saw her mother standing next to the door of the terminal. Emily took a step toward her daughter, then closed the space between them swiftly when her eyes landed on Paisley.

"Kathleen, you've come home! I've prayed so much for this day. And who is this little bundle?" She reached out to embrace them both with wet eyes, that turned confused when her daughter leaned back, not accepting the hug. Her mother's bright smile dissolved.

"Mother, please listen. This is important." Kathleen's voice cracked on the last word. It took every ounce of her will to not grab her mom and bawl in her arms. She spewed her words out quickly before she lost her nerve. "This is Paisley Rose McBride. She was born on September ninth. Her father, Jackson McBride, and I were married last December. He was a combat medic in Vietnam. He died when his helicopter was shot down. Please take care of our daughter. I can't do it alone."

She busied herself removing Paisley's bag from one shoulder. Reminding herself to breathe, she continued. "Here are her things, including the formula she drinks. And there's a copy of her birth certificate and health record the bag. Uh... she's a little behind on her immunizations." Kathleen felt heat creep up from her neck to her cheeks. She peered at Paisley as if soaking up her image and laid her daughter in her grandmother's arms, then hung the baby's bag on Emily's shoulder.

Only then did Kathleen look into her mother's eyes. "Please don't ask questions. I know you and Dad will give Paisley the wonderful childhood you gave me."

The tears washing down Emily's face almost undid Kathleen. She had to hurry. With one last long look at her daughter, she stepped around her mother and rushed to the terminal's counter.

"When's the next bus leaving? I don't care where it's going."

Chapter 41

The gray-haired, rotund woman behind the counter blinked, then checked the daily schedule. "If you hurry, there's a bus leaving in five minutes. It's headed to Pikesville, Kentucky."

"I'll take it," Kathleen said. Unshed tears blurred her vision.

The woman studied her for a moment, then leaned closer and whispered, "Honey, if you're in trouble, I'll call Sherriff Williams. He'll help you."

"Please, just give me the ticket," she begged. Kathleen glanced over her shoulder, dismayed to see Emily in the same place, only she'd turned to watch her daughter.

Ticket in hand, she exited through the only door putting her face-to-face with her mother.

"Daughter, please don't go. Stay." Her mother begged.

Kathleen continued walking, though each step

felt like she was walking in wet concrete. The last words from her mother were, "I pray for you every day. I know God is watching over you until you come home."

Running, she boarded the bus bound for Kentucky, grateful to find an empty row in the back. She dashed down the aisle as the driver closed the door. *Good, no one will sit beside me.* Once seated in the window seat, she stowed her bag in the outside seat, her face wet with silent tears.

As the bus rolled out of the terminal, her arms ached, not because Paisley was in them, but because she wasn't. The void in her body was a black hole sucking her into a spiraling downfall. How can a family of three become no family at all? Can life really be so cruel? Kathleen's bitterness grew from a shoot to a full-grown tree.

Wrapping her arms across her middle, she bit her bottom lip to keep from screaming. Rocking back and forth, she jerked at a baby's cry from the front of the bus. Paisley! She stood, ready to rush up the aisle, when she saw a baby on the shoulder of its mother. *How can I endure this?* She feared if she hit the bottom, her bones would shatter into a million pieces.

It took four bus changes and three days to get back to Morgantown. She walked the half-mile from the bus terminal to her apartment, then slept for a full two days, getting up only for the bathroom or to swig down a glass of milk and eat a spoon of peanut butter.

The jangling of the phone woke her around noon on the third day back. Kathleen fumbled with the phone, dropping the receiver, which caused the cord to twist into a mess. Finally, she gave a breathless hello.

A cherry voice reminded her of a routine-cleaning dental appointment she'd made six months ago. Was that tomorrow? She didn't even know today's date. "Right. I'll be there," she said in a sleep-laden voice, knowing she had no intention of doing so.

Wide awake now, Kathleen's gut told her she needed substance. After finishing a bowl of cereal and a piece of dry toast, she sat staring at the crumbs on the small plate. Finally, she pushed herself from the table with an urge to be busy.

"First things first," she mumbled, then cringed at the phrase of someone planning a new life. Everything within her wanted her old life back. A sudden urge to keep busy engulfed her.

She grabbed a notebook and pencil to calculate course hours. By taking eighteen hours in the spring semester and a full load both summer sessions, an August graduation was possible. Then she'd escape again.

She reached up to put the notebook back on top of the fridge when she kept it and caught a whiff of her stinky underarm. She was ashamed of how many days it'd been since she'd had a shower. Turning the left handle to be as hot as she could tolerate, her tears mixed with the water and her moans drowned out the sound of the spray from the shower head. She stayed there until the water turned cold. Afterward, she fought the urge to call into bed again. But there was something she needed to do. She called Mahira first.

"How was your visit with your parents? I'll bet they were thrilled with Paisley."

Kathleen worked to keep her voice close to

normal. "I called to ask you and Ainsley to come over tonight. I'll tell you about it then."

"I love to. And I'm sure Ainsley will as well. I'll ask her. We're having lunch today. Is six o'clock a good time? Paisley should be still awake, right?"

"Right." Kathleen cringed at the thought that she didn't know what her daughter was doing at any moment. Hanging up, she went to the bedroom and set her alarm for 5:00 p.m. Then, once again, shut out her world with a deep sleep.

Mihira arrived first with Ainsley just seconds behind her. Both searched the living room for Paisley. Kathleen saw the question in their eyes. Best to get this over with.

"Paisley's not here. I left her with my parents. There's no way I'm fit to raise her," she announced, surprised her eyes remained dry.

Ainsley exploded, "Are you crazy? If this is a joke, I'll tell you right now, it's not one bit funny!"

"Oh, honey," Mahira said in a strangled voice. "Surely you didn't."

It was a grueling half-hour. Kathleen kept most of her reasons to herself, stating over and over it was the right thing for Paisley. When the three of them said a teary goodbye, she wondered if they'd ever want to see her again.

Kathleen slept through most of Christmas Day, barely noticing the soft snow gracing the holiday. The most recent call she had from Mahira was two days ago, inviting her to spend the day with her and Jai. She declined and cut the conversation short, as she had with every call from her friends since getting back to Morgantown.

The week after Christmas, Kathleen had Salvation Army pick up the crib and rocker from her bedroom. The gap left in her room matched the hole in her heart. Every waking moment came with a painful longing to hold what she'd given away. She often shook the snow globe Jake gave her or held a small sweater she'd kept back when she packed her daughter's things. Its smell brought her comfort.

In January, Kathleen busied herself with the heavy load of course work required by taking five courses. Each morning, she filled her green thermos with black coffee and packed a lunch to avoid eating in the cafeteria. She barely noticed the winter weather, often not dressing warmly enough or forgetting an umbrella.

All the efforts to block everything and everyone from her life failed two weeks into the semester when she came face-to-face with Professor Wells in the hallway.

"Kathleen, it's good to see you. How's the baby? I'll bet she's really growing."

Kathleen choked back the words *I wouldn't know. I gave her away.* "She's fine. She's four months old now." Not a complete lie. But was she fine? Her heart tightened as a cascade of thoughts tumbled from her head. Had she had croupe again? Was she teething more? Did she still wake up at night?

"I'm glad. You've been through a difficult time. But God has blessed you with a daughter. Please bring her to my office sometime. I'd love to meet her,"

"Mm-huh. I'm late for class." She walked away,

refusing to feel guilty about her rudeness. She only had the energy to focus on herself and her mission.

Kathleen didn't attend her graduation ceremony. On the last day of her final class, she began packing. Two days later, she made another call to the Salvation Army to take her furniture, bed, lamps, and bookcases. She walked to the rotary phone sitting on the kitchen cabinet and dialed Mahira's number.

Her friend picked up on the second ring with a cheery hello. Kathleen's heart hurt at the thought of saying goodbye to her. She struggled to find her voice.

"Hello? Who is this?" Mahira asked.

"It's me, Kathleen." She heard a gasp from the other end of the line.

"I'm so glad to hear from you. It's been so long. Is everything all right?"

How like Mahira to show concern. She suddenly realized how much she'd missed her these past months. "I'm fine." Kathleen launched into the words she'd practiced. "I'm leaving today. I've been accepted into the master's program for library science at Old Domain University in Norfolk."

Steadying her voice, she said, "I'm calling to... to thank you for being my friend. Please tell Ainsley about my call and tell her I appreciate her friendship as well. Must go now. I have a six-hour drive to Norfolk."

Kathleen placed the receiver back on the phone, but not before hearing Mahira begging for her to stay on the line. Shame blistered her throat. Self-loathing had become her shadow.

Before leaving Morgantown, she went to the post

office to check her box and turn in the postal key. Inside lay an envelope with Mahira's return address. *Why would Mahira write to me?*

She stuffed the letter into her jeans pocket and started her trip to Virginia. If she made good time, she would arrive in Norfolk by mid-afternoon—plenty of time to run by the library sciences building to meet with her adviser before she checked into a hotel.

Soon she'd need to find an apartment, but first, she wanted to learn a little about the city. Once again, she was grateful for Jake's military benefits and the funds Owen had bequeathed her. Money wasn't something she needed to worry about.

The drive went smoothly. Kathleen made only one stop to put gas in her car and drive through a fast-food burger place. By three o'clock, she sat across the desk from her adviser.

"We're happy to have you here, Mrs. McBride. We're very proud of our library science degree." The adviser smiled. "I'm here to help you understand the requirements for the degree and make sure your time at Old Domain is rewarding."

"I'm sure it will be." Kathleen just wanted her information packet, not a long visit. Yet, she found herself saying, "Please, tell me about the university." Twenty minutes later, she regretted being gracious. Her facial muscles were tired from smiling.

"Excuse me," Kathleen interrupted. "Is there a time limit on visitors' parking at this building?" She crossed two fingers in her lap and hoped there would be. Anything to get away from this endless description of the university. Clearly this woman loved Old Domain.

"Why, no there isn't." She narrowed her eyes at Kathleen and asked, "Do you need to be somewhere? Because I have an important question, one I always ask new students who are entering our program." The adviser picked up her pen. "Why do you want to be a librarian?"

Kathleen's response spoke about loving the idea of being a resource for learning and helping people find the information they need. But her mind was saying, *It's the best way to hide from the reality of the world.*

Chapter 42

"**K**athleen, we have a shipment of new children's books arriving this afternoon. The children's librarian would like them cataloged and ready to shelve by Monday, before the book fair starts on Wednesday." Mrs. Petterson, her supervisor, offered a sympathetic smile. "I'm sorry for the rush. Betty admits to putting the book order in too late."

"It's fine. I can always pop in Saturday morning to finish the cataloging."

"I appreciate your helpfulness, but I hate to see you give up your Saturday. A young, pretty girl like yourself should spend days off going out with friends, especially of the male type." Her South Carolina accent was always the strongest when she teased.

Kathleen gave a smidge of a smile. "I really don't mind." No one knew she was a widow. She had removed her ring when she moved to Norfolk.

In truth, she did mind. Not because she wanted a day off, but because she was getting restless with her job—and with her life. It started a few months back and had grown stronger lately. Time was flying by, yet she stayed stuck in the past.

How could she move forward when her heart stayed on the day she put Paisley in her mother's arms? How could she hope for a normal life when she no longer had Jake or Paisley? Bitterness returned with a vengeance, and she felt the familiar pain in her stomach—painful burning she was well-acquainted with. Bent over with gut pain, she remembered a doctor's visit from a few months ago.

"You've developed an ulcer. I can give you medication, but it won't help unless you get rid of the stress in your life." Her doctor scratched out a prescription, then flipped the pad to a blank sheet and wrote a name and phone number. "Here's the name therapist I think will help you."

Kathleen filled the prescription and stuffed the name of the therapist deep in the recesses of her handbag. Then, a few weeks later, when her nerves were tight and her gut burned as if it were in a pizza oven, she thought of her doctor's advice. She dug deep into her purse, scrambling through the contents until she found the crumbled sheet with the name and number of a therapist.

With trembling hands, Kathleen called the number and explained her need. She'd seen Dr. Owens that day. The irony of the doctor's name wasn't lost on her. Dr. Owens—like her friend Owen—had offered wise counsel. Counsel she hadn't followed.

Sunday morning, after two long days of cataloging children's books, she hoped for a day of rest. Yet, her restlessness drove her to keep busy. She spent four hours cleaning the kitchen with a vengeance.

Still unable to rest, she moved to her closet. After an hour of organizing and casting out clothes, she found a pair of old jeans stuffed in the back of the closet. Kathleen pulled them out, intending to put them in the pile of clothing for Goodwill, when a folded envelope fell to the floor.

Her forehead crinkled as she reached down to retrieve the letter, then felt her breath halt when she discovered the return address. Mahira! It was the letter she'd received before leaving Morgantown over two years ago.

Sitting on the floor with crossed legs, she opened the letter, wishing there was better lighting in the small closet.

Dear Kathleen,

I know you're surprised to find a letter from me when I live only a few miles from you, but you've shut yourself off from me and Ainsley. There are no words to help you with your losses except for God's Word. I hope you continue to read this letter because I believe with all my heart, the Holy Spirit will lead you to a place of forgiveness and peace.

Too often, when life's circumstances put us in a state of despair, we let our problems take root and live a life of bitterness and strife. Our Lord Jesus says we don't have to do this. He offers peace, hope, and faith to anyone who believes in Him.

You once shared with me you had the Bible Jake read while he was in Vietnam and that he had underlined certain verses. He'd found peace and strength in these words during the war.

Look at his Bible and find the verses that meant so much to him. Have you ever considered that they could mean as much to you?

God sees our brokenness, our flaws, and our scars. These marks, left by life's struggles, don't take away from the beauty when God looks at you. He sees only His creation and offers a path to Him through the death and resurrection of His son. Believe in Jesus, dear friend, and find His forgiveness. Let Him restore your soul and renew your life. He will show you the path He has for you.

I pray for you daily, as does Ainsley.
In His love, Mahira

Kathleen sat on the floor, pondering what she'd just read. *Is it true? Can I find forgiveness after all I've done?* She stood and moved to the dresser in her bedroom, opening the bottom drawer where she'd put winter clothes. Beneath them lay Jake's Bible. The day it arrived, she'd stashed it away, not wanting to open it. Now something pushed her to look inside.

Holding it against her chest as though it might dissolve, she sat in an overstuffed chair in the living room and ran her hands over the cover. Kathleen visualized Jake holding it in his tent, reading from his cot.

The desire to read it grew stronger and stronger. Verse after verse spoke to her as though someone actually knew her—her sorrows, her fears, her shame.

Kathleen's eyes filled so many times, she had to stop and wipe away the wetness before continuing. *... for God so loved, ...we walk by faith, ...heals the brokenhearted, ...cares for you, ...our refuge and strength*. All underlined, some with notes written in the margin. She gave a teary smile, seeing Jake's handwriting.

Slowly, the hardness of her heart melted like chocolate left in the hot sun. Kathleen had the overwhelming desire to know Jesus. Her prayer was simple—*Jesus, I know now that I need your mercy and grace in my life. Forgive my sin of unbelief. Show me what to do next*. The answer came immediately. *Make things right*. She was stunned to hear the same words her therapist used over and over.

Chapter 43

The next morning, Kathleen booked a flight to Charleston, West Virginia. Her second call was to her supervisor to request a week off. Then, she searched the bottom of her closet and pulled out a tattered, rectangle box. Removing the lid, Kathleen carefully lifted the most treasured doll from her childhood.

Chatty Cathy was dressed in a pink and white striped dress with a white pinafore. She pulled the cord in the back of the doll and was delighted when it spoke to her. Kathleen smiled at the thought of giving it to her daughter.

She found her seat on the plane and stowed her carry-on in the rack above her. After fastening her seatbelt, she stared at her hands in her lap, marveling at what had happened in the last twenty-four hours. Goosebumps raised high on her arms when Kathleen thought of the night before.

The timing had to be God's doing because today was Paisley's third birthday. This date had riddled her with self-loathing for the last two years. Now, she felt a peace she didn't understand. She said a quick prayer. *Lord, you started this. Please see it through.*

The flight landed on time, and soon Kathleen was driving a rented Chevy toward Farrowlee. A soft wind and slight chill made it a perfect September day. She rolled down her window and breathed in the earthy scent of the mountains, enjoying the winding road that offered familiar vistas. Her old self would have been frightened to return home, but her new self carried the hope of reconciliation.

Around the last curve of her trip, Farrowlee came into view. It felt surreal when she parked the car and walked to the front door of her parent's home. After a moment's hesitation, she heard the soft whisper of *Fear not, I am with you.*

Two knocks and her mother opened the door wearing a pink apron she remembered from her childhood. There were so many words she could have used, but only one left her mouth. "Mom."

She watched as tears filled her mother's eyes, then slid down her cheeks.

"Daughter." Emily said in a choked voice. "You're here. I've prayed so much for this day." She opened the door wider for Kathleen to step in, then embraced her in a long hug.

Kathleen stepped back, amazed at her mom's acceptance. "How can you even look at me after all I've put you and Dad through?"

"Because we turned you over to Jesus and prayed the verse in Genesis 28:15 over you every day. *I am with you and will watch over you wherever you go. And I will bring you back to this land.* It brought us both hope and peace." She offered a wide smile and continued. "Would you like to see your daughter? She's outside with her Pops."

Kathleen could only nod as her heart marched double-time. She followed her mother through the house to the back door. Emily went down the stoop, but Kathleen stopped at the door. She stared at the little girl on a tree swing, taking in the sight of her daughter's long, blond curls and listening to her infectious laugh so like Jake's.

She briefly saw her father staring at her, but turned her eyes back to her daughter, unable to take her attention from this beautiful child. Her and Jake's child.

When Paisley saw Emily, she scrambled from the swing and ran to her. She saw her grandmother's teary eyes and asked, "What's wrong, Nana? Did you scrape your knee like me?"

"No sweetheart. These are happy tears. I want you to meet someone special. Do you remember all the pictures we have of your mommy?"

"The mommy we pray for every night?"

"Yes, that one. God answered our prayers because she's here."

Paisley leaned around her nana and stared at Kathleen. "Are you my mommy?"

For a moment she feared how Paisley might react if she said yes, but God reminded her to not be afraid. "Yes, I am," she responded, in a wobbly voice.

Paisley walked closer, surveying her face. "You're crying, too. Are they happy tears like Nana's?"

Kathleen crouched down until she was eye level with her child. "They're happy tears like your grandmother's."

"Did you know I scraped my knee? Would you like to see my Band-Aid? Do you know I have a daddy named Jake? He's in heaven with Jesus." Paisley didn't wait for answers. "Today is my birthday. We're going to have a party as soon as Uncle Walt gets here." She squinched her face into a frown. "Sometimes he's slow. But Nana says to be patient because he only has one leg."

Kathleen gave her mom a questioning glance, who responded with a whispered, "I'll tell you later."

The blare of a car horn drew the attention of everyone. "Uncle Walt!" Paisley ran around the exterior of the house to the front yard. "Now we can have cake and ice cream. And open the presents." Kathleen smiled when the last word came out as "pwesents."

Emily followed Paisley while Kathleen waited for her father. He came to her, put his arm around her waist and walked with her, saying, "Welcome home, Kathleen." She marveled at the grace of her parents.

They arrived at the front yard in time to see Walt bend and gave the three-year-old a bear hug. "Hey, Rabbit. I'm told someone has a birthday today."

"Silly. It's my birthday."

As he stood, his eyes landed on Kathleen. "Hello, Kathleen."

"Hello. What are—"

Walt interrupted, "We'll talk later." Paisley tugged on the sleeve of his right arm with all her might.

"Right now, I think this young lady would like to go to a party."

Kathleen followed them inside as confusion clouding her thoughts. *Why is Walt in Farrowlee?*

The next few hours were filled with opening gifts, blowing out candles, ice cream melting next to slices of cake, and the delighted squeals of a three-year-old.

Kathleen watched the activities around the table with a thankful heart. In the depths of her mind, she filed away moment after moment as treasured memories.

"Time to put this little lady down for a nap," Emily said quietly in mid-afternoon.

"I'll clean up," Henry announced as he stood up from the table littered with cake crumbs, spilled milk, and crumbled bits of wrapping paper.

Emily smiled at her husband. "Why don't you spend some time with our daughter?"

As if on cue, Walt stood and started toward the front door. "I think I'll enjoy one of those rockers on the front porch."

Alone with her father, Kathleen felt a surge of guilt. "Daddy, I'm so sorry. I need to... to ask your forgiveness. I've behaved so badly." She couldn't go on. *How can she explain all the paths she'd taken?*

Henry leaned over and took her hand. "Daughter, your mother and I forgave you a long time ago. When you're ready, we would like to hear your story. But know there's nothing you can tell us that would take our love from you. Jesus taught us this."

His kindness humbled Kathleen. The only words she could muster were "Thank you."

When a giggle came from upstairs, Henry said, "I need to help your mother. I think the princess had too much sugar." He put his hand on her arm and gave it a slight squeeze. "Thank you for coming home, Kathleen."

She watched him walk up the stairs, a myriad of emotions stirring within her. A sudden tug at her conscience reminded her of what had become her mantra. *Make things right.* She walked out the door to find Walt.

True to his word, he sat rocking in one of the two rockers on the porch. "Can we talk?"

Walt nodded, then tilted his head to the other rocker. "I'm sure you'd like to know what's going on." Walt's kind eyes linked with hers.

Kathleen sat down next to him, twisting her body until she faced the man with whom she'd spent the most miserable night of her life, and said, "Actually, I came out here to apologize for how I treated you in the past."

"No, I'm the one who needs to apologize. I was wrong to take you to the crash site. It's plagued my soul for the past five years." He looked down, then returned his gaze, eyes moist. "I felt I'd ruined your life by my selfishness." He shook his head and continued. "I wanted to take you to the crash site, not because you wanted to go, but because I wanted to get to know you and used the wrong opportunity to do so."

"But how...?"

"I saw you in the class where I was a TA. You looked and talked like someone I wanted to know—to be with." He paused, drumming his fingers on the arm of the rocker. "I asked the Lord to forgive me for causing you and your parents such pain. Eventually, I asked them for their forgiveness, though it took me some time to do so. I loved my time with them and feared they might not want to be around me any longer." He pulled his hands through his hair with a long sigh. "My greatest shame is what I did to you. I tried many times to find you and when I couldn't, my only path was to pray for your safety and hope for a chance to see you some day."

After heaving another deep sigh, he continued. "When the accident happened and I lost my leg, I became bitter and angry with God. During my time in the hospital and most of my time in rehab, I stopped praying, for me or anyone."

His smile returned as he continued. "I thank God for an amazing physical therapist who loved the Lord and helped me put things into perspective. And your parents who supported me through the hospital stay and a long time in rehab. God hadn't taken my leg, and He'd been there with me through all the challenges of learning to live as an amputee. It took me some time to grasp this reality. Eventually, I understood my identity was in Him, not in a man with only one leg."

He stopped, folded his hands, and leaned closer to her. "The one thing in my life that never left me was the pain of what I did to you." A smile broke across his face. "Now, you're home. The place I begged God to send you... and I can ask forgiveness."

The similarities between their lives stunned Kathleen. It was exactly how she felt until Mahira's letter explained the path to Jesus. It took her a moment to realize Walt was still talking.

"I'm here today because of a trip to Farrowlee

to write a story about mining. Emily and Henry have since become good friends. Their faith sustained me through many rough days. And, of course, there's Paisley." He turned his gaze to a doll left on the wicker table between the two rockers, then back to Kathleen. "You have an amazing daughter. She's sweet, loving, and wise beyond her years." Walt paused. "Enough about me. Tell me about you. You seem more peaceful than the girl in the waitress outfit."

"I am, but that's a story for another time. Right now I want to focus on getting to know my daughter and renewing my relationship with my parents. I don't want to go my way any longer."

Kathleen fixed her gaze on the mining town in the valley below the house. "With God's help, I hope to raise Paisley and be near her grandparents so she can have the same childhood experiences I had living in Farrowlee." She turned back to Walt and continued. "On the trip here, I kept thinking about Charleston. I'm praying I can find a job at a library in the city. It would be close to here."

Walt's smile spread wider across his face. "When I finally made it back to work after the accident, I wrote a news story about the plight of the mining families in our state and other states. APS picked it up and, as a result, many mines were saved from closure, including Farrowlee Mine. Recently, I was contacted by the *Charleston Gazette* to offer me a job as assistant editor. I've lived there for a month now." He gave Kathleen a tentative look. "There's a great zoo in Charleston. Maybe we can take Paisley there sometime."

"I'd like that," Kathleen said in a soft voice.

Chapter 44

This is the way. Walk in it.
—Isaiah 30:21

1983

*T*he May air was warm, yet a chill squeezed Kathleen's heart and flowed through her bloodstream to all her extremities. She stood on a small rise, her shoes wet from the morning dew. Memories swarmed in her mind like bees searching for a new home. She thought of all the miles she'd traveled and all the people in her life who had befriended her and kept her safe until she found her way home. She followed a timeline in her mind, humbled by how God had watched over her.

The noise of approaching footsteps jerked her from the memories. Kathleen turned to find a man near her age standing beside her, staring at The Wall.

"Daunting, isn't it?" he expressed with a bittersweet smile. "Is this your first time?" He turned to face her with eyes that carried a sadness behind them.

"Yes, it is."

"Visiting someone or here as a tourist?"

Kathleen hesitated. Few knew this story. As a believer, she'd learned over the past years to trust that God placed individuals in her path for a reason. Some became fast friends who came along beside her in her walk with Christ, offering their support as her faith grew. She encountered others only briefly, yet God often used them for her good.

"I'm here to visit my husband." She noticed the cane in the man's left hand.

"I came to pay my respect to Lenny Lewinsky and three other buddies who died on the same day in the 1969 offensive later named Hamburger Hill. We were on patrol, and I'm the only one who made it back to base, thanks to a medevac team." His smile faded, and he glanced at the monument. "There were seventy-two casualties and over 370 wounded, including me, during the ten-day offensive."

Kathleen murmured, "It must have been awful. I'm so sorry about your friends. God must have a purpose for sparing your life that day." She observed as he struggled with his composure.

Changing the subject, he explained, "The names on The Wall are listed in chronological order, according to the date the of the soldiers' death. It allows veterans, like myself, who were in the battle to see their friends forever united on monument. Find your husband's name in the Directory of Names placed at the end of each wall. It'll help you locate exactly where to look."

She watched him walk toward the parking lot, using his cane to help with a significant limp in one leg, knowing she would pray for this veteran in the days to come.

Kathleen forced her mind back to the task ahead. A few steps later, her shoes slipped on the wet grass. She berated herself for how she'd dressed this morning—a black double-knit pant suit with black pumps.

When her pumps hit the concrete, she stood at the vertex of The Wall, overwhelmed. Tears filled her eyes when she moved close enough to view the massive number of names—a reminder of the loss of lives in Vietnam.

On a podium at one end of the monument, Kathleen found the Directory of Names. She touched the bound, waterproof book, larger than the size of a family Bible—another reminder of the enormous loss. Opening the cover, she read the first page.

The directory is in alphabetical order by last names. The number next to the name denotes the panel, and the letter is for the East Wall or the West Wall.

Kathleen flipped the pages until she landed on M. Sliding her finger down the page, she stopped at Jackson Mason McBride. Engraved beside his name was the location—68E.

She found the correct section only a few steps from the podium. It was the third panel at the end of the East Wall. She stepped closer and saw Jake's name literally at eye level.

At first, she had little reaction to seeing his name engraved among so many. Slowly her eyes moved beyond the names, and there she was—a perfect reflection of herself in the shiny black marble. The connection was immediate. She was once again with Jack.

Suddenly, it wasn't her reflection on The Wall. Instead, she saw the younger Kathleen dressed in the clothes she'd worn to their wedding, a long, white granny dress with lace around the high neck and puffed sleeves. A wreath of flowers circled her long hair, which fell from a part down the middle of her head. On her feet were a pair of white huaraches. She gasped and closed her eyes. When Kathleen looked again, she saw her thirty-one-year-old self.

The sound of Colin's ceaseless chatter diverted her attention. She smiled at the sight of Walt holding their five-year-old's hand and trying to answer Paisley's many questions about the monument. His thoughtfulness touched her when he offered to take the kids for ice cream, giving her a few minutes alone before joining her.

When they reached her, Kathleen held her hand out to her daughter, now eleven. "Paisley, come see the name of your father."

Book Club Questions

1. What are the major themes of this book?

2. What were Kathleen's defining traits? What were Walt's?

3. How did Kathleen's and Walt's choices impact this story?

4. How would you describe Owen's character and what shaped it?

5. How did the secondary characters in the book influence or impact Kathleen and Walt?

6. Which character can you relate to or empathize with the most and why?

7. What was your favorite scene or passage and why?

8. What was your least favorite scene or passage and why?

9. In what ways, if any, did you see God's providential hand in this story?

10. As a historical fiction, how did the author blend historical facts and fiction in this book? Did you find the book accurate and authentic?

11. Did you learn anything new or interesting about the time and place of the story?

12. Did you find anything striking or memorable about this book?

13. Did the story have enough tension to hold your interest?

14. How would you describe the author's writing style in a few words?

15. If you could travel back in time to the historical setting and period of this book, what would you do or see?

Acknowledgments

*I*t's been a joy to write this series about the life of several families over four decades. I fell in love with the mountains and people in the state of West Virginia during our two trips there to do research. Thank you to the residents there who graciously shared their lives and knowledge of their state's history.

Many thanks to my sweet author friend, Cheryl, whose encouragement and suggestions improved my stories. I thank God for her presence in my life.

I'm grateful for Tranquility Press and for Teresa Lynn, my editor, publisher, and friend. Her guidance and expertise have taught me so much about the craft of writing. I admire her patience and sweet spirit.

Thank you to my readers whose comments humble me and make me want to continue writing.

To my husband, thank you for doing the household chores, giving me time to write this series, and for driving me across the state of West Virginia. You are truly my blessing.

And to my Lord, Jesus Christ, I give all the honor, glory, and praise. Without Him, none of this can happen.

Brenda O'Bannion is a writer and retired educator. She writes faith-based historical fiction with a little romance thrown in. Her latest series, Wonderful West Virginia, explores the lives of a family over four decades.

She has also written a parallel memoir of her grandmother and herself. Added to her list of books are a children's chapter book and two children's picture books.

Brenda is a member of the Centex Christian Writers Group and Faith, Hope, & Love Christian Writers.

Book clubs often invite her to present her books at their meetings. Brenda has also presented at educational conferences around the state on the topics of autism and bullying, both of which are a part of her children's books.

When not writing, she enjoys reading, attending Bible studies at her church, leading a Women's Life Group, and volunteering at low-income apartment communities. She lives in Georgetown, Texas with her husband.

Visit Brenda's website at
www.brendaobannion.com
or join her on Facebook and Instagram.

Brenda's books:

Wonderful West Virginia series

Book 1, ***The Land Between Us,*** follows two families during the Great Depression who find courage, love, and hope in unexpected places.

Book 2, ***Farrowlee Mountain***, finds an Irish famiy navigating troubles at the mine they work for as war brews in Korea. Where will they find peace?

Book 3, ***Winding Roads***, follows Kathleen as she runs from tragedy at home and in a far-off place called Vietnam--until she finds the one place of true refuge.

9 781950 481521